The Glimmer Saga
#1

Glimmer

———

D E McCluskey

D E McCluskey

Glimmer
Copyright © 2022 by D E McCluskey

ISBN 978-1-914381-04-1

Cover art design by:
Forsaken Folklore

For Annmarie…

I know I haven't written
You a poem yet.
So, I thought this might help!

1.

THE LIGHT FROM the flickering candles cast a warm, gentle glow over the room. It was like liquid gold dripping comfortingly from every corner, making even the darkest shadow a thing of beauty and intrigue. The moonlight shimmering through the large window staged a wonderous battle between the silver and the gold, almost like a choreographed ballet.

In the centre of the room was a four-poster bed. The beige curtains were drawn back to the posts and tied with a deep blue ribbon. Wrapped up, warm and safe within the plump covers of the bed, was a young girl of maybe nine years old. Her hair was dark and tied back with a swathe of the same deep blue ribbon that held the curtains. In the centre of her hair was yet another blue wave, again, the azure streak the same colour as the ribbons.

An older woman was in the large chair next to the bed. She was holding an old leather-bound book. Her hair was the same colour as the little girl's, and the look in their eyes spoke of their relationship.

Mother and daughter.

The décor of the room told of majesty and privilege, but the furnishings, although lavish, were also soft and whispered of loving attention to detail.

'Will you tell me the story again, Mummy?' the little girl asked with childish excitement, tinged with more than a modicum of fatigue. 'Please!'

The mother chuckled and opened the book. 'Again, Cassandra? You do love this tale don't you, darling?'

The child, Cassandra, nodded and shifted position in the bed, allowing room for her mother to climb on and lie next to her. The older woman, taking Cassandra's hint, smiled and snuggled into the giggling child.

'It's my favourite,' she replied.

'Don't you get scared?'

'Scared? Why would I be scared? They are stories of our family, my ancestors. Why would they want to hurt me?'

Why indeed, her mother thought as she opened the tome in her hands.

'I love that smell. It's the smell of tales from long, long ago, isn't it?'

The woman smiled at her little girl, the love practically dripping from the deep blue of her eyes. 'It is if you want it to be, baby girl.'

'Then I want it to be! Can you begin, Mummy? I'm sleepy, but I want to hear the story.' The child wriggled about beneath the sheets before finally finding a position she was happy with and then lay still, her big eyes looking up at her mother.

The mother smiled as she took in the delightful smell of the old paper. When she was a girl, it had smelled like adventure to her too, as her mother and father had often sat and recited similar tales at bedtime. They were fond memories indeed. Now, she was passing on the adventure before Cassandra became the big sister to the little Azurian currently residing in her belly.

The little girl reached over and put her hand on her mother's belly. 'Are you listening too, little one?' she whispered as the epic tale of the Glimmers began.

'A long, long time ago, in an age long since passed, there stood a castle. It was no ordinary castle; it was the castle of the Glimm!'

2.

THE CASTLE WAS old, it had been built many, many centuries before. It was true to say that it had seen better days, glorious days in fact. Days when people by the thousands had run through the great halls and had worshipped at the Altar of Glimm. Days when children gambolled around the vast gardens picking the fruit that was in abundance in the orchids and vineyards. When the castle formed as a central attraction to a large, bustling village.

But those days were passed. Long passed. They were nothing more than a shadow in the mind's eye of the castle's current custodians. A misty dream of a long ago, forgotten childhood.

An old man pattered through the vastness of the Great Hall, taking a moment to bow towards the altar in the centre of the room. He muttered to himself as his footfalls echoed through the otherwise emptiness of his surroundings.

The man was thin, his thick grey hair was long and unkempt. It fell about his shoulders and back before the unruly mass merged with the grey of the long and shaggy beard he wore. His emaciated body was wrapped in a muslin sheet that was tied around his waist; his feet and chest were bare.

In his hands, he carried an object, a small metallic ball. The ball itself would have fit into the palm of one of his hands, yet he carried it in both with deep reverence.

His path was illuminated by candles, some of which were nearing their end, others fresh. Their light danced around the Great Hall, illuminating his way towards a large, ornate wooden door.

'Come, Brother, it is time!' he yelled into the candle lit twilight behind him.

'Yes, Brother, I do believe it is,' a disembodied voice answered from the darkness.

Moments later, a second man, very similar in appearance to the first, emerged from the gloom. He, too, was labouring with a round metallic object in his hands, once again giving it his utmost respect.

Both men converged at the door. They regarded each other before bowing lower than anyone would have expected men of their apparent age to be able to bow. The first man shouldered the heavy door, putting all his weight behind it in an attempt to open it. His partner, seeing his struggle against the obstinate obstacle, leaned in too.

The scrape of metal against metal screeched through the air. It screamed its hellish echo off every wall, but the door opened just enough for them to squeeze through.

The room beyond was pitch black. Even the miniscule light that was clambering in from the outside room fought a losing battle with the oppressive obsidian within.

The metallic balls both men held, touched. It was just the slightest of kisses, but it caused an explosion of deep purple.

The brightness illuminated the entire chamber.

This hall was a contradiction to the other room. Although almost twice the size, it was clean, free from dust or decay. The walls were adorned with pictures depicting scenes of reverence as well as fun. Portraying folk who were religious but also lived life to the fullest. There were plenty of women and children depicted within these pictures, and the two brothers stared at them for the longest time, both faces filled with longing and yearning.

Eventually, they made their way towards the single altar in the centre of the chamber. It was easily twice the size of the one in the corresponding room. The white sheets adorning the structure were pristine; the creases in the thick, luxurious fabric were fresh and sharp.

Both men fell to their bony knees onto the thick maroon carpet that surrounded the holy table. As they did, the metallic orbs fell dark. The ominous, oppressive darkness once again took dominance.

Then, the orbs began to glow.

One shone a deep, warm red. The other a cold blue. Again, the room was cast into a heavy maroon glow. Both brothers leant forwards, their shaggy bearded faces brushing the lush carpet of the altar. They remained there for a few long moments before finally rising.

The maroon of the orbs pulsated, creating a slow, hypnotic throb.

'Brother, as we are the last of our line and we are both childless, it our solemn duty to preserve our ways as best we can.'

'Brother, I propose here today, at the Altar of the Great Lord Glimm, the father of our race, that we cast our essence into these orbs. We do this to preserve our customs, our knowledge, our magic, and our laws.'

Both men struggled to their feet and drew short but dangerous looking daggers from within the folds of their gowns. They both stared at the weapons, muttering something that was akin to a blessing under their breaths. Then, as one, they offered their other hand to each other. Each brought their daggers forth and cut deep. The knives sliced through the flesh of their palms like a hot knife through cold butter. It didn't take long for fresh blood to flow from the wounds.

The Glimmer Saga #1
Glimmer

Dark, scarlet beads dripped from each hand, covering the glowing orbs beneath, smothering their pulses. It was in that semi-darkness that each brother leaned forward and trickled saliva from their mouths, allowing it to drip, to mingle with the blood coating the balls. There was an audible hiss from both artefacts, and they began to pulse once more.

This time, the illumination was twice as bright.

The men shied their eyes away from the glow, still muttering blessings underneath their breath. When they were facing away from each other, they cut deep X marks into the flesh of their foreheads, between their eyes.

They allowed the blood from the wounds to trail down their faces and mingle within the grey of their beards.

They stood as still as statues for maybe an hour, maybe longer, there was no other living soul there to document.

Countless prayers and blessings tore through their minds before finally, after what could have been an age, they turned to face each other. They bowed low, once again displaying a suppleness that would take a lifetime to achieve, before removing an orb each.

They held their glowing spheres aloft and, as one, uttered three words each. 'Behold the Glimmers!'

The brothers turned and walked off in opposite directions.

3.

CASSANDRA WAS SAT up in her bed. The story was having the opposite desired effect on her, and she was now alert. Her bright blue eyes were wide, excitement blazing from within them. The reflection from the candles in the room danced in their radiance, animating them even more. 'Where did they go, Mummy? What are the orbs? Why did they cut themselves?'

The questions came hard and fast.

Her mother laughed as she rested her hand gently on her swollen belly, relishing the small kicks and wriggles from within. 'My little Cass. So many questions. You must remain patient; all will be revealed in time. Good things come to those who are willing to wait! Heed these words, Cassandra, then and only then, a fine princess and queen you will make.'

The little girl tutted and flopped back down into the lush pillows beneath her head. 'Mummy, *please* finish the story!'

Her mother laughed. 'OK, Cass, I'll finish the story if you promise that you'll go straight to sleep afterwards.'

Cassandra looked at her. The little girl was aware that her mother was the queen of Azuria, and she knew that both queens and mothers needed to always be obeyed. Even with this knowledge, she still crossed her fingers beneath the blankets before answering in a sweet voice. 'OK, Mother, I promise.'

Her mother, knowing that her little girl was crossing her fingers, smiled again. 'Right then, if you're comfortable, I'll continue.'

'I'm comfortable, Mummy,' Cassandra whispered.

The mother re-opened the large book on her knee, once again relishing the musty smell of the paper and allowing it to take her back to her own childhood, only for a moment or two, as she knew that living in the past, especially with a young child and another on the way, was a dangerous thing.

'The two brothers knew that they needed to spread their knowledge. They were the very last of their order and, as such, knew that on their passing, the knowledge and skills of all the Glimm would be lost with them. The two orbs, or Glimmers, one blue and one red, had been sealed with their essence, their magic. Now, their very last mission was to find custodians for the precious globes. They were aware that the new custodians would not be able to fully understand the magic that would be at their disposal, but they would understand the power each held. The last mission they must undertake before they could rest with their beloved and benevolent Great Lord Glimm was to make sure the Glimmers were held apart. If any one person were to hold both Glimmers, they would become all powerful. The people of this world were young and therefore were not ready for that level of responsibility.'

Here, the mother paused and looked at her daughter. She was still wide awake, but she could see the first vestiges of sleep sneaking through her veneer. She smiled and continued …

4.

ONE BROTHER TRAVELLED many, many miles to the north. His journey was cold, but due to his magic, he never once felt the biting wind at his skin or the ice clawing at his heels.

Eventually, as he neared the end of the land, he saw exactly what the Glimmer had told him he would. It was a small settlement, nothing more than a few huts with rudimental defences surrounding it. The brother bypassed the guards with ease and made his way towards the largest, most central of the dwellings, the one that was situated on a small hill.

Again, he slipped unnoticed past the guards, as if he were a ghost. A small, wry smile creased his hidden lips as the primitive men shivered as he passed.

Inside the dwelling, the walls were adorned with animal skins and weaponry. The people here were primitive, primal, but the brother could see a fantastic future for them. Riches, advancement, and civilisation.

He smiled contentedly.

There were many people inside the main chamber, and each of them was startled at his appearance. A few of the men brought their weapons to bear and grabbed for him, but none could hold him, none could harm him. Unmolested, he continued his pace towards the throne that was set against the back wall.

A man was seated on the throne, and he watched the brother's progress with interest. His attention focused on the mystical talisman he was carrying in his hands. He nodded as his best men attempted to stop this old man, all to no avail.

Eventually, he stood to greet this stranger, his hands resting on the hilt of a large weapon at his side. He spoke, but even to the brother's learned ear, the language was harsh and the dialect was primitive. He adjusted his finger on the Glimmer in his hand, and it flashed a bright blue light.

Everyone in the room gasped, and in that instant, the leader could understand everything the brother spoke.

'Do not be afraid, my brethren. I am here to bestow upon you a great gift. I bring to you the secrets of the Glimm. Trapped within this orb is everything you need to bring your tribe to prosperity and peace.'

The chief sheathed his weapon and faced the newcomer. 'Who are you that you can stroll into my village unharmed and offer me this ...' he looked at the Glimmer in the brother's hands, and another blue flash illuminated his face. '... gift?' he finished.

'I am of the Glimm! I am one of the last two of my people. I offer you our full knowledge and guidance. All you need to do is protect this Glimmer, and your village will prosper.'

The brother bowed his head and offered up the blue glowing orb to the chief.

The chief looked around at his people, unsure of what to do. Obviously afraid of the glowing magic, he did not want to lose the faith of his tribe. He looked around the room, but no one caught his eye. He looked again at the bowed man before him and accepted the gift.

The moment the Glimmer was out of his possession, the brother stood. As he did, the men in the crowd drew their weapons.

The brother, unfazed by the threat these men posed, centred his attention on the chief, the custodian of the Glimmer. 'This Glimmer is known as the Azure. It will keep you safe and show you the way to prosperity. You must remember the ways of the old ones, The Glimm. Your tribe will forever be known as the Azurians.' With that, the brother disappeared, leaving the chief holding the glowing orb.

Everyone in the room bent their knee and their head to their new idol.

~~~~

Hundreds of miles in the opposite direction, on the opposite coast, the second brother had made his way into a similar camp. He was holding, with the same reverence, the Glimmer that was glowing red.

Several of the guards and the warriors of the tribe were attempting to capture him, but as with the other brother, their efforts were all in vain. Each time they gripped his thin clothes or his wild hair, their hands would pass through him, allowing him to continue unhindered towards his final destination.

He passed into a great hall that was similar to the one his brother passed into hundreds of miles away to be greeted by a chief sat on a large throne made of wood and bones.

'What is the meaning of this intrusion? Are the Gods so displeased with us that they send a demon to torment us?' the chief shouted as he stood before his throne. There was panic in his voice and in his actions. Seeing the panic in their leader stirred the warriors into a similar frenzy.

'I am no demon. I come bearing gifts,' the brother said in the tribe's natural tongue.

'If you are no demon, then how are my men unable to apprehend you? You speak my language, yet you are clearly not of these parts,' the Chief observed.

'I am of the Glimm! I come bearing you offerings of power and magic.'

The chief relaxed as his attentions fell upon the glowing red orb the stranger was holding.

'Power?' he asked. 'Of what kind of power do you speak?'

'Thousands of years of knowledge of the Glimm are encased within this Glimmer. If you keep it safe, it will offer you security and guidance. The sum total of our years is encapsulated within.' The brother bowed his head and offered the globe towards the man on the throne.

'Am I able to touch this offering of fire?'

'It is yours to do with what you will.'

The chief poked at the offered orb, his face awash in the red glow, creating a red mask that covered his curiosity. Eventually, he accepted the gift and held it aloft, above his head. Everyone in the room fell to their knees in reverence.

The brother took a step back and regarded the room, a surge of relief and pride coursing through his body. 'This gift has not been given lightly! It is a gift of power and a gift of responsibility. You who now hold the Carnelian Glimmer must do it with a sense of good. The orb should not be used for ill. Remember the ways of the old ones. Remember the ways of the Glimm. You will forever be known as the Carnelians!'

No sooner had the words left his mouth, the brother disappeared.

~~~~

Both brothers reappeared at the original altar. The room had not changed. As they beheld each other, they embraced.

'Our burden is complete, old man,' the first brother uttered, his voice dripping with triumph and excitement. 'We are now free to join our brethren before us.'

The second brother kissed the first on both cheeks before pulling a dagger from the folds of his clothing. It was the same one he had used to cut his hand. He smiled as he watched his brother do the same.

They held their knives aloft, both blades glinting and dancing in the candlelight. 'Today sees the end of the Glimm,' the first brother announced.

'It is a glorious day,' the second brother replied.

'Long live the Glimm,' they both chanted.

Then, with no further diatribe, they each buried their knives deep into the chest of the other, piercing each other's hearts, killing them instantly.

Both men fell onto the altar, still in their embrace. Fresh blood pooled around them like shrouds, sinking into the fabric of the cloth adorning the altar, staining it forever with their sacrifice.

5.

'WERE THEY DEAD, Mummy? Forever dead?' Cassandra asked, her eyes wide.

Her mother, seeing that the child was far from the sleep she needed, closed the book and stroked her hair. 'Yes, Cass, they were dead forever. Dead, but only in this land. There are some who say that the Great Lord Glimm himself came and took them. Taking their souls up to Koll'Su to be with him, to live forever with the angels and the cherubs.'

'Is that where Daddy is? Koll'Su?' the little girl asked; her eyes, although now tiring, were tinged with sadness. Her father's death had been so recent that Cassandra hadn't had time to take process it.

'Yes, child,' her mother soothed, still stroking her head. 'He's in Koll'Su with all our ancestors, and they all love him very much.'

'Will I go to Koll'Su when I die?'

'Yes, my sweet, of course you will. You're a good soul, but you needn't worry about that anytime soon.'

'Will Daddy be there when I go?'

The mother smiled again. 'Yes, my sweet. He'll be there to welcome you with open arms, as will I.'

'What about my ancestors? Will they all be there too? And will they all love me as much as you and Daddy?'

'Yes, child, they'll all love you, just as we do. Now, it's time you went to sleep. Princesses need their sleep more than anyone else, as they need to grow their brains.'

This alerted the little princess again. 'Will my brain grow during the night?' she asked in excited tones.

Her mother laughed as she struggled up from the bed, holding her swollen belly. 'Goodnight, sweet child,' she whispered as she made her way to the doorway, blowing out candles as she passed.

'Goodnight, Mummy, I love you.'

'I love you too, sweet pea,' she whispered as the door closed behind her.

6.

WHAT THE BOOK didn't document when relaying the story was the great war. The war to end all wars, they called it. It raged for nearly two hundred years. It took far too much from the two regions and gave almost nothing back.

Over the years since the brothers bestowed their gifts, the two villages thrived. They developed into great powers within the land and became prosperous provinces rich in resources.

For hundreds of years, the direct descendants of the chiefs ruled the lands of Azuria and Carnelia, overseeing the development of the communities, the building of customs, the devising of governments. Both cities decided, irrespective of each other, to develop regal systems. The chiefs became kings, who married queens, who begat princes and princesses.

Over the years, as knowledge and science grew, modernism took hold. The Glimmers that had once been held with utmost respect began to be forgotten.

The people neglected what these orbs had done for them as they had begun to do things for themselves. The magic and the knowledge they possessed became overshadowed by the people's own intuitiveness and scientific acumen.

The demise of the Glimmers from the countries, as they now were, was helped by two occurrences that happened within a few years of each other, one in Azuria, the other in Carnelia. Both events resulted in the Glimmers being stored under lock and key in the deepest dungeons.

The first occurrence happened in Carnelia. The king of the time was holding court, and they were discussing the drainage system and how they could get the best results from the construction of an underground sewer. There were experts droning on about how the irrigation of the soil could also benefit from the system, and the king had gotten rather bored. He spied the Glimmer in the corner of the room, where it was on display, as it had been for centuries, on a plinth.

He began to admire it from the other side of the room, marvelling at how its red glow had not diminished, not even a little bit, since he could remember, even as a small boy running about the castle. There had always been a taboo surrounding it, and it had always been out of bounds for him to play with. But he was the king now, no longer a small prince who could be told what he could and couldn't do.

He stood from the table as the speaker was in mid-waffle. The man stuttered for a moment before the king waved him to carry on. 'Don't mind me, sir. I just have a curiosity I need to quench. Please, continue.'

The speaker continued, not taking his eyes from the curious king.

As he made his way to the corner of the room where the oddity stood, everything else in the room faded into obscurity and the red glare emanating from the orb filled his senses. Without thinking, almost as if he was guided, he reached out and touched it.

When his fingers caressed the smooth surface, he was underwhelmed. Due to the red glow of the ball, he'd always assumed it would have been hot to the touch, but it wasn't. It wasn't even warm, more room temperature. Another thing that surprised him was he had expected to feel something happen when he touched it, a buzz, a shiver, something. All he felt was disappointment as nothing happened.

At least that was how it seemed at first.

A dark cloud began to form above the castle. It was so dense that daytime turned into night. The people working in the fields outside the castle and the people working inside, all ran, blessing themselves, crying out to the Great Lord Glimm to watch over them. They held their fingers up towards the darkness in a feeble, superstitious attempt to ward off the evil that was happening above them.

A single roar emanated from the cloud. It sounded like walls crumbling, thick walls, castle walls. Once again, the people ran away from the sounds of destruction, ducking for cover.

A single crack of lightning built up within the cloud before escaping and descending unnaturally slowly upon the castle. The populace, the ones who weren't huddled away praying, witnessed something strange that day, something that they would tell their children and their children's children about.

The fork of lightning broke free from the confines of the cloud and struck the castle. But it didn't disappear!

The zigzag of bright red light hung in the air as if it were searching for a window, for any way inside. Eventually, it found what it was looking for and breached the walls.

The king was still holding the Glimmer in his hand when the red lightning burst forth. It shattered the window with a shower of slivered glass.

It struck the orb.

It was then that he felt something. Maybe the same something he was expecting to feel when he first touched the thing.

Every hair on his body stood to attention as a buzz coursed through him. His eyes began to shake, and his toes began to throb, all at the same time. His puzzled brain yelled at him to let go of the orb, to let it drop to the floor, to smash the thing into a million different pieces, but something stopped him. He felt something, what he later described as an inner peace. It was a transcendence to another place, a strange place.

Opening his eyes, he was shocked to witness that the boring council meeting room had been replaced by a strange, dark candle-lit room. In the centre of the room was an altar, and stood before the altar was a man.

His hair was thick and grey. It matched his wild and unkempt beard. He wore a simple outfit of white muslin wrapped around his thin body. His arms were held out towards the king, and there was a serene and genuine smile on his face.

'Welcome!'

The word was not spoken aloud, but he could hear it, in his head.

The king dropped the Glimmer.

The instant his contact was lost, the strange electrical bolt dissipated, leaving an odd smell in its wake. The king was back in the meeting room, and he watched, open mouthed, as the orb rolled towards the corner of the room.

Since that day, the Glimmer had been locked in a box and placed in the darkest corner of the castle's deepest dungeon.

~~~~

A few years later, a similar event took place in Azuria.

It was during a jousting competition to celebrate the king's engagement to his young bride-to-be. The day was warm, which was unusual for the Kingdom of Azuria, but it was seen as a blessing for the happy couple. The populous attended by the thousands to witness their hero king take the lance against the best their knights had to offer.

Dressed in his Azurian colours, blue and white, King Fredricco strolled into the jousting arena to tumultuous applause. The men agreed that he looked heroic, and the women agreed that he looked dashing. He gestured towards a stand where several dignitaries were seated, and a young and very pretty lady stood to take her bow. The crowd cheered and whistled again. Fredricco was a popular king, and his wife-to-be was said to be one of the most beautiful women in the land.

Today, everyone agreed with both of these notions.

'Today, we celebrate my engagement to the beautiful Margrite!' the king informed the crowd. 'We shall commence three days of festivities that will culminate with Princess Margrite becoming Queen Margrite of Azuria. And long may she hold that title!'

The crowd went wild again; it was a publicly funded event, and everyone loved a party.

'Before I declare these celebrations open, I would like you to witness a token of my love for this woman.' The king turned to his left and gestured towards a young boy in the crowd. 'Squire. If you will.'

The young man, dressed in chainmail that depicted the flag of Azuria, made his way through the crowd. He was the proud custodian of a small box. Everyone in the crowd watched as he made his way to the Royal Stand. He held the box towards the princess and bowed his head.

'As a token of my undying love and adoration, I pass to you the symbol of our nation of Azuria. It is a Glimmer. It had been passed from king to queen throughout the ages. I now pass it to you so we may pass it to the offspring we bear. Today, my love, I beseech you to accept my gift.'

The squire slid the lid off the box, and the crowd breathed a collective sigh as the blue glow from inside illuminated her already beautiful face.

'I accept your gift, my love!' Princess Margrite shouted so the whole crowd could hear. This was a novel idea of the king, as normally, the possession of the Glimmer passed without ceremony or with the object being handed over symbolically, but King Fredricco, ever the showman, wanted to make a display of it.

It was a display that he would come to regret.

As Margrite reached inside the box, the sky turned dark. There had not been a single cloud prior to this. Everyone, including the princess, and the king on the jousting field, looked upwards, each wondering what could have elicited such a dramatic change in the day.

A heavy cloud hovered over the castle grounds.

It was a cloud like no other.

It shimmied, not unlike the turbulent sea when the winds acted upon it, but it seemed to move independent of the direction of the wind.

The cloud darkened still. It had a look of ink spilling into clear water. A noise could be heard; it was faint but getting louder. It was akin to a high-pitched squeal, or more precisely, many high-pitched squeals.

The cloud then shifted of its own accord, the ink rolled within the glass, and the cloud began to descend upon the castle. Hundreds and thousands of tiny dots constituted the haze as they swooped and swarmed towards the unsuspecting crowd below.

A single scream was enough to start the panic. A single shriek, closely followed by a shout of, 'BATS!'

Leathery wings swooped upon the crowd below. They tangled in people's hair and fluttered their wings in faces. The crowd began to stampede. There were screams of terror and anger as the throng fled from the marauding mammals.

The princess seemed to be the target of the attack as the hub of the cloud headed towards the Royal Stand. The seating area was swamped in swarming darkness, and the muffled screams could barely be heard over the hubbub of the squalling creatures.

The king wasted no time in rushing through the melee towards where his princess was lost in the bat induced mist.

Cutting a swathe through the attackers, he made it to the Royal Stand. He jumped over the bodies of stricken spectators and charged past loyal subjects who were mostly batting the vermin away from their faces. There was an inordinate amount of blood everywhere.

Eventually, he got to the area where Margarite had been sitting as she held the Glimmer. This was where the congregation of the bats was at its thickest. With visibility at close to zero, he could just make out the screaming voice of his bride-to-be from somewhere within the obsidian.

He took a deep breath, gagging at the stench of the winged devils. He swung his sword and cut through the dark veil before him. There was no resistance as the blade slipped effortlessly through the darkness, and he managed a brief, tantalising glimpse of Margarite.

He swung again and again, each time it was like slicing through water. A few of the bats would die and fall from the air, only to be replaced moments later by others.

He continued to swipe at the darkness until he eventually felt his weapon strike something solid.

Almost instantly, the dark curtain of bats began to weaken. It faded, thinner and thinner, as they started to flurry away.

That was when the king saw what it was his sword had struck.

The princess lay on the floor of the Royal Stand, the glowing blue Glimmer next to her. The blue light emanating from it turned the spreading pool of scarlet surrounding it purple. His face fell as horror and grief overtook him.

As the storm of bats flittered away almost as fast as they had appeared, the king's eyes fell upon the body of his love. A deep cut ran the length of her neck, from her ear to her shoulder, and dark, fresh blood pumped from it. The propelling of the blood was in almost perfect timing with the rapid beating of his own heart.

He ran to her and held her, screaming for someone to help.

As the bats disappeared, the king surveyed what was left of his celebrations. The jousting field and the surrounding stands were littered with small, writhing black mammals, but the worst part was what was between the animals. There were bodies, human bodies, his subjects and loyal courtesans, strewn around the area, some moving, others not.

With his eyes stinging from holding back tears, the king shouted for assistance once again. In his shocked state, he never noticed the person who took his princess from his arms.

Princess Margarite survived the attack of the bats, although she was scarred for life from the king's own blade. The cut had damaged her nerves, and the left side of her face was pulled and disfigured.

But the king loved her for who she was, not just for her appearance.

The wedding was postponed but did commence months later, and King Fredricco and Queen Margarite lived to produce five beautiful, healthy children and survived to a very old age together. On quiet nights, she would often regale him with the tale of what she saw all those years ago during the attack of the bats. She would tell him about a large, empty room, empty except for an altar and a strange man standing next to it. A man with unkempt hair and strange clothing who looked like he was welcoming her to wherever she was.

The Glimmer was boxed up and taken away.

It languished in a glass box within the crown jewels vault for hundreds of years.

7.

THE DEVICES both kingdoms had in common, the very things that should have brought them together in a common bond, were locked away and feared.

The secrets and the whispers that came with the imprisonment of the devices was what escalated the tensions between the two kingdoms. The seeds of paranoia began to take root. The individual governments employed spies to work within their neighbouring kingdoms. These spies reported twisted half-truths to the ears of power. Tales of magic that were beyond control. Enchantments that could harness the very weather and control the lightning from the sky. There were tales of communications with animals and armies of monkeys and bats trained in the arts of warfare, ready to attack on command.

Disinformation was rife. It passed back and forth between the kingdoms, and the paranoia grew. What was once an open trading agreement between the nations had grown into distrust and dislike.

Each kingdom thought the other's Glimmer was more powerful than theirs.

Communications began to break down, and finally… war was declared.

It was a war that was to last for over two hundred years.

Both kingdoms were devastated and decimated by the conflict. The fighting took everything from both ways of life.

Generations of men, women, and children were born into the war and died without ever seeing resolution, or indeed peace. It devoured property; it consumed collateral; it took the food out of mouths; it stole everything it could.

And for what?

For the duration, neither kingdom, never once, gained an upper hand. They were too evenly matched. Neither was taken, no king was ever toppled, and the whole affair was fruitless.

Considering the hostilities began because the power of one Glimmer might have surpassed the other, the artefacts themselves were never used in engagement. Both parties were too scared of the very things they were fighting over to consider using them against the other side. In fact, *during* the two hundred years of hostilities, the reason for the fighting was forgotten.

It became a war just for the sake of it.

After far too long, and far too much loss, it was decided that the only way either kingdom could move forward was for a truce to be forged.

A ceasefire was negotiated, it was signed, and both kingdoms agreed to the terms. As neither side lost anything in the negotiations, an era of peace was embarked upon. A peace that had held, sometimes shakily, for nearly five hundred years. Neither side absolutely trusted the other, but trade was once again opened, and travel between the cities was again allowed.

In fact, the family of the sleeping child lying in the bed with her pregnant mother watching over her was instrumental in negotiating the very same truce that both kingdoms still lived under.

~~~~

The mother, the Queen of Azuria, stood and watched her child sleep for a few moments. A tear welled in her eye before falling from her face as she caressed her swollen stomach. The

28

tear was for all she had lost and for what would never be there for the baby in her belly, or the child asleep in her bed.

Children needed a father, and Azuria needed a king. She didn't think she was strong enough to be there for her family and her kingdom.

She was wrong!

8.

AS CASSANDRA AWOKE, the light streaming in from the thin crack in the curtains told her it was already morning and that the sun was shining today. A ball of excitement knotted in her stomach; something big was happening today, but in her sleep fog, she couldn't quite remember what it was.

A commotion from outside her room roused her curiosity, and she prised herself from the comforts of her bed and hurried towards the window overlooking the vast courtyard of the castle.

The child who had been enjoying the bedtime story had grown into a beautiful sixteen-year-old girl. She was blessed with the good looks of her mother, and everyone who met her noted she had inherited her good nature too. She also had the strong leadership skills of her late father.

Her brow ruffled as she watched the people milling about the courtyard, busying themselves, attending to horses and dogs. There were also several dignitaries present, all dressed in hunting clothes. In her sleepy state, it took her a moment to realise what was happening.

'The hunt!' she spat. 'No, I've slept in.'

Frantic not to miss the event she had looked forward to all year, she dashed around the room, throwing clothes everywhere until she found her outfit. Dressed and ready to go within ten minutes, she sprinted towards the courtyard to join her friends and family.

As she rushed onto the cobblestones, she was dismayed to hear the blaring of the horn indicating the start of the hunt. 'Hang on. Wait for me,' she yelled as she battled through the masses of people thronging in the yard, all of them hoping to give the queen a cheer and a good send off on the Great Hunt.

Historically, the hunt had been for the good of the people of Azuria. It was a time when the kings, queens, and knights of the realm would ride out into the surrounding countryside to hunt for food supplies, allowing them to stock for the coming winter. Nowadays, it was a grand gesture, an excuse for a little pomp and circumstance.

Queen Alverna turned on her horse to witness the princess's mad dash and her fight through the crowd. 'Cass, you're too late. I tried to wake you, but you were in a deep sleep.'

'But, Mother, it's the Great Hunt. I can't miss this.'

Her mother smiled as the horn brayed again, signalling the opening of the main gates. As the crowd began to cheer and shout, the queen struggled to be overheard.

'I'm sorry, sweetheart, but you must look after your brother today, you know how he gets when I'm away. It's too late to delay it now.' She offered an apologetic smile at her disappointed daughter. 'I'm sorry, Cass, just watch Alexander.' She then pulled the reins, and her horse turned to join the rest of the Hunt-Tribe exiting the castle grounds.

Cassandra watched them go with a heavy heart.

A small boy pulled on her arm. She looked down at him and frowned at the tears in his eyes. 'Alex, what's the matter? Why are you crying?'

'I wanted to go on the hunt.'

She laughed, not condescendingly but in appreciation of the charm of the good-natured boy. 'You know you're too young to ride with the Hunt-Tribe.'

'But I'm the Prince of Azuria, my place is next to my queen. I should be there to protect her at all times. It's not fair. I'm a better rider than most of them,' he sobbed, wiping tears from his eyes.

Cassandra put her arm around her brother and squeezed him. 'Of course you are, but as you say, you're the Prince of Azuria. If you were out there, protecting Mother, who would be in here protecting the realm?'

Alexander looked at his sister, his tears dried up in an instant, and he straightened his back as if he was growing into the role Cassandra had just described for him. 'You're right, Sister. I do have to protect the realm.'

Cassandra bent and whispered into his ear. 'I'll let you into a secret. The hunt is boring; all they do is jog along on their horses talking politics. The first time I went, I thought I'd feel the rush of the wind in my hair as I galloped through fields, jumped hedges and ditches, and fought ferocious beasts one on one.' Alexander was looking up at her, his eyes lost in a dream of faraway glory. 'But nope. All they do is yap, yap, yap, then one of the hunt hounds will catch a scent. There will be a little running, someone will shoot at a small beast with a bow and arrow, they will miss! Everyone will cheer, and that's it, done for another year.' She stood up straight and watched as the people in the courtyard began to disperse to do their chores and tasks for the day. 'Come, Alex, I'll race you to the kitchens. No doubt they'll be steaming the puddings for the feast tonight. Maybe we can get a pot to lick.'

The child was back in Alex's eyes at the thought of steamed pudding and licking the mixture from the pot. He laughed and sped off without notice. 'Bet you I win,' he shouted.

She laughed before speeding off after him.

9.

THE HORSES CAREENED through the countryside, frightening the smaller animals as their hooves thundered through the bushes and the undergrowth. Their riders, unaware of the carnage they were causing to the animals' habitats, were busy talking about important business of the realm.

Queen Alverna had once loved the Great Hunt. She had adored the adrenalin-fuelled gallops with her husband at her side. She, with her young girl's eyes and fast beating heart, and him, with his handsome profile and intensity in his ride. He had never allowed business talk until after the beast had been caught, or at least shot at, and they were on their way back to the castle.

Secretly, she always loved the way her husband never allowed the beast to be slaughtered. He always said that it deserved a better chance than being run down by a pack of riders accompanied by hunt hounds.

She had also never been a fan of talking business, even though it had been thrust upon her after her husband's death. She had always found it to be a bore. An exercise of patting each other on the back, even for projects that failed. The people in charge of these projects were receiving rewards for trying. It seemed like madness to her, and in truth, she wanted nothing to do with it.

Today, she was running behind the pack, enjoying the beauty of the countryside, the smell of wet leaves, and the mild weather that was an Azurian spring. A fat merchant was riding next to her and had been regaling her with a report about something or other. She had no idea who the man was or what the conversation was even about.

'So, Your Majesty, I'm of the belief that the security forces in the city must be improved. Just because we've had an extended period of peace, this should not mean we let our defensive stature slip,' the man continued, even though she was paying him very little attention.

It was then she realised that this might be an important conversation and something she needed to listen to. 'Are the Carnelians not our allies now the war is over?'

'Yes, Your Highness, they are. But one should not slip into complacency just because we have cordial relations. If I cannot get funds allocated to employ more men to guard the city, may I have permissions to …'

As the man continued to waffle, something caught her eye, thankfully diverting her from this most boring conversation. 'What was that?' she asked no one in particular before galloping off ahead of the boring man.

'Right, well thank you for your time, Your Highness,' he called after her, shaking his head.

She had already forgotten about him, far more concerned about what she had seen. 'Commander,' she called to the uniformed man not too far ahead. 'Commander, are you seeing what I'm seeing?' She had to shout to be heard over the hooves of the entourage as she advanced through the pack towards the military escort.

The commander slowed his horse some yards ahead of her and turned to regard the queen charging towards him. The three men flanking him had not taken their eyes off the strange event that was occurring before them between the trees. All conversations had stopped as everyone watched the queen gallop past them towards their escort.

'I see it, ma'am. I was just about to employ men to investigate it. In the meantime, if you and the other dignitaries could hold back, I'm sure it won't take long.'

The hunt hounds had gathered around the horses' legs. All of them doing their very best not to look at the phenomenon before them, their tails were tucked firmly between their legs and most had fallen into a strange, skittery silence.

The black mist hanging in the trees looked like it was seeping from the very forest that surrounded it. Wisps, dark, smoky fingers, probed from it as if it was a sentient being and was testing its surroundings.

'If you would be so kind as to step back, ma'am,' the commander urged her again. 'We'll have this investigated as soon as we can. The hunt will resume as normal shortly.'

'Yes, Commander, of course. Whatever's best,' Alverna replied, turning her horse away from the men. The merchant who had been talking to her earlier sidled his mount next to hers and offered her a nervous smile. She replied in kind, although her eyes told him that she wasn't interested in continuing their conversation.

Silently, the members of the hunt party watched as two guardsmen approached the odd, undulating haze. Both men looked fearless, but their horses didn't. They were troubled by the darkness and whatever lay beyond it.

As she watched, the two men disappeared into the mist. A strange feeling overcame her. It ran through her body, causing her to shiver. The merchant offered his cloak. 'No, thank you,' she replied courteously. 'I'm not cold.'

'But you need to keep your strength up,' he replied, not relenting his offer.

The party had fallen silent; even the commander was quiet as he stared into the mist. She could tell he was worried about the men he had deployed, but he was also worried for his wards. The entire party was under his protection, including her.

The remaining men of the guard had positioned themselves into a defensive posture surrounding her. Their manoeuvre squeezed out the merchant from this protective circle, much to his obvious disappointment.

She noted the silence in the woods was definitive, absolute.

Not a bird sang in the trees, the dogs were silent, there were no nervous whinnies from the horses. She coughed, not because she needed to but because she wanted to test if her hearing was still working; it was that quiet.

It stayed like that for a short while. *The calm before the storm,* Alverna thought, scaring herself in the process.

Then suddenly, there was a sound.

The queen's horse was first to react. Soon, everyone was reacting, including the guards, the commander, and the dogs. It began as a muffled shout, nothing coherent, but it sent the same shiver up her back as she had experienced earlier. There was something about the shout, something that made it seem more like a scream.

It was high pitched, and it was female. It tore from the mist like an arrow from a bow, affecting everyone in the group. The dignitaries began pulling their horses away from the phenomenon. Subconsciously, or not, putting distance between themselves and the alien sounds coming from the mist.

The scream came again, this time sounding closer.

'Protect the queen! Get her as far away from here as—'

The soldier didn't have time to finish his command as something dark and huge bolted from the mist. Acting on instinct and training, the commander charged towards the darkness and buried his longsword deep into whatever monstrosity was spewing from the dark maw.

The group reared, the horses and their riders all panicking.

When the excitement and the hideous scream from the mysterious beast had died down, it took a moment for everyone to register that the monster the commander had so courageously attacked was nothing more than a horse. A horse that was sporting the colours of Azuria. The stricken animal lay on the ground dying with the commander's longsword protruding from its ribs. When he realised what it was, he dismounted to inspect it. He looked at all the eyes that were upon him, human, dog, and horse alike, and flicked his foppish hair back from his face before putting his boot on the animal's neck and removing his weapon from its body.

Tangled in the horse's stirrup was what was left of a severed leg. This appendage was also dressed in the Azurian colours. Its boot was still attached to the stirrup. All the eyes shifted from the commander towards the offensive, bloody stump. Hanging from the leather straps, it looked bizarre, almost as if it wasn't real, like something from a mannequin used for combat practice. The difference being mannequins didn't bleed.

The silence descended upon the group again as, one by one, they all stared into the mist.

The queen looked hard into the cloud. She was sure the darkness, the one that had taken one of her men, was advancing. The scene was strangely serene. No one panicked or ran away, which was something she would have expected from most of the merchants and dignitaries present. *I'm glad Cass isn't here,* she thought as the mist continued towards the group.

Another scream came from within, and this time, everything changed. It brought with it a catastrophic chain of events.

The merchant who had offered the queen his cloak shrunk from the scream, backing his horse from the advancing mist. As he did, the horse stepped onto a dead log on the ground. The log snapped loudly, and the horse spooked. The fat merchant pulled the reins too hard, and it reared, tossing the man from his saddle like a ragdoll. Hysteria rippled through the group, and all the guests began to flee, steering their mounts through the trees in a haphazard fashion. The merchant was trampled by one of the horses. The screams he emitted as his bones snapped beneath the powerful hooves were ignored as self-preservation took over and the dignitaries bolted from the clearing.

The mist was still moving, encroaching on the fleeing party at a faster pace now than it had been, as if in pursuit of its potential victims. Wispy tendrils grasped at the thick tree trunks and branches, facilitating its advance on the party, or what was left of it.

'Protect the queen,' the commander shouted again as he raised his sword to face the unknown adversary.

The protective circle around Alverna tightened, and the five men guarding her unsheathed their longswords. She also unsheathed her own weapon. It was her husband's longsword, and she knew how to use it.

Two of the fleeing guests inadvertently drove their horses into the advancing mist and were quickly swallowed. Muffled screams were heard from the darkness shortly thereafter; two of them were human, the others, equestrian.

'What the hell is happening here?' the commander shouted as he stood his ground, watching the advancing mist. 'Get the queen away. Do it now,' he barked.

The five guardsmen reared their mounts, turning away from whatever foe they faced, and forced her horse in the opposite direction, the direction the rest of the hunt party had fled. On turning, they were more than dismayed to find the darkness had now encircled them. The shifting, undulating entity had surrounded them, cutting off any and all routes of escape. Distant screams echoed from all directions, all of them issuing from within the mist. Alverna guessed they were from the rest of the party.

'Sir, there's no way out. We're surrounded,' one of the guards reported over the muted cacophony of the muffled screams.

'Dismount and prepare to engage,' the commander ordered. 'Ma'am, we'll get you out of this. One way or another, we *will* get you to safety.'

The guards, to their credit, were ready. Swords were raised at whatever they were facing, whatever was within the fog causing the unholy screams. Alverna dismounted her steed and stood shoulder to shoulder with her men. The commander looked at her, aghast that his queen was ready and willing to fight with him. He went to her and took her by the shoulder, roughly spinning her around. 'Ma'am, I can't allow this. You're the queen and I will not—'

'Will not what, Commander?' she asked.

'I … erm, I meant no …'

'No, I don't suppose you did,' she hissed. 'I'll not sit upon my horse as my people die around me. I know how to use this weapon, and I'm willing to use it against whatever is in there. I want to get back to Azuria, Commander, back to my children.'

There was a steely resilience in her eyes, and the commander smiled. 'If you're staying, ma'am, then you heed my every word and you don't question my orders, not even once. Do you understand?'

The queen adjusted her grip on the hilt of her husband's sword and looked past the commander towards the surrounding mist. She winked and tipped him a smile. 'Understood, Commander. Now let's deal with this and get home.'

'Men, circle formation. Nothing gets through, do you hear me? Nothing!'

The men shouted their acknowledgement, as did Alverna, as the mist advanced.

10.

CASSANDRA AND ALEXANDER were leaving the kitchens, their bellies filled with leftover steamed pudding, both sporting satisfied grins. They were heading back to the royal residence; Alexander had studying to do, and Cass was determined not to let him skip on anything just because their mother was away for the day.

'Do I really have to read twenty pages?' he asked, his face pained.

'Yes, you do. And the quicker you do it, the quicker we can go fishing in the stream.'

His face changed in an instant. 'Really? Today?'

She nodded. 'Yes, and as mother is away, you can do your reading in the meadow next to the stream. There's no reason to keep you indoors on a day like this.'

The boy threw his arms around his sister. 'Oh, Cass, you're the best. I wish you were the queen.'

'Don't say that, Alex. Mother's the queen, and long may she reign,' she half chastised the child while stifling her laughter.

'I know, but just for today, I wish you were the queen.'

She chuckled and hurried her brother along.

11.

THE MIST SKULKED towards them like an animal stalking its prey through the trees. It guzzled the foliage and wildlife around, but what worried Alverna most was the ground it was swallowing. In less than a minute, it had halved the distance between them and was still coming.

'Stand your ground and protect the queen as much as you can,' the commander shouted as it edged closer.

'None of you worry about me!' she countered. 'Keep yourselves safe and let's get through this together. That's a royal decree, by the way,' she joked. 'I'm not missing the hunt feast for anyone.'

The men laughed at the joke. Her husband had always taught her that when you faced certain death, face it with a smile and the Great Lord Glimm would be merciful. This was a situation that called for humour if ever she had been in one.

The mist continued, enveloping everything in its path. Visibility was restricted as it surrounded their tight circle. All seven of them gripped their weapons, ready to defend against whatever was causing the muffled screams.

Alverna swallowed, it hurt her throat, but she hardly noticed. For the very first time in her life, she was petrified. She could see no way out of this situation as the mist crept so close that it almost touched her nose. Then, without warning, it wrapped itself around her, absorbing her into its icy embrace.

She felt rather than saw the guard next to her swing his sword towards some unseen adversary before a heavy swooping sound made her stagger back from her defensive position. A stifled cry followed by a wet snapping told her all she needed to know.

There was a humming in the air. It was a heavy, oppressive throb that ached inside her head. She could just about make out large, undefined shapes that were lurking in the murky depths of the sea of mist before her. There was another scream, and another guard was ripped from his position. Mercifully, his shouts were muffled by the shifting mist. Sweat lined her palms. It dripped from her hairline as she adjusted her grip on the hilt of her husband's sword. 'Commander? Commander, are you still standing?' she half shouted, half whispered, hoping beyond hope for a reply.

'I'm here, ma'am,' he replied to her relief. 'I can't see you! Visibility is absolute zero.'

'Same here. I think two men have been taken.'

'I think there may be more than—'

The commander never finished his sentence; his last words merged with his own wet scream into the cold, dense fog.

Alverna shifted her position, hoping to see what had happened to the commander. Something large bashed into her. It knocked the wind out of her and pushed her backwards. Her husband's sword, her only defence, spilled from her hands. She fell. As she did, something snapped beneath her. She had no idea what it could have been, but she had more pressing issues, like the fact that whatever had rushed her, and knocked her down, was now on top of her.

A thin, warm wetness dripped onto her.

She braced herself for the attack, closing her eyes and turning her head to protect her face. But the assault never came. After a moment, she risked opening an eye. Still trying to push the weight of her would-be attacker from her, she saw that the beast was mere inches from her face. The wetness dripping on her was blood. It dripped from her attacker's face, from its open mouth. She wanted to scream but couldn't risk it. She didn't want the hot, coppery liquid entering her mouth. To her dismay, and to her sorrow, she recognised her attacker, understanding that it wasn't a beast at all.

It was the commander.

His eyes were wide and pink. Thick, fresh blood was pouring from his nose and mouth. His skin was waxy, and it took her a moment to realise the man was dead.

With a shriek, she pushed the cadaver off her. The body fell onto its back on the forest floor. That was when she saw the wound in his chest. Thick, almost black blood and bright, ugly pink intestines slopped from the large wound. Steam rose from it in the cool of the afternoon. Alverna offered a small, panicked prayer as she watched his soul rise from the wound to disappear into the ether.

As there was no longer the threat of swallowing blood, the scream that had been trapped inside her finally found an exit.

The sound was muffled by the mist, and she guessed there was no one left to hear it anyway.

The thing that had snapped beneath her earlier, she now learned to her dismay, had been her ankle. As she tried to lever herself up from the ground, hoping to get away from whatever was causing this horror, her screaming ankle wouldn't allow it. She fell unceremoniously onto her backside, clutching the swollen joint.

Gritting her teeth, she pulled herself backwards, resting her body against a sturdy tree. She was exhausted and terrified, not for her own life, she was fully resigned to her fate after seeing the dead commander, but for her children. Cassandra and Alexander. They would now be orphans.

Knowing they were a useless gesture; she wiped the tears forming in the corners of her eyes and looked around. To her astonishment, the mist was retreating. It wasn't just abating; it was disappearing faster than it had appeared. Within moments, she found herself out of the swirling black hell and back in the small clearing. Around her were the strewn bodies of six guards, the commander included. All of them slaughtered, each with large, gaping holes adorning their chests and abdomens, similar if not identical to the one that had killed the commander.

She was alone.

Only, she wasn't as quite as alone as she thought.

The heavy thrumming noise she felt rather than heard earlier was back. It pulsed the air around her. She could feel it in her teeth, in her chest, in her head. She tried to shift her body, wincing at the pain from her twisted ankle. The noise grew heavier and, at the same time, louder.

Dark shapes began to appear in what was left of the mist. She tried to use the tree trunk behind her as a crutch to aid her standing up. Whatever it was coming for her, she was damned if she wouldn't meet it standing up.

If today was her day to die, she was going to do it like the queen she was!

It was, however, a useless gesture. The sharp shards of agony shooting from her ankle were crippling her. There was no way they were going to allow her to stand upright. As she gave in to the pain, dropping back down with a disgusted grunt, she looked around her. Her sword, the one that had been her husband's, was lying beneath the lifeless corpse of the commander. She reached, attempting to move him out of the way, to gain some purchase on her possible salvation. After a short struggle, her head began to swim as her ankle screamed at her. The sword, however, gave, and she managed to pull it free.

Small victories, she laughed to herself.

Using both hands, she held the weapon aloft, pointing it towards the thinning mist with the strange dangerous shapes lurking inside. A whisper tickled her ear. She flicked her head, surprised at what she'd heard. She scanned the trees, but all she could see were the slain guards, trees, and fog. She fancied the whisper had come from trees themselves, or maybe the mossy ground, or even the clear sky above her, but realised all that was folly; it was her mind playing games with her head.

'Alvernnnnnnaaaaaaa!' the whisper came again.

She knew this time it was not in her head. It *was* coming from the mist.

She grasped her sword tighter, not liking the way the hilt slid in her sweat-lined palms. She held the heavy weapon aloft anyway. 'Who's there? Show yourself, you coward!'

'Alvernnnnnnaaaaaaa!'

Something stroked the back of her hair. She snapped her head around, bringing the sword with her. Her ankle screamed louder than the whisper, but somehow, she was able to put it to the back of her mind. She shouted into the mist again. 'Who's there? Show yourself! In the name of Azuria, I command you to show yourself.'

A red glow issued from the thickest area of haze. Two large red circles were cutting through the murk. Her heart thudded against her ribs as she squinted.

A terrible thought dawned on her.

Wolves!

The two spheres were joined very quickly by another pair, and then another. Soon, the mist was full of them, red, glowing, and pulsing in the coming darkness. The thrumming in the air was horrible, making her head swim. She closed her eyes and uttered a small prayer to the Glimm. *Whoever you are!* she thought with more than a touch of cynicism. The Great Lord Glimm, who she had been taught from an early age to pray to. She had always thought there was too much unknown about their god. Who was he, and why did they pray to him?

This was no time to begin debating theology, there were far more pressing matters requiring her immediate attention. The foremost being the hungry pack of wolves, who could mysteriously stab people through the heart and manifest an ugly, crawling mist.

The eyes were now everywhere, surrounding her, remaining just inside the mist, out of sight. It was a strange phenomenon to her. She knew wolves hunted as a pack and would keep their distance, but once the prey was defenceless, they became bold and would attack ferociously. *Also, there's enough easy prey scattered around for the wolves to feast on for a month. Why aren't they content with that?*

The eyes began to advance.

She pressed her back to the tree and gripped her sword tighter. She was ready to swing at the first, second, and even third beast who would spring out from the mist and attack her.

The throbbing noise intensified.

It was coming from everywhere. From the trees themselves, the ground, the sky. It escalated into a buzz, thrumming through the soil she sat upon. It was in her head, in her bones.

The silhouettes in the mist began to grow, and she noticed they were not wolves. They were far too tall to be from the canine species, plus, they seemed to be … hovering!

Taking another dry swallow, she attempted to shift her position, but her ankle had swollen, and any movement, no matter how small, sent her head spinning with pain.

Her whole body was shaking. 'Show yourselves, you cowards,' she screamed into the mist, tasting blood in her throat as she did. The fog receded again, revealing more of the devastation of her hunt party. Dead horses and lifeless dignitaries were abound, each sporting wounds, penetrating their chests and abdomens. She tried not to look at them as she focused on the dark silhouettes before her.

The buzz in the air grew again, as the shapes moved out of the mist. She had never before seen anything quite like what the mist revealed.

12.

'SOMETHING IS WRONG!' Alexander turned his face towards his sister as they both waded out into the stream, each armed with fishing rods, reels, and a copious amount of bait.

Cassandra looked at her brother. It was always her opinion that he looked far too serious for a boy his age, his features too old for his years. But there was something different about him now, something deep. A flutter of panic passed through her, chilling her, it had nothing to do with the bite of the cold the water. 'What is it, Alex?' she asked, not really wanting to know what the boy was thinking but needing to all the same.

He stared at her, his young face running a gauntlet of emotions.

'Alex, I asked you a question. What isn't right? What's wrong?'

His ten-year-old blue eyes widened, and he shook his head. His stare was fixed on her.

'Alex, you're scaring me. What's not right?' she demanded.

As suddenly as it had appeared, the strange look lifted, and he smiled at her. The innocent boy was back, but Cassandra was still not happy.

'Alex?' she scolded. 'Tell me.'

'I … I just think we've brought the wrong rods to catch salmon. I think these ones are for trout,' he replied, holding up the thin rod. 'I don't think they'll hold the salmon. They're too wild, but we can try.'

Cassandra could feel her heart pounding in her throat and ears as she looked at her brother, but she couldn't help breaking into a smile. She shook her head and waded further into the cold stream, holding her rod and reel above her head. 'Well, it's all we've got! They'll have to do. Now come on and let's catch some fish for the feast tonight.'

The siblings, neither of them knowing they were about to become orphans, laughed as they waded through the stream looking for the best place to catch salmon.

13.

ALVERNA COULDN'T BELIEVE what she was seeing. Her eyes widened, filling with a petrified wonder as her grip on her husband's sword wavered, much like her grip on sanity. 'What the Glimm?' The question dripped from her mouth, and she was unaware she had even spoken the words aloud.

The figures that had been hiding within the mist revealed their true magnificent and terrifying form to her. She now understood how her guards and the hunt guests had received their wounds.

Huge red eyes glowed from small black heads. Long, curved bodies hovered a foot or so from the forest floor. Small, gossamer wings beat furiously. It was this that caused the bone shaking hum she could feel rippling through her body. The bloated, glowing bodies of the beasts were striped yellow and black, and at the bottoms of their huge, impossible bodies was the most fearful thing she had ever seen in her life. Long, lethal stings protruded from the bodies of the unnaturally large insects. Each sting dripped with a thick, semi-permeable liquid. Even though there was no way of knowing, she was sure the sap dripping from these beasts was toxic.

Ignoring her screaming ankle, she dragged herself from the floor, putting all her weight on one thick branch behind her while holding her sword uselessly towards the beasts. 'What are you?' she screamed over her pain. 'Who sent you?'

She swiped at the nearest one, but it was too far away from her blade to have impact.

They kept on coming.

Hundreds of them emerged from the murky depths surrounding her. She was trapped. Her back rubbed against the tree as she looked around; to her dismay, there were as many behind as there were before.

One of the beasts moved forward, advancing a little closer than the others. Alverna could smell the toxicity of the sap dripping from the end of its sting, like a fierce alcohol. The insectoid face stared at her with black, alien eyes. With the last of her failing strength, she swiped again at the hideous creature. This time, the strike was true. The blade cut through the creature's bloated body. The scream it issued was high-pitched and painful to hear.

Thick ichor flowed as its wings slowed their beat. It fell to the ground and curled, its wounded thorax and sting meeting its own face.

There, it died.

Buoyed by this small victory she raised her sword again. The ichor was dripping from the tip as she swung, warning the other insects to stay away from her.

They ignored her, or at least three of them did.

Two approached from behind. Their thick legs gripped her, their incredible strength making short work of pinning her to the tree and forcing the sword from her hands.

She thrashed, trying to free herself from her repulsive captors. It was all to no avail. Their strength was superior to hers, and the agony in her ankle, coupled with the terrors she was witnessing, made her head spin.

A third beast hovered forward from the crowd. As it drew closer, it regarded its dead colleague on the floor. Alverna snarled into its hideous face. She was building herself up to spitting at it, a useless tactic, she knew, but it was the only defiance she could manage.

Then something strange, something her brain had trouble fathoming, occurred.

The red eyes of the beast began to change. The antenna at the top of its head began to recede. Its whole body began to transform. With a series of grotesque and sickening cracks, the beast became less insectoid, and more … human!

She blinked as the transformation completed in less than a minute.

A woman was now stood before her. Long, silver hair flowed in the afternoon's breeze. Her features were of an undiscernible age, not young but also not aged enough to be considered old. Alverna could see that she had once been pretty, a great beauty maybe, but her wild and unkempt appearance had put paid to any fairness she may have owned what looked like an age ago.

The woman smiled at her.

'Who … what are you? What do you want?' Alverna spat. Her breathing was shallow and laboured as she struggled against the beasts restraining her. 'Do I know you?'

'Alvernnnnnnnnnnnnnnnaaaaaaaaaaa,' the woman whispered; it was the same whisper that had come from the mist.

Was that only moments ago? she asked herself. 'What do you want? Unhand me at once. We can work this through; I am the queen of—'

'I know who you are, Alverna,' the woman said. Her voice was a deep whisper that reverberated around the clearing. 'I know *exactly* who you are. I chose you specifically for my purpose.'

'And what purpose is that?'

'Revenge!'

'Revenge?' Alverna repeated, genuinely confused. 'Revenge against who?'

'Everyone!' the woman replied. She laughed then, and the twinkle in her eye spoke of a youth long lost. She produced a longsword from her long purple robe and brandished it at her.

Alverna took a moment to look at it, noticing that it bore the markings of Carnelia.

'What is the meaning of this? Azuria and Carnelia have been allies for hundreds of years.'

'This has nothing to do with Azuria and Carnelia.' The woman smiled. 'Yet, it has *everything* to do Azuria and Carnelia. You, Queen Alverna, are no ally to me. You are nothing more than a means to an end.'

'Who are you?' Alverna stuttered, repeating her question. The oddity of the situation had drawn all the fight from her. She looked at the legion of fireflies hovering around her, and a single tear fell from her eye. It created a track through the dirt that covered her face.

There was something hanging from the belt of the stranger's cloak. She only got a flash of it hiding in the folds of the material, but the red glow coming from it could not be hidden. She recognised it from somewhere but was not sure where.

'My name is long since forgotten, but as you have the right to know your executioner's identity, I will tell you. It has no bearing on the situation. My name is Endellion.' As soon as the words left her mouth, she swung the Carnelian sword she held. The swing was filled with determination, and it was true.

The lethal metal did its work.

In compliment to the maintenance of the sword, Queen Alverna's head was severed from her body in one swing.

Endellion bent and picked it up, she looked into the wide, lifeless eyes and laughed. 'Take her body to her horse,' she commanded the fireflies. They did her bidding without hesitation, their wings beating faster as they rose into the air, carrying Alverna's headless body with them. They flew her to where her horse was standing, shaking, and steaming, surrounded by the huge creatures. They laid her body over the saddle. Endellion carried the head to the horse and opened one of the saddle bags. After removing and discarding the contents, she inserted the head inside. She then took the Carnelian sword and drove it through the queen's body, careful not to spear the horse beneath.

'Home,' she whispered into the beast's ear before slapping it hard on the rump.

The horse whinnied and sped off into the trees, in the direction of the Kingdom of Azuria.

Endellion grinned as she watched it run.

14.

NIGHT FELL ON the kingdom of Azuria, and the hunt-party had not yet returned. People had gathered in the great hall, excited and ready to commence the festivities, but even though the food was already on the table, no one had touched a bite.

Even the scavenger dogs that occupied the palace had sensed there was something wrong and had taken off to see what bounties could be found elsewhere.

The atmosphere was dire. The royal aides were doing their best to keep everyone's spirits up, especially Cassandra's, but it was a difficult, if not impossible, task. Something was amiss, that much was obvious. The hunt-party had never been late in the entire recorded history of the event.

Alexander was in a corner of the hall with four of his friends; they had been playing the same game of tag for over an hour. Cassandra was looking at him, envious of his innocence of the situation. The situation that no one was talking about.

Something had gone wrong at the hunt.

The boy looked up and waved at her. She caught it and returned it with a forced smile, hoping he couldn't see through the façade of her emotions. She didn't want to ruin his game, his night, and, quite possibly, his life.

'Princess, we must send out a patrol. It's obvious they have run into difficulty out there,' Anthony, her mother's closest advisor, whispered into her ear. 'Whispers abound. The people need to know why there is no celebration.'

Cassandra looked at him. Her stare persisted longer than was comfortable for either of them before he bowed his head.

'Let us allow Alex another hour of playtime before the grief of this night takes his innocence away,' she whispered.

'Very well, Your Majesty,' Anthony agreed as he backed away from the young girl, the one he now thought of as his queen.

Cassandra snapped her head around and glared at him. Her look was as fierce as the fire in her eyes. 'I'm not Y*our Majesty*, Anthony. I am Y*our Grace* at best. Please, do not forget that,' she scolded.

'My apologies, Your Grace.'

A shout from the courtyard rang through the great hall, and everyone present stopped what they were doing and looked towards the disturbance. Cassandra, however, had to look the other way. She needed to see where her brother was and what he was doing. She was disturbed to find him standing on his own in the corner, all his friends, it seemed, had left him, and he was looking over towards where the people were congregating to see what the shout was about. His face told her a number of truths. Not the least of them, the fact that he knew. He knew he was now an orphan! He knew their mother would never again tuck him into bed and tell him tales of the Glimm.

'Anthony,' Cassandra called over to the man who was now *her* advisor. 'Get Alex out of here, he doesn't need to see this.'

Anthony looked at her. 'What, Your Grace?'

'Alex! Get him away from here. I fear there's nothing good about that shout. I fear, with the delay of the hunt-party, it can only mean one thing. My brother does not need to see what happens next.'

'Yes, my lady,' he answered and gestured towards two maids who were trying to see what was happening at the window but knew they couldn't leave their stations. Twice he tried to catch their attention. 'Take Prince Alexander to his chambers.

Princess Cassandra doesn't want him to witness what is occurring here.'

'What *is* happening, my lord?' one of them asked, quite forgetting who it was she was talking to.

'None of your business. Now do as I bid and remove the prince.'

The maid turned toward Anthony and her face flushed red. 'I'm so sorry, my lord. Right away.' She took hold of the other maid's hand, and they made their way towards where the young boy was standing on his own.

The pallor of his complexion was alarming to the girls, and to his sister as he cast a gaze towards her while being ushered from the banquet room. She could see the pleading in his eyes, and it was all she could do not to turn away from him. She wanted to, but knew that if she did, she would lose his confidence for the difficult times ahead, maybe even the rest of his life. She knew he needed her now like he'd never needed anything or anyone else in the world. But at this moment, she needed him gone. She mouthed the words 'go to bed' over to him, and the sadness in his face broke her heart.

After a moment's hesitation, he accepted the offered hands of the maids.

Cass's heart left the room with him as he turned, just once, to look at her before disappearing.

Her attention then returned to the pressing matter of what was happening over the other side of the room.

The commotion was coming from the courtyard and had already reached almost fever pitch. She pushed her way through the throng, towards the door where everyone had gathered. She thought it funny, she didn't even know for certain what was happening outside, yet she now thought of these people as hers. Several soldiers had congregated by the gates to the castle, creating a perimeter around something that was in the centre of the courtyard. As she walked out of the great hall, every pair of eyes turned to look at her. She felt the weight of every Azurian's gaze. Her skin prickled as her face flushed a deep crimson.

She battled through the crowd. In truth, it wasn't much of a fight as the people moved out of her way with ease. None of them wanted to look her in the face or even meet her eyes as she challenged them. Their heads either bowed low or turned away as a path opened before her.

There was something in the centre of the yard.

She could only just make it out.

It was a horse.

It was her mother's horse.

She felt every beat of her heart as her vision tunnelled and her head began to whirl. As she got closer to the petrified beast, the world spun, and she thought a blackout was less than a hairsbreadth away.

The brown and white pelt of the beast was matted in something dark that reflected the dancing lights of the candles.

Then she saw it.

A headless body was laid over the bridle of the horse's back. It was wearing the same clothing her mother had worn when she left that morning.

It took her a few moments to put the pieces of the gruesome jigsaw together.

The courtyard was silent.

The last thing Cassandra remembered before the threatening blackout finally took her was the broadsword bearing the symbol of Carnelia jutting from the lifeless, headless body of the Queen of Azuria, her mother.

'Don't let Alex see this,' she whispered to Anthony, who was at her side as she faltered. 'Don't let him see this. He's too young!'

With these words, she fell into a dark and dreamless sleep right there on the cobbled floor of the courtyard.

15.

EIGHTEEN HOURS LATER, Cassandra opened her eyes. She was in her own bed, and the late afternoon sun was streaming in through the window, as the thick, blue curtains were held back with golden rope.

Someone was fussing around inside the room. She could hear the tinkle of water pouring from a jug coupled with the smell of cooked meat. Her stomach gurgled, and her tired face broke into a smile. 'Mother, what time is it? Have I slept late?'

The silhouette in front of the window stopped what it was doing and turned to face her. She eased herself up in the bed, fluffing her own pillows, ready to accept the breakfast. 'Why did you let me sleep so late? And on such a nice day too.'

Without speaking, the silhouette removed the cover from the metallic bowl next to her, and the aroma of sausages and eggs filled the room. Her stomach responded to the smell with another loud, agreeable grumble.

The silhouette carried the breakfast to her. It was then that she realised it wasn't her mother, it was a maid.

This realisation brought the events of the previous day crashing back to her reality.

Her mother was gone.

She was never going to return.

She had seen things no sixteen-year-old girl should ever see.

'Your Majesty. I'm so glad you're awake,' the maid whispered with a sad smile. 'I have someone who's very anxious to see you.'

With that, the door to her chambers burst open and a tearful Alexander rushed in, brushing past the maid and diving onto the bed.

'Cass, is it true what they are saying? Is it? Please tell me it's not true. Mother ...'

She took the boy into her arms and looked up at the maid, her smile lost now and her eyes welling with tears. 'Please, give me a moment with my brother.'

The maid nodded before turning and exiting the room.

'They said she had no head, Cass. But she did have a head, I know she did. I saw it every day.' The boy was sobbing into his sister's nightgown, his tears melting into the stitching, merging with her own, which were now flowing freely. 'Did she have a head?'

Swallowing her sob, Cassandra breathed a deep, shaky breath. 'Of course she has, Alex. Whoever told you that was lying, or you misheard them.'

'Is she really gone?' the boy asked, removing his face from her nightshirt, and looking at her with blue eyes tinged with red.

She held his head tight and rested it once again on her chest. Stroking his dark hair, she offered him as much comfort as she could afford. 'She has, Alex. She's gone to be with father in Koll'Su.'

'I thought you'd gone too when you wouldn't wake up. I thought you'd gone and left me all alone.' His small voice was muffled against the fabric of her gown, but the sorrow and longing were not lost within the confines of it.

'I've not gone, Alex. You can see me and feel me here. Should we play today? Just you and me? We'll go to the stream and fish and run and ... just be together all day.'

Alexander looked up at her again. 'You can't today, Cass. You banged your head when you fell. You have a bandage around it.'

She lifted her hand to feel her forehead, and sure enough, there was a swathe of material coving her head. No sooner had she touched it, pain filtered into her brain, and she felt weak.

The maid appeared again.

'There'll be no playing for you, Your Majesty. You must rest, at least today, and probably tomorrow too.'

She called me 'Your Majesty'... she thought abstractly. *Shouldn't I be Your Grace?* After that thought left her head, the weight of knowledge of who she now was to these people descended on her.

'I have to walk through the gardens with my brother,' she answered. 'We have much to talk about. He needs me.'

'I must protest …'

'I have a ten-year-old brother who has just lost his mother. I have a duty to him. You may assist me, but I *will* walk with him through the gardens,' she snapped, instantly feeling bad that she did.

The maid bowed her head and stepped back. 'As you say, Your Majesty.'

I really am queen now, Cassandra thought.

'Alex, we'll walk in the gardens. I may not be able to play and run, but I will accompany you. Your queen needs your protection.'

A smile spread across his face, so wide that it was hard for her to imagine what he looked like without it.

16.

AS THE SIBLINGS strolled through the gardens hand in hand, there was a much larger security detail in place than usual. Armed men were stationed around every corner, behind every bush or tree, and all of them were watching the royals' every move closely. In her heart, Cassandra couldn't believe that Carnelia could perform such an overt act of war against her nation. There had been peace for hundreds of years.

There was absolutely nothing to gain from it.

Alexander was subdued, much as she'd expected him to be.

When they reached their favourite spot, the bench that overlooked the orchard, she sat on the bench—so placed for users to enjoy the view, which was especially delightful at sunset. A sigh of relief escaped her as her brother sat next to her.

'Are you all right? Does your head still hurt?'

She removed her hand from her still bandaged head and smiled. 'Yes, it does. It throbs and aches, as does my heart.'

He looked at her, his face was a mask of pain.

'I miss her already,' he sobbed as a tear trickled down his face, acting as an exclamation point to his statement.

'So do I,' she whispered. She wanted, *no,* she thought, *I need to stay brave and strong for him.* 'You know Mother is now in Koll'Su with Father, and they're looking down on us as we speak, and they are smiling. Their love will get us through this.

So please don't be sad, Brother. I need a strong, brave knight to look after me. You know I'm the queen now, don't you?'

A small smile cracked on his sad face as he looked at her. The low sun was shining in his eyes, and he had to shade them from it. 'I'm the bravest knight in the kingdom, and I'm the best rider too,' he boasted.

'I know you are, Alex. I know you are.' She took him in her arms and hugged him tight. The moisture of his eyes once again soaked through her gowns.

'I have heard people talking, Cass.'

She eased him away from her and looked into his eyes. 'What are they saying?'

He thought about what he was going to say for a while before continuing. 'They are saying that bad men from Carnelia did this to Mother, and they wouldn't be surprised if they were going to try to do the same to me and you.'

'Who said these things?'

'Just people.' He shrugged. 'I'm scared, Cass, I want Mother to be here.'

Cassandra took her brother back in her arms and hugged him tight once more. 'I'm going to find out exactly what happened, Alex. But please, let me assure you, there will be no one coming for us. I doubt that Carnelia did this, they have nothing to gain from it. But I promise, I will find out.'

'I still want Mother here, though.'

She lifted her head and watched as the gentle but cool breeze stroked the tops of the trees in the orchard below them. This time she couldn't quell the tears falling from her own eyes.

'So do I, Brother. So do I.'

17.

THE NEXT FEW days were busy for Cassandra. Almost every waking moment was spent dealing with the intricacies of the transference of power, her rushed coronation, and the state funeral of her mother. There was also Alexander's emotional wellbeing to consider, plus dealing with her own grief.

Over the past ten days, she had been awoken, at what she considered as an unearthly hour, and made to sit in boring meetings from breakfast until evening meal. Being the queen was nowhere near as much fun as she thought it might have been.

When she finally dragged herself back into her chambers after twelve or thirteen—sometimes even fifteen or sixteen—hours of official meetings, Alex was always there with his excited face, happy to see her and ready to spend quality time with his sister and only remaining relative.

She was physically and mentally exhausted.

But something still played on the back of her mind. Something was not right.

She had sat through hours of security and strategy meetings, where they talked of how to deal with the Carnelian outrage, how they should respond so as not to appear weak in the sight of their enemy, and how to move forward with this situation.

But something still bothered her.

It finally dawned on her in the middle of her mother's state funeral. They'd already had a private, personal ceremony for themselves and their closest friends and family, but the nation called for, and deserved, a state funeral to give the populace the opportunity to mourn.

As she sat with Alex at her side, nodding and smiling to the dignitaries who were offering her their deepest condolences, she realised what it was that was nagging at her.

There had been no contact from Carnelia.

Anthony, her mother's closest advisor, and now *her* closest advisor, was sat next to her. He was a wizened and loyal old man.

'Anthony, has there been *any* contact from our friends in Carnelia?' she whispered, nodding and smiling as a line of people paraded before her, none of whom she knew or had even met before.

'There's been nothing, Your Majesty. It's making the council very nervous. If this atrocity was an intention of war, then we should have heard something by now. It is quiet, perhaps too quiet.'

'Has there been anything from our ambassadors?'

'We pulled them from Carnelia on the morning of the death of your mother, but word from them was that it was business as usual in their kingdom. Nothing out of the ordinary. It's all very strange.'

'There must be someone who knows what's happening. I'm amazed King Thaddius hasn't sent an envoy.'

'It has been noted and discussed, Your Majesty. It'll be addressed after the funeral is complete and you are fully installed on the throne.'

The rest of the funeral was a tedious affair. Cassandra kept stealing glances from her brother, who looked both as sad and as bored as she felt.

When the ordeal was finally over and they were making their way to the great hall for the celebratory dinner in honour of

Queen Alverna's life, Cassandra took Alexander's hand and veered him off in the opposite direction.

'Your Majesty, where are you going? You can't just ...' Anthony shouted after them. She knew he was far too old to chase them.

'Go ahead and start without us. Me and Alex just need a little fun.'

Anthony shook his head but smiled warmly as he watched the youths gambol off through the corridors on their way towards the gardens.

'Cass, why did the Carnelians kill Mother?'

Cassandra was shocked by the question and was not prepared with an answer.

'I ... erm, I don't know. I'm not even sure they did.'

'All the evidence points to the fact they did. Everyone says so.'

She stopped walking and looked at her brother. 'Alex, you're the Prince of Azuria. You're heir to the throne. I know it sounds mean, and a little premature, but you must begin to grow into your role.'

The young boy looked at her, his bottom lip trembling, just a little, but it was a tell-tale sign of how fragile he was. His blue eyes were glued to her as he nodded.

'And,' she continued, 'that means not listening to gossip and false words from fools who don't know what they're talking about. You have to look at the evidence. You have to look deeper. If there's an inkling that something is wrong in any situation, then you have to look deeper. Remember that and you will be a gallant knight and a fantastic servant of the realm.'

A decision was made in her head at that precise moment. It was a decision that would shape the fates of both kingdoms.

18.

THE COUNCIL WAS in full session. The royal seal was hanging on the door outside, acting as a reminder that the queen was present, and any interruptions required a very good reason indeed.

Cassandra was sat at the head of the table, and Anthony was seated to her left. The room was filled with men and women she barely knew and some she had only met briefly at the state funeral. It was an odd feeling that these wise and dignified men and women would take heed to anything she had to say. Anthony had trained her well in the etiquette of the room and how not to offend anyone.

What she hadn't been prepared for, however, was the levels of anger and threat. Grown men and women shouting and yelling at each other, parchment documents being thrown across the table, and people standing, pointing, accusing, and threatening each other. She couldn't believe what she was seeing. 'Is it always this … volatile?' she asked her aide.

Anthony smiled. 'Not always, Your Majesty, sometimes there's actual bloodshed.'

Her shocked face made him laugh.

'It's funny how quickly those who are allies to our kingdom are vilified by actions that they either were or were not the perpetrators of,' she observed.

'Warriors love their war, ma'am. This is a strange time. Nothing like this has happened in hundreds of years. It needs to be dealt with. An appropriate response is required.'

'I already know what we are going to do!' Cassandra said aloud, loud enough for everyone in the room to take note that the queen was speaking.

The hubbub died instantly, and everyone turned to look at the sixteen-year-old girl who was looking a little unsure of herself at the head of the table. Inside, she was struggling with what she had just done, but she stared back at them, one by one. She hoped the defiance she felt was mirrored by her external presence. She looked at Anthony next to her. She expected him to be angry, to be pulling a face, one that told her she was being a petulant child and to sit down and know her place, but that was not what she saw. He was smiling like a proud father, like he approved her stance.

As the room silenced, one man, dressed in the rich tunic of a dignitary, turned to look at her. The scorn on his face felt like a physical blow. He made a mistake then, one that she guessed not a lot of others would be making anytime soon; he underestimated her.

'Please forgive me, Your Highness,' the dignitary said. The smarm and sarcasm was dripping from his voice. Clearly, the moment in the council hall had gotten the better of him. 'But the adults are speaking right now. This situation needs addressing by people who know what they are doing.'

Cassandra's face blushed, and she looked down at the table. The man shook his head and continued. 'So, if *Your Majesty* wouldn't mind us continuing, we might be able to formulate a plan to keep you on the throne that you so thoroughly deserve.'

Anthony pushed his chair back to stand up, to address the man who had been so rude to the queen. But Cassandra put her hand out and stopped him. She looked at him and whispered,

'Thank you, Anthony. But if I'm to rule, then I must fight my own battles.'

He lifted his eyebrows, nodded, and sat back down.

'Sir?' Cassandra said as the dignitary turned his back to her to address another man in the room.

'I said, SIR!' she shouted. The dignitary stopped talking and looked back at her. 'You *will* look at me when I address you.' Her voice boomed through the chamber, but, Anthony noted with a smile, she did not shout.

The man looked at her, and his face fell. It was as if he was witnessing the child at the head of the table become a queen before his very eyes. He looked scared, humble, apologetic, and regretful all at the same time. If Cassandra hadn't been concentrating so hard on looking regal, looking like something she did not feel she was, then she, too, might have cracked a smile.

'You will address me with respect *every time* you speak to me, and you will keep my counsel on everything I say. Do you understand me, sir?'

The man looked like he wanted to be somewhere else, anywhere else, as he bowed his head, accepting the dressing down.

'I'll let this transgression go, just this once. I understand it must be difficult talking to a sixteen-year-old girl as your queen, but that is the situation we find ourselves in. If you *cannot* get used to that, I have no further need of your counsel. You will be stripped of your privileges, and I will have someone else in your post in an instant. Do you understand what I am saying?'

The man looked around the room. He was looking for a lifeline, for someone to back him up. Not one councillor was forthcoming. A thin sheen of sweat lined his forehead. 'Erm, yes … Yes, I understand.'

Cassandra shot him a fierce look as she raised her eyebrows. 'Yes, what?'

The man looked mortified as he bowed low—it was commented on after the meeting that no one had ever seen him bow so low in his entire life.

'Yes, Your Majesty.'

Cassandra flicked her eyes, dismissing him, and he sat down quickly, shuffling the parchments before him.

'I understand what you are trying to do here, and I appreciate all your efforts, I really do. But I have made up my mind. I know how we are going to address the Carnelian issue.'

The room fell silent; she had the undivided attention of every person at the table.

'I will lead an expedition to Carnelia.'

There was a murmur through the room. Even Anthony looked shocked at her statement.

'It will be an expedition of peace. I will take a full contingency of guards. I may be green, but I am not stupid. I'll go and present myself to them, ask the pertinent questions that no one has otherwise been able to answer. I will ask them if they killed my mother. The answers I get to these questions will determine if we go to war or not. If I return, then we will have peace between our nations. If I fail to return, then war it will be. I leave the day after tomorrow.'

She stared around the room. It seemed no one had anything more to say.

'General,' she addressed the man sitting on her right. 'Please make the necessary arrangements.' She stood, and everyone followed suit a moment later.

'If we have no other business, I'll take my leave and break the news to my brother.' And with that, she turned to leave.

Anthony followed.

As the doors closed behind her, she heard, with a smile on her face, the room burst into shouts and arguments. She turned towards her trusted advisor. 'Anthony, tell me, was I right to chastise that man like that?

'You were, Your Majesty,' her aide said with a nod, laughing. 'That man is indeed a cretin, but he has some decent ideas from time to time. Good things come to those who are prepared to wait for them,' he said with a smile.

'That was my—'

'Mother's favourite saying. Yes, child, it was,' Anthony finished for her.

She thought about finding a saying of her own, but really, she liked that one too much!

19.

THE COURTYARD WAS once again filled with people and horses. A large contingency of soldiers, laden with equipment for a long-haul march and dressed in the blue uniform of the Kingdom of Azuria, adorned the forefront of the crowd.

Alexander was watching from the window of his chambers, overlooking the gathering. His mouth was twitching as he counted the soldiers. There were twenty, all of them sat astride large, muscular steeds. His eyes widened as he spied what he was really looking for. His sister, mounted on their mother's horse, dressed in attire that was appropriate for a queen to ride in. When he saw her, he ran. Halfway down the stone stairway, he stopped and turned back, remembering something important that he needed. The box was in the corner of his room where it had been for quite some time, ever since he'd found it on one of his many adventures and took a liking to it. Looking at it had made him feel funny, and he wanted Cassandra to take it with her. Maybe it would bring her good luck in her mission.

With the gift in his hands, he ran into the courtyard and caught up with her. She was mounted and was inspecting her longsword, the same sword that used to be her mother's, and her fathers before that. When she saw him charging through the crowd, she smiled. She turned her steed to face him, sheathing her sword at the same time. 'Alex, I'm so glad you made it. I thought you wouldn't be up in time.'

'There is no way I was going to miss you leaving. I wish you didn't have to go.'

'Me too, but we've been through this, you know I have to. It's important for the future of our kingdom and the relationship with our neighbours. You'll be in charge while I'm gone, Little Brother.'

His face lit up. 'I will?'

'Yes. You'll oversee the whole of the kingdom.'

He straightened his back and puffed out his chest. 'Then I will be a great ruler. I'll be fair and true.'

She laughed as she reached down and ruffled his unruly hair. 'I'm sure you will. Anthony will be there to advise you, O fair ruler.' She raised her eyebrows as she looked at him. 'Even though you're in charge of the kingdom in my absence, you still must do whatever Anthony tells you to do. Do you understand me?'

His shoulders sagged a little as he let out a small sigh. 'Yes, Cass, I understand.'

'Good, now give me a hug before I leave, and I'll see you in a few days. Remember, I love you, Alexander, and I'll be home soon. Remember what mother used to say. Good things come to those who are willing to wait for them.'

~~~~

Barely holding in her tears, she reached down as the boy reached up. She was just about able to wrap one arm around him. He managed both. This simple gesture warmed her heart. As she looked up, she saw Anthony watching from the crowd. His face was troubled, and his folded arms told her of his anxiety. Their eyes locked for a moment, and he nodded his head, accepting his responsibility for the boy. Suddenly, she felt a lot better, knowing that Alexander was in good hands.

As the hug came to its natural conclusion, she sat up straight and fidgeted with the bridle, it was just something to do to avoid her brother seeing the tears that were running from her eyes. It was a seven-day ride to Carnelia, and she didn't know how long she would need to be there before they could set off home again, hopefully with the peace treaty between them still intact. *And my head still on my shoulders,* she thought with a shiver.

'Oh, Cass. I nearly forgot. I got you a little something for the journey. It's just something to remind you of home.' He bent down and picked up the small box he'd been carrying and held it up to her. 'I found it in one of the dungeons. It reminds me of the stories mother used to tell us when we were children.'

She looked down at him and smiled. *You are still a child, Alex. Please, stay that way for as long as you can.* This thought almost brought her tears back again.

She took the offered box and opened it. Instantly, her face began to glow blue as the light radiating from the object inside illuminated everything around her. She was intrigued by the orb nestled within the wooden container. 'Alex, where did you find such a thing?'

He looked away from her at the question, as if he was shying from explaining his little adventures. 'Oh, you know. Just in one of the dungeons in the castle. We sometimes play down there. I thought it might bring you good luck or something.'

She put the lid back on the box and hid it within the folds of her cloak. 'I'm sure it will, fair brother. Thank you.'

With that, the commander of the guard blew his horn, signalling the start of the expedition. Cassandra looked once more down at her brother and smiled. 'I'll see you in a few days, Alex. Remember to be good and true, and to listen to what Anthony tells you. OK?'

Anthony stepped out from the crowd and put his arm around the boy. Alex shrunk into the embrace, smiling at his sister as he did.

She instructed her horse to turn and head off with the rest of the party, offering one more look back at her brother, her whole

73

family. She tipped him a wave before riding out of the courtyard and out of the castle.

As she galloped away, she shouted something that she hoped her brother could hear over the noise of the crowd. It was just a little something to lift his spirits.

'Farewell, King Alexander! I'll see you very soon.'

20.

FIVE DAYS INTO the expedition, the journey had been uneventful. There had been long, hard days of riding followed by camping on rough terrain, enduring multiple weather fronts, and a rough diet of wild animals and shrubbery; but in all, it had been an entertaining and enjoyable mission.

Cassandra was welcomed at the fire pit during the evenings, when the guards would cook the meat and vegetables and make coffee laced with honey and rum.

There, many tales were told.

Some of the older guards regaled her with stories of her father, his skills with a long bow and sword and how he never once shied from a fight. Some entertained her with tales of her mother's bravery and how heartbroken she was at her father's mysterious passing. Some of the men even told her tales of herself when she was a toddler and how she had longed to ride the horses.

Others told stories of long ago, during the great war with Carnelia. Accounts of daring escapes and epic battles and, eventually, tales of how the war had ended when both sides realised neither of them remembered why they were fighting in the first place.

She laughed, she cried, but most of all, she listened and learned.

Tonight, the coffee and rum were good, and the roasted meat was fantastic, but the talk and the stories were not. There was a change in the men, an unease that made them edgy, even testy with each other. She had witnessed several verbal arguments, and once, a guard had to come between two others to stop them from drawing swords.

As she huddled closer to the warmth and safety of the fire, the commander came and sat next to her. He, too, looked distant and nervous.

Cassandra smiled as he leaned forward to cut a chunk from the roasted beast suspended over the fire. He sat back, his metal plate filled with juicy meat, he took a swig from his laced coffee, and let out a long sigh.

Eventually, he turned towards her and returned her smile. 'Not long now, ma'am. Another two days' ride and we should be in the Kingdom of Carnelia.'

'That is a blessing, Commander,' she replied with a nod.

'It is. But something is niggling the men.'

Cassandra nodded, her face half illuminated by the flames. She hoped the darkness would disguise her own fears.

'Oh, no, Your Highness, it's nothing bad.' He smiled to reassure her. 'It's just that we would have expected to have at least encountered some Carnelian patrols by now, or even some of their army on manoeuvres, but there's been nothing.'

'Is that an ill omen, Commander?'

'I'm not sure,' he replied, looking into the flames. 'But there is one thing I will tell you.'

'What's that?' she asked with a waver in her voice.

'This meat is fantastic.' He stood with a grin and clapped the queen on the shoulder before walking off to do an inspection of the camp.

She smiled at the comradery shown towards her before finishing off her own meal alone at the fire. When her plate was empty, she stood and dusted off her riding trousers, washed her plate and cup, and retired to her tent.

The camp was set up in three circles, with her tent dead centre, protected on all sides by three rows of guards. She signalled the commander and untied the canvas flaps on the sides. Once inside, she slipped into her bed clothes and lay down with a heavy sigh onto the semi-comfortable camping bed.

The sounds of the men outside her tent, busying themselves cleaning up, washing dishes, and protecting her, lulled her into a secure and fatigued sleep.

21.

IT WAS DARK, pitch dark. Cass awoke from a strange, stifling dream where a blue cloud had enveloped her and she couldn't breathe. The cloud had dispersed now that her eyes were open. *Are they open?* she thought, as she couldn't even see her own hand when she waved it in front of her face.

The only sounds she could hear were her own rapid breathing and the thudding of her speeding heartbeat. She took a moment, forcing herself to breathe deeply, to shake the remnants of the dream from her system, and to calm her nerves. It was then she became aware of the silence outside. It was too quiet. She held her breath, hoping to eliminate the sound of her breathing so she could listen. To her relief, she could hear rustling. It was the sounds of the men on guard duty outside her tent.

She lay back onto her bed and fluffed her pillow, confused as to why she was so jittery. She closed her eyes, but sleep evaded her.

Something *was* wrong, but she didn't know what.

She sat up and reached for the storm lamp at the side of her bed. She found it, then located the box of tinder that lay next to it. She lit the lamp but kept the flame at a minimum, she didn't want to alert anyone to her being awake. If they knew she was active, they would wake more of the men to attend her. She didn't want this as she knew they needed their sleep.

Once the tent was adequately lit, the first thing she noticed was the small box that Alex had given to her as a leaving gift. It was in the corner, stacked on the top of a few of her personal belongings.

Somehow, the box called to her. It wasn't in a mystical or even magical way, she just longed to look at the blue glowing orb as a sudden, sharp stab of homesickness penetrated her. She craved a connection with her brother.

Scrambling over the covers on her bed, she reached the box and closed her eyes. Her cold fingers fumbled at the latch on the top and opened it.

It was then she heard the first of the many screams she would hear this night.

Her eyes were dragged from the beautiful deep blue to look at the canvas roof of her tent. There was something terrifying about the sound of men screaming. It spoke to her of true horror. She knew nothing trivial would make her guards scream like that.

Her blood felt like it had frozen in her veins. Goosebumps had risen over every inch of her skin, exposed or not, and her heart was pumping in her ears.

The scream was accompanied by a strange buzzing or thrumming. It was hard to hear, but the feeling it caused in her stomach could not to be ignored. Neither could the cold sweat that was now lining her body.

'Protect the queen!' The shout tore through the night. 'Go and find out what that thing was.'

'Wake the commander, I may have casualties.' The second shout echoed through the night.

Within moments, an on-going commotion was happening outside her tent.

She needed to know what was happening. Quickly, she dressed, tucking the small box she was holding into the folds of her robe. She undid the ropes that kept the tent flaps closed and peered into the night.

There were two men talking excitedly, and to her relief, she could see the commander walking briskly towards them.

'Report,' he ordered when he was within hearing distance.

The two soldiers snapped quickly to attention, and one of them began to talk. Cassandra couldn't understand everything he was saying as he spoke rapidly, excitedly, about something that had occurred, but she did get parts.

All the while, the strange buzz could be felt in the air and through the ground.

'We were on the rounds, sir, each taking a different point of the star, as per orders. There was a noise, and a strange mist was forming out in the bush over by Barzell's position. He signalled he was going to look. That's when he was attacked, sir. We think he's dead. He entered the mist and never returned. We think there were ... things in there.'

Cassandra could see that the soldier was frightened as he indicated the bushes surrounding the camp. She followed his pointing arm and noticed soldiers emerging from their tents. None of them looked sleepy; their training had taken over, and they were alert and ready for what was coming at them.

'Things?' the commander snapped, looking out of the camp.

The soldier looked more than a little sheepish. 'We're not entirely sure, sir. They were there one minute before disappearing back into the mist, but they were there.'

'What are *they*? Carnelians?'

'I ... I don't rightly know, sir. It looked like men, but then ... not men.'

'I don't understand what you're saying,' the commander raged. 'Spit it out, man. What do you mean? Not men?'

'Well, they were bigger than men, and there was a strange kind of drumming noise, like that buzz we can hear now. Only ... it wasn't exactly louder, but heavier!'

The commander considered the information he was given. 'Wake the rest of the men and protect the queen. I'll take a team out to see if there's a threat and to find Barzell.' As he turned on his heels, he indicated four men to follow him into the bushes, towards the fog that was gathering there.

Cassandra watched them go as another team, all of them carrying blazing torches, surrounded her tent.

Is it just me, or is that fog glowing? This thought gave her a shiver. She wanted to burst out of the tent and alert the commander and his men. Tell them no, order them not to enter the mist. She fumbled at the rest of the ropes on the flaps of her tent, but her cold fingers didn't have the dexterity required to untie the knots. 'Commander,' she shouted. 'Don't enter that mist.' He either ignored her warning or never heard it, and they continued out of the camp. 'Don't go into the mist,' she shouted again, hoping to be heard over the thrum in the air. 'That's a ... a royal decree. Do you hear me?' Her frustration was getting the better of her at the knots when two guards came over to help.

'Here, ma'am, allow me,' one of the men said as he fumbled at the twine.

'Don't worry about the knots,' she commanded. 'Alert the commander. Tell him I've ordered him not to enter the woods. Can't you see the glow from over there?'

The soldier stared at her for a second or two before looking back towards the commander. His face was confused.

Cassandra shook her head and barked at him. 'Are you deaf as well as stupid? Tell the commander not to enter the mist.'

The man ran off towards the group of six who were getting smaller as they neared the bushes and the fog that was hanging off them.

From the small hole in the tent flap, she could see that most of the camp was up and moving. This made her feel more secure. She knew that every one of these men would give their lives to save her from anyone or anything. She also knew that she would never ask any of them to do it for her.

The distance to the bushes couldn't have been more than half a mile, and the soldier running in that direction had a lot of catching up to do.

'You there, yes you,' she shouted to the nearest soldier, who turned to look at her peering through the small hole in the tent flaps. 'Can you give me a hand here?'

'Your Majesty, it may be better for you to stay inside, just for the time being. There's been a breech. We need to ascertain if it's safe, and if not, we need to be able to ferry you to safety. Please sit back and … what the …' The soldier seemed to forget that he had been talking to the queen and walked off, out of her view.

Cassandra, in frustration, pushed on the tent flaps to get a better look at what the soldier had seen. As she peered around, she quickly regretted that decision.

Morning was breaking, and pale sunlight was filtering through the dark sky, shading the thin clouds into a breath-taking pink. Some of the men were returning from the bushes on the other side of the camp carrying something between them. It wasn't until they were closer that she could make out what it was.

It was a soldier.

One of her own.

He looked dead.

She could make out their direction only by the trail of dark blood that had slipped from his wounds on their journey. She altered her position again, watching as the men laid their stricken comrade on the ground. As they did, she saw exactly what it was that had killed the man. There was a hole in his stomach. It was wide enough to see right through him. She could literally see the grass underneath him through the bloody maw.

Shocked, she fell back into the tent. Her was head reeling. She could hear the guards fussing about the man, whispering, and talking between themselves. A dichotomy descended over her, she wanted to both hear and not hear what they were saying in equal measures.

'I've not seen a weapon that could penetrate so deeply and so cleanly,' one of them said.

'We need to get the queen out of her tent and away to safety. What do you think?'

The silence from the other soldier was deafening as he contemplated the proposition. That was when the thick, almost palpable thrum in the air returned. She felt it in her bones. The deep, heavy buzz was coming from everywhere.

There were more screams; a lot of them. They were coming from far away, from the direction of the bushes and the mist. 'Commander,' she muttered and threw herself back towards the flap at the end of the tent, desperate to see what was happening.

The blood curdling screams came again, and she had second thoughts about looking.

'Holy Glimm …' she heard a soldier shout; it was closely followed by, 'Look at the size of those things.' And then one more: 'What the Glimm are they?'

Cassandra was shaking, it was a strange feeling as it was in competition with the vibrations of the buzzing in her bones.

More screams. Then came the sounds of longswords being drawn and more shouts of 'Protect the queen!'

Bless you, she thought, petrified, as she remained secure in her tent.

The buzzing got louder, and the shouts of the men, obviously now in battle, escalated to a frenzy.

She could feel the death and destruction all around her, and she was stuck in her tent, useless, unable to help

Something solid hit the canvass wall above her, and a small scream escaped her. She chastised herself for being a cliché. Reluctantly, she turned to see what it could have been. The indentation on the roof of the tent began to slide, leaving behind it a trail. A dark stain appeared around the indentation, spreading as it slid down the slant of the roof.

She couldn't move. From the size and the shape of the thing, she had an idea of what it could be.

A human head!

Panic rained down on her.

Even though sounds of a ferocious battle were coming from everywhere outside, coupled with the sickening, resonant buzzing, she knew she wouldn't be able to stay in this tent much longer. *Better to die fighting than stuck in here listening to men die for me,* she thought.

She battled with the ropes on the tent. Once more, to her frustration, she was unsuccessful in untying them. She drew her mother's broadsword from its sheath next to her bed and swiped at the knots. The well-tended blade made short work of cutting through the twine. As the canvas opening swung loose, she was free to leave her prison. She watched as the entrance flapped, and hesitated. *If go out there, what will I see?* Her breathing became rapid and shallow as the panic that had been threatening accelerated its peril. She closed her eyes, drew a deep breath, then exited the tent.

Striding boldly towards her freedom, she screamed and jumped back as she was quickly accosted.

Relief washed over her when she realised it was a soldier, one she recognised.

'Come with me, ma'am,' he said rapidly and breathlessly. 'We're under heavy attack. We have to get you to safety.'

'Where's the commander?' she demanded, but the soldier ignored her question.

'Hurry, ma'am, I don't think we have much time.'

She scanned the tent for her belongings. Looking to see if there was anything she should take with her.

'We don't have time for belongings, ma'am,' the solder said, anticipating what she was doing. 'I must insist we leave right now.'

She took the man's gloved hand and was pulled roughly away from her sanctuary.

On exiting, the first thing she noticed was the beautiful pink sky. *The day is going to be a beautiful one ...* she thought absently before the noise of the battle drew her. There was a wall of five soldiers around her tent, all of them had drawn their swords. Their faces were terrified.

The buzz was more oppressive out here, and she could feel movement through the air, as if something was swooping and flying towards her. *It sounds like a firefly,* she thought.

The soldier grabbed her head and pushed it down before hauling her towards the back of the tent. Five horses were tethered maybe a hundred meters away. They were bucking and whinnying, frothing at the mouth, as they reared their legs and rolled their eyes wildly. 'You need to get to those horses, ma'am,' the soldier shouted as she felt his hand on her back, pushing her in the direction of the scared beasts. 'Whatever you do, don't look up. Go now!' he shouted. It was more of an order than a request. Either way, Cassandra didn't hesitate.

She took off in a stooped run.

Something swooped over her, and a blood curdling scream came from somewhere behind her. In a moment of panic, she turned to see what it was, just in time to see the soldier, the same one who had rescued her from the tent less than one minute earlier, being picked up, screaming, into the air. A slurry of blood gushed from him as a wet, ripping noise filled her ears. A body was dropped unceremoniously to the ground. There, it lay, crumpled, wrapped in its own innards. The soldier, her saviour, lay lifeless on the thick, lush grass.

She shivered but continued towards the horses.

The two huge fireflies then turned in the air and hovered. Their over-sized obsidian eyes and antenna were looking at her.

She didn't know what to do. She knew if she attempted to get to the horses, the fireflies would be on her in an instant and tear her apart like they had done to the poor soldier. Even if she did get to the horses, they were far too spooked by the beasts in the air and would be too dangerous to ride anyway.

'Queen Cassandra, this way,' another soldier shouted from behind.

She turned and caught a glimpse of a blue uniform ducking behind her tent. Without hesitation, she followed him, keeping low, hoping that would fend off any aerial attacks. The soldier's face was covered in blood. The blood was mixed with a thick golden liquid that was glowing in the twilight of the morning.

'What are those things?' she asked, struggling to speak as she thought her throat was beginning to close over.

'I don't know, ma'am. I've never seen the like of them before. I just watched one kill two of my men with very little effort. I think the stings are poisoned.'

'I don't think it matters,' she replied with a chuff. 'If one of those things pierce you, you're done for anyway.'

As if to emphasise her words, one of the beasts flew low, its huge sting passing just over her head. The soldier, throwing caution to the wind, stood, and struck at it with his longsword. The strike caught the flying beast in its abdomen. It emitted an unholy squeal as thick, golden liquid, which looked to be the cause of its fire, spilled down the soldier's sword, covering his face and his neck. He wiped at the strangely beautiful gore and looked at her. 'That's the third one I've gotten,' he boasted. 'But every beast I slaughter is replaced by another two.'

Cassandra was looking to the sky. It was now a deep, dark blue with only a few clouds. The pink hue of earlier was dissipating in tandem with the brightness of the rising sun. She couldn't believe a battle of this ferocity could be occurring beneath such a beautiful morning vista. To accentuate this thought, another beast swooped down towards her, the sting on its abdomen dripping with venom. The sunlight caught it and cast a pretty pattern on the bloody canvass of her tent.

The spray of blood stung her eyes and entered her mouth. The warm coppery taste caused her to gag, and she fell back against the outside of the tent. She wiped her face subconsciously as she slid down the sloped wall, landing on her rump on the grass. The heavy buzz was coming from everywhere now, joining with another, even more unpleasant noise—the wet sound of the soldier's death throes as he was torn apart by the beast's sting.

She didn't want to look but had to. She had a duty to the man, another one, who had so bravely offered his life to save hers.

She backed away from the gruesome scene, instinctively knowing that the sight of the monster contorting as its sting entered the soldier's corpse again and again could very well be one she took to her grave. It was hideous but was only the forerunner to the horrors she was about to witness as she backed away from the attack and out into the open field.

More men, her men, were strewn over the campsite. There were severed body parts covering the ground between the dark, stained tents. In places, it was hard to tell if the grass was green and not a stained dark red.

She could not see one soldier who had survived the attack.

As she surveyed the camp, she noticed that the body parts were not exclusively human or horse. There were insectoid limbs too, wings, heads, and golden glowing gore littered among them. She fell to her knees, resigned to whatever fate was to become of her. Waiting for certain death to swoop on her from the sky and tear her apart like her men and the horses.

She looked upwards and was horrified to see the clear blue sky was gone. It was now dark, almost black, but with a strangely hypnotic yellow glow. It was filled with hovering shapes that where mostly silhouetted by the sun.

There were hundreds of them hovering above her.

A noise from behind dragged her attention from the hovering legion, and she turned to see the commander and two of his group being led by some of the hideous beasts. Their faces were bloody and beaten, and she couldn't help but notice, and be proud of, the golden stains all over their tunics.

'Commander, are you hurt?' she shouted, standing to greet him and his men.

'No, Cassandra, he's not hurt. Not yet anyway.'

The thin, whisper came from behind her, and she snapped her head around, bringing her weapon to bear, to see who was calling her by her name.

A single firefly, this one larger than the others, descended from the ranks and hovered before her. She looked deep into its black insect eyes. Then something happened, something that should have been impossible.

The beast's features began to change.

They became … human!

Cassandra wiped her bloody face. She thought that the horror of the battle coupled with the blood stinging her eyes was causing her to hallucinate. But when she removed her hands, the firefly was morphing into a female form.

The half-lady floated to the ground, her wings disappearing as she landed before her. She was wearing a long, flowing purple gown. In her hands, she held something that Cassandra recognised at once.

It looked like the gift Alexander had given her, only this one was glowing red.

'Why, hello Cassandra,' the woman whispered.

'How do you know my name? And what is the meaning of this attack? Are you from Carnelia?'

'So many questions, my dear. Let us not jump into a philosophical discussion right now, eh?' the woman hissed. 'We have so much to do before we sit and talk.' She cocked her head, her older features, the ones that Cassandra thought as once being beautiful but no longer, changed as a smile covered her face.

'I'm afraid that you are now my prisoner, and I insist that you yield to my thralls and come with me.'

'Where are we going?'

'All will be revealed in time, Queen Cassandra.'

'What about my men?'

The woman shifted the glowing ball in her hand and closed her eyes. 'They will be coming too.'

The winged beasts leading the men forward grasped them beneath their arms and lifted them onto their curved abdomens, giving them a makeshift seat. Thick insectoid limbs crisscrossed over them, strapping them in for the ride. With their cargo secure, the humming beasts rose into the air and flew off in the direction the other insects were flying.

The woman offered a hand, inviting her forward.

She had no option other than to accept the invitation.

Smiling, the woman shifted the ball in her hand again, and two more fireflies descended into position. She climbed onto one of them and indicated to Cassandra to alight the other.

She looked at her ride and scowled.

The woman laughed. 'Oh, don't worry, they're perfectly safe as long as you do as I ask.'

As she climbed onto the awaiting beast, she looked at the smiling woman. 'Who are you, and what do you want?'

The woman grinned; her ancient beauty shone through.

You must have been devastatingly beautiful at one time, Cassandra thought.

'My name is Endellion, and as regards to what I want, my young Cassandra, that you will have to wait and see. In the meantime, why don't you sleep?'

She felt the strong arms of the firefly secure her as the woman shifted the ball in her hand again. As she was lifted into the air, everything went black.

22.

CASSANDRA OPENED ONE eye. There was a dull ache in the small of her back, and it was singing in chorus and rhythm with the sharper ache in her head. She felt a little like how some of the soldiers had described how it felt the next morning after a bellyful of ale. There was a queasiness in her stomach that matched her aches.

The throb in her back she put down to the uncomfortable bed she was lying in, and the confusion in her head, to the strange, unfamiliar surroundings she'd woken in. The room was dark and gloomy. From what she could make out, it looked circular. There were two windows on opposite sides. From the lack of shadows, she guessed it was sparsely furnished.

A dim illumination was streaming through the windows, indicating to her that it was either early morning or early evening, but in her disorientation, she had no way of knowing which. She lifted her head from the lumpy pillow, and her body screamed at her. As she moved, she could feel her brain moving with it, only a microsecond later. This brought on dizziness, followed closely by nausea and a rapid thudding in her temples. Saliva began to build in her mouth, and she only had a moment to realise that it was the precursor for vomiting before her stomach heaved. She threw herself off the bed and only just made it to the window, where she thrust her head outside.

She was there for a while. The memories of everything she had seen in the camp and the battle with her slow-moving brain writhing inside her skull induced more violent heaves. When she was done, she fell back onto the bed, manoeuvred herself into as comfortable a position as she could, and fell into a deep and dreamless sleep.

~~~~

A deep buzz thrumming around the room roused her from the blackness. She could hear it and feel it, but she was loathe to open her eyes. She didn't even want to move her head. The bed she was in felt a lot more comfortable than it had when she woke earlier. She tried to relax back into it and sleep again, but the buzzing continued around the room.

Suddenly, she opened her eyes and bolted upright.

She recognised it. Everything from the camp rushed back to her. The memories of her men being torn apart flooded back to her. The sounds, the vibrations in the air advertised the advent of … *fireflies!*

She jumped from the bed and ran to the window, where full daylight was now streaming through. The light illuminated the sparse circular room.

The feel of the fresh air on her face and the view were dizzying.

She was high over a forest.

Very high.

All she could see for miles were thick, lush trees with what looked like the foothills of mountains. She turned and ran to the window on the opposite side of the room and looked out of that one. Once again, the same view hit her. Nothing but trees and mountains as far as the eye could see.

She was in a valley, but one she didn't recognise.

The buzzing was still in the air. She thought it had gotten louder, more ominous. The ache in her head was gone, but it had been replaced with horrible vibrations that rattled her teeth.

She leaned out of the window, craning her neck, attempting to see around the other side of the circular building, to see if she could see where the fireflies could be.

There was nothing there.

Making her way over to the other side of the room, she looked out of that window again. She banged into a small table that was holding a pitcher of water and a cup. The pitcher fell, shattering, spilling its contents over the floor.

The sound of the container smashing caused a change in the pitch of the buzzing, and Cassandra felt her heart stop. She froze, she stopped breathing and closed her eyes.

The buzzing was closer now. The reverberations in her teeth travelled down her spine, rocking the core of her body. She didn't want to open her eyes, as she dreaded seeing those hideous things again.

'What do you want from me? Why am I still alive?' she shouted. 'Where am I?' The last shout was more a demand than a question.

'You're in my home, my queen. I call it the Forest of Su. Should I call you Cassandra, as you are definitely *not* my queen?'

The smooth, seductive voice came from behind her, from the other window. She recognised it instantly, even though last time she had heard it, she had been in a heightened state of anxiety.

Cassandra turned slowly. She knew the woman was behind her, but it was still a shock to see her in the room where, previously, she had been alone. She tried to see how, or where, the woman could have gotten in. There were no doors that she could see, only the two windows, and from the limited time she had spent looking—and vomiting—out of the window, she hadn't noticed any ladders. Then she remembered the woman transforming from a firefly into the intriguing older lady before her.

The woman smiled a beautiful but sardonic smile. 'I'm sorry, but your authority is not recognised,' she indicated the room, 'here.'

'I've never heard of the Forest of Su,' Cass said, trying to sound calmer than she felt.

'That, my dear, does not surprise me.'

'Who are you?'

'Who I am you will not know. My deeds will have been long forgotten or overwritten by now. But what I want is easy.' She stepped closer, and Cassandra couldn't help but move away from the leering woman until she banged into the bed. 'I want to be you!'

Cassandra looked at the mad woman; her eyes told of the hundred, if not thousands, of questions she needed to ask, but there was only one she could voice. It was the most burning of all the questions.

'What?' she spat.

The old woman laughed. Once again, Cassandra could see the beauty in her face that must have been so prevalent a long time ago. 'You'll see, my pretty, you'll see.' With that, she removed the clip from her silver hair and allowed it to flow like a silky river past her shoulders and down her back.

Cassandra noticed the edges of the hair were still tinged red, a red that matched the glowing orb she carried hanging from her belt.

Carnelian ... she thought.

The moment the thought passed through her; the woman smiled. 'I know what you are thinking, sweet child. You're thinking my allegiance is to the Kingdom of Carnelia.'

Cassandra looked at her with dead eyes. 'The thought did cross my mind.'

She laughed again, this time louder and with more humour. 'Believe me, you couldn't be further from the truth.'

'Who are you with then? And what do you want with me?'

She reached down and caressed the glowing ball at her hip. Cassandra watched as she closed her eyes and shimmered, as if her essence were no longer there.

'Bring me my powers, old man!' she demanded to no one that Cassandra could see.

She turned to see if there was someone else in the room that she had missed when a great wind whipped around her. Cassandra's hair was blown, as was her body, and she was pushed backwards again by the force of the phenomenon. As the wind died, it was replaced with a wave of warm air that radiated from the almost translucent woman before her.

A sadness enveloped her as the wave passed, but strangely, she didn't think it was her own sadness. It came from … somewhere else entirely. Cassandra looked up from the bed towards Endellion. During the maelstrom in the room, she had changed, she was no longer the same woman who had revealed herself moments ago.

She was now … her!

Looking at her hurt Cassandra's eyes and her already confused brain. It was like looking into a mirror. A dark one. One that did not reflect her own movements but the movements of something malignant and evil that still resembled her.

She watched as the woman, who was now her, fixed the glowing orb back into the small sling hanging from her belt and walked slowly towards her.

She was stunned at the transformation. Not a single trace of the old woman could be seen. She was now the perfect doppelgänger of her, a young woman with flowing dark, blue-tinged hair. The only thing that set them apart was her clothes. They were a long way from the dirty, blood-covered riding clothes Cassandra was wearing. Endellion wore a long, flowing regal gown that would not have looked out of place in the Azurian great hall during a glorious ball. Her eyes were full and filled with youth, and her face was devoid of the wrinkles that had been such a feature prior to this makeover. Her skin glowed, and her lips were full of lustre.

Quite simply, this young woman was beautiful.

The transformation had not only occurred in her facial features; Cassandra could see the fullness of her figure beneath her gown. Where before there had been ghosts of curves that a younger Endellion might have sported, they were now replaced with the real thing.

'What are you?' Cassandra whispered at the transformed figure before her.

'I have told you my name, child. I am a normal woman, just like you. But I have lived a very different life. However, all of that is about to change.'

'You won't get away with this, whatever it is you are trying to do. The Kingdom of Azuria will not sit still for this outrage. There'll be war between our nations. A war of your making.'

Endellion laughed. The simple act of smiling changed her face from beautiful to stunning within the wink of an eye. 'Oh, my sweet, young, innocent child, you make me laugh. As I have stated, I am not an agent of Carnelia, although I do herald from that dreadful place.' She leaned into Cassandra, so close that she could smell the perfumed powder on her skin. 'But hear me, child. War *is* something I am counting on. Only, it won't be the in the name of Endellion, or even Carnelia. It will be in the name of … oh, let me see …' She made a pantomime of contemplating a conclusion to this sentence, rubbing her chin and rolling her eyes, all the time with a playful but sinister grin. 'You!' she concluded.

Cassandra's face fell. 'What are you talking about? I would never—'

'You are right, of course,' she interrupted with a musical laugh. 'But you are wrong too.'

'Why? Why would you do this to me?' Cassandra asked, struggling to spit her words out. 'What will you gain?'

Endellion looked at her with Cassandra's own eyes that were laced with malevolence. She shook her head. 'You naïve girl. You ask what I could gain from becoming the Queen of Azuria?' Endellion laughed again. 'Only everything I have ever dreamed of, my child. *Everything*!'

'Why not just kill me then? If you are to rule in my place, why not dispose of me?'

Endellion—or was it now Cassandra?—smiled. It was a gentle smile, almost loving. 'I can't kill you yet, my child,' she whispered. 'The Glimm have evaded my questions regarding me being able to keep this image if you die. So, as I do not want to jeopardise my plans, you will remain here, as my prisoner, until I see fit to let you go or death takes you naturally. Either way, I should have enough time to see my plans come to fruition.'

With that, Endellion danced out of the window, turning from the young woman into a firefly in another sizzle of wind.

Cassandra was alone in the room, confused, angry, and scared. Pondering what would happen next.

23.

THE CELL WAS dark and damp. The stink of putrid water and decaying flesh hung heavy in the air. The walls were black and wet with the slime of age and neglect, but unfortunately for the Azurian soldiers held captive inside them, the age had not deteriorated the structure. The rooms were impenetrable; the brick was thick and solid. However, none of this deterred the soldiers from meticulously searching every inch of the walls and bars to find a weakness to exploit.

'There has to be a way out,' one of the men, scrambling in the dark, grumbled to himself. 'I've never, not once, been in a room that I couldn't get out of.'

'Will you shut up? You've been mumbling like that for the whole time we've been in here.'

The first soldier stood and squared his shoulders. 'Yeah, and what of it?' he challenged.

The other soldier accepted the challenge and squared up himself. 'I'm just a bit sick of it. Can't you sing a different tune?'

'I don't hear you …' the first soldier began before giving up halfway through the sentence and pushing the other man to the ground.

The commander was inspecting the metal bars of the cell, looking for any decay in the bricks or the mortar between them. He marvelled at how the construction had stayed so well built over the years he estimated it had stood. He stopped as the scuffle began on the filthy, straw covered floor. 'The pair of you, stand down, now,' he ordered. 'Fighting between ourselves will not get us out of this predicament. We need to find a weakness, and we need to get to the queen.'

The two men, as per their training, snapped to attention at the sound of the commander's voice. Both agreed with what he had to say.

'We got in here, so I'm sure we can get out.'

'Sir, what will we do against those fireflies? We don't have weapons.'

'We'll cross that bridge when we come to it. Now search.'

The three men returned to the task at hand, testing the walls, ceiling, and bars.

A few moments later, their work was interrupted by locks turning in the door outside their cell and the ugly sound of old metal grinding on more old metal. The rusted handle to the cell was turning.

'Someone's coming,' the commander whispered. 'Get on the bunks and be ready to follow my lead.'

Both soldiers dutifully followed his orders.

The commander found his way back to his bunk and lay back, closing his eyes, pretending to doze. The old hinges of the door squealed as they were punished from lack of lubrication. He expected to hear either the heavy footfalls of the jailer or the horrible throbbing buzz of a firefly. He preferred the former, they had a better chance against another human than one of those monstrosities.

What he heard surprised him.

Instead of a heavy tread, he heard light, almost dainty footfalls into the cell area. *That's a woman,* he thought. He opened one eye, ever so slightly, and peered through the gloom towards the door. He was expecting to see the witch from the battlefield, the one who had commanded the fireflies, and once again, he was ready for her.

A dim glow cut through the dark of the cell, illuminating the person who had come calling. The commander jumped from his cot and was at the bars in a flash when he saw who it was.

'My queen.' He knelt on one knee as Cassandra flitted into the room, looking both ways as if expecting a jailer. 'How?'

He was joined by the other two men, equally relieved and impressed by the sixteen-year-old girl rescuing them.

'I've no time to go into details now, Commander, but I've disabled the witch. However, the fireflies are still under her control. We must leave now.'

She produced a set of keys and went through them one by one until eventually finding the right one to open the thick iron door of the cell.

The commander rushed out and held her, his rough hands grabbing her by the shoulders as he looked her up and down. 'Are you OK? Did she hurt you in any way?'

Cassandra shook her head. 'No, I've been treated with respect. But we don't have much time, we need to get out of here.'

'Have you had a chance to look outside? Do you know where we are?' he asked as he searched the small jail for anything they could use as a weapon. He handed a large wooden broom to one of his men while the other picked up chunks of masonry from underneath a table.

Cassandra removed the red glowing ball from beneath her gown and rubbed it with one hand. As she did, a pulse radiated from it, filling the room with heat for a moment. All three soldiers stopped what they were doing and stood stock still, looking into the glow. Their faces were vacant and expressionless.

She smiled at their compliance. *Fools,* she thought with a laugh.

'Yes, Commander, I did see outside. We're held in a Carnelian fortress; we were brought here as prisoners after we were attacked and our men slaughtered by the bastard Carnelian army. We must get back to Azuria and warn them against the pending invasion.'

When she had finished, she put the glowing ball back into the folds of her gown, and the three men snapped out of their trance.

'Come, my queen, we have to get back as soon as possible. We must ride with haste to warn of the treachery of Carnelia,' the commander gushed as he pushed past the girl, heading for the door. 'Men, guard the queen. I'll look outside.'

'Yes, sir,' they both replied.

Cassandra looked at them, her forehead wrinkled with worry, but if either guard had taken a moment to look closely, they would have seen the humourless grin that lay only a gossamer layer below the surface.

Her hidden Endellion was showing.

24.

FOR TWO DAYS, she had been trapped in her prison. She had measured the time by watching the sun rising in one window and setting in the other. The witch Endellion had left her rations of food and water, enough to sustain her for a while, but there was precious little for her to do.

She had searched the entire room, twice, looking for trap doors or secret passageways, anything that could help her escape. But her frantic scrabbling had been fruitless. There was a small area that looked like it had once been a door but had long since been bricked up. She banged on the walls, first with her fists and then with the legs of one of the small tables she had smashed in anger and frustration. It was all to no avail. Apart from releasing quite a bit of dust into the room, it had no impact on the integrity of the brickwork.

She lay back on the uncomfortable bed. Tears were close, but the stubbornness of her anger was not allowing them flow.

She eyed the window, trying to imagine how many times over the last two days she had leaned out of it, screaming until she could taste blood in her mouth. That had been to no avail either.

She had even hung out of it, as far as gravity would allow, looking for any kind of handhold or grip she could use. The circular tower's exterior was smooth and vertical for the unfathomable distance to the tops of the trees below—and who knew how much further down beyond them.

It was hopeless.

The fresh supplies the witch had left for her were running sparse and in danger of rotting. All she had left were some dried meats and fruit that she had, until now, turned her nose up at. Water was in good supply, and there were means to get more by holding her bowl out of the window when it rained, but even doing that, she could see herself running seriously low if she were still captive during the dry season.

She pondered, sometimes too much, on what Endellion had planned for her beloved kingdom, in her beloved castle, with her beloved … 'Brother,' she sighed, relaxing her body into the bed and closing her eyes, attempting to sleep.

Her slumber took the immediate predicament away. In her dreams, she could be anywhere she wanted to be, anywhere other than where she was.

But sleep was as sparce as her food. Once again, it was held back by that most troublesome gatekeeper, anger. She had never felt so much rage before, and this, coupled with the lack of food and water, caused her extreme fatigue.

She lay on her bed, studying the ceiling above.

25.

AFTER FIVE DAYS of hard riding and very little sleep, the party of the commander, his two men, and their pretender queen arrived at the outskirts of Azuria. The horses were tired and in dire need of a rest and plenty of water. To be honest to himself, the commander thought his men were too, and he included himself in that. The only one who didn't look bedraggled by the journey was the queen. She looked as fresh as the day they had set off on their ill-fated mission.

As it was dark, the two soldiers were carrying flaming torches as they approached the walls of the city. A heavily armed party of guards had ridden out to meet them, not knowing if they were friend or foe.

'Who are you? Identify yourselves and identify your purpose here,' the gruff voice of the guards shouted from the darkness.

'It is me, Commander Isrith of the Royal Guard. We've returned from our failed mission to Carnelia.'

'Isrith? Is that really you? Come forward into the light and let me see you,' the guard ordered.

Isrith did as he was told, holding no malice towards the guard for his caution. As he stepped into the light, the man recognised him instantly and signalled for the others on the wall to stand down.

'We'd feared the worst when there was no word.' He looked beyond the man before him at the small party behind. 'Is the queen safe?'

'We were ambushed by Carnelian dogs,' he began. 'They slaughtered the regiment, only we three survived. We protected the queen from their arrows and longswords.' He nodded his head slowly. 'They're the scum who killed Queen Alvernia. The same villains tried to kill Queen Cassandra.'

He gestured towards Endellion, who trotted her horse forwards enough to enter into the light for the guard to see her fully.

'Your Majesty, it's so pleasing to see you alive and well.'

Endellion smiled Cassandra's brightest smile. 'It is only down to the bravery and training of these three men that I did survive. They are a credit to Azuria, and I want them recognised for it.'

Isrith turned to face her. 'Ma'am, that's not necessary. We were merely doing our duty. I'd rather the families of the men who fell be rewarded for their efforts.'

'I'll see to it that they are. Commander, will you please accompany me to my quarters. It's been a gruelling ride, and I need my rest in safe surroundings.'

'Of course, Your Majesty,' he replied, bowing from the back of his horse.

The guards led the returning party into the castle. The journey was conducted mostly in silence. They were all tired and emotionally drained.

Even for the late hour, there were people on the streets of the kingdom, some working, some revelling, but all of them stopped and watched as their queen rode past accompanied by the guards. It put a sly smile on Endellion's face, although she hid it behind Cassandra's gracious one.

~~~~~

The castle loomed in the short distance, and Endellion's heart began to beat faster. Were her plans finally coming to fruition? All the years of exile, scheming, and self-doubt that she could do this were beginning to pay off. Here, right before her eyes, within her grasp, was the fruits of her labour.

Castle Azuria was hers.

When they passed through the gates, there were more people working within the grounds, and once again, they stopped what they were doing and paid their respects. Finally at their destination, an equestrian master and his staff came and relieved them of their horses.

As Endellion dismounted, with the help of the master, a young boy came tearing out from the throng of people who had gathered to see her return.

'Cass, Cass …' he shouted. There were tears in his eyes. 'Cass, I'm so happy that you're …'

Endellion thanked the master and the guards before turning her back on the small boy and entering the royal residence.

'… back,' he finished, watching her leave after brushing past him as if he wasn't there.

~~~~

The shock on Alexander's face was there for all to see as he watched his sister leave. Anthony rushed through the crowd, too late to greet the queen but not too late to comfort Alexander's distress.

The young boy looked at his counsellor. 'Anthony,' he sniffed, 'she didn't even look at me.'

The older man took him in an embrace. 'Don't you worry, Prince Alexander. It seems your sister has had quite a traumatic experience. The messengers from the wall have reported her torments at the hands of the Carnelians. She'll be tired and emotional. It's my bet that she's already asleep.'

105

'Should I leave speaking to her until morning?'

Anthony nodded. 'I would. Leave her be tonight, and I'm sure she'll be her normal self tomorrow.'

'I hope so,' he whispered.

26.

'GUARD, SUMMON THE council straight away. This outrage by Carnelia must be addressed as soon as possible.'

'But, ma'am, I thought you needed to rest.'

Endellion turned to him, and he backed his protest down straight away. There was something in her eyes that told him not to second guess her. 'Yes, Your Majesty. I'll summon Anthony right away.'

'Anthony?' she asked, cocking her head questioningly.

'Your chief aide, ma'am. Anthony will rally the council, and you can be in session within the hour if you wish it.'

'An hour will suffice.'

'As you wish, Your Majesty. I'll arrange right away.' The guard nodded and walked off in the direction they had just travelled.

Endellion looked both ways along the corridor where she was now alone. It was then she realised that she didn't know where she was going. She had never been in this castle before. 'Guard,' she shouted again, down the corridor towards the soldier.

'Yes, ma'am?' he called back, stopping immediately and turning her way.

'I need you to accompany me to my chambers. After everything I've been through over the last few days, I'm feeling rather jittery.' She laughed; it was a small, nervous sound, as if she knew she was being silly.

The guard bent his head in reply. 'Of course, ma'am. It's this way.' He indicated the way as he caught up with her. Endellion smiled and linked his arm.

They walked, mostly in silence, for a few hundred yards and then up two flights of stairs before stopping outside a large wooden door. 'Here you are, ma'am, safe and sound at your residence. Is there anything else I can help you with?'

'Not right now. If you could muster the council together, that would be excellent.'

'Right away, Your Majesty.' He saluted before walking away.

'Oh, just one more thing,' Endellion shouted.

'Yes?' he asked with a smile.

'Could you come and get me and accompany me to the war room when the council has assembled?'

The guard's mouth tightened as he cocked his head. 'War room?'

Endellion shook her head and laughed. 'Sorry … I'm tired, I meant the council room.'

The guard smiled again and nodded. 'I will, Your Majesty. I'll return within the hour.'

'Thank you, sir,' she replied, pushing open the large wooden door.

Once inside, she closed it and stood with her back to it, relishing the barrier between her and the guards whose job it was to protect her. She looked around to see if anyone else was inside the chambers. After a quick scan, she was convinced and relieved she was alone. With a heavy sigh, she removed the glowing orb from the folds of her gown and caressed it as if it was the most valuable jewel in the world. As she did, her facial features began to change.

The pretty youth of Queen Cassandra melted away, replaced with the harshness of age and the haggardness of exile.

Endellion was back.

She sighed, an exhausted breath escaping her cracked lips. She entered her sleeping chamber and sat down heavily on the bed. Her old, calloused hands caressed the smooth comfort offered by the bed covers, and she cursed herself for calling the council meeting so soon. She lay back on the luxury; her long, thinning hair fanned over the pillow as she wriggled her old, used, and wasting body into a position of comfort. She closed her eyes, and a delightful and welcome doze descended over her.

Within seconds, or what felt like seconds, there was a harsh rapping on the door. She sat bolt upright, not even aware she had napped.

'Yes? Who is it?' she shouted, reaching for the Glimmer within her gown.

'It's Commander Gordun, ma'am. Commander Isrith has asked me to accompany you to the council room.'

'Yes, right! Give me a moment and I'll be ready. Are the members of the council present?'

'They will be by the time we get there. They're eager to find out what occurred on the road and what the role of Carnelia has in this debacle.'

'Fantastic. All will be revealed in the room.'

'Yes, ma'am,' he replied as Cassandra opened the door and took his arm. The commander led her down the corridor, out of the residence, and into the political wing.

27.

THE COUNCIL ROOM was full.

As Endellion entered, disguised as Queen Cassandra, the first thing she noticed was the smell. It was the aroma of bravado and war. It was as if the bickering and arguing councillors were secreting a thick, cloying stench, a cocktail of pheromones and sweat.

She loved it.

The next thing she noticed was the heat. It was overly warm in the room, probably due to the overriding tension.

The instant she made her entrance, all talking and bickering ceased. Every pair of eyes fell upon her.

Endellion loved this power.

It was everything she had courted, craved, and dreamt about in the seemingly endless years of exile. She took a moment to drink it in. The smell excited her. Eventually, she turned to the commander on her arm. 'Thank you, Commander Gordun. Now, if you would be so bold as to find Isrith and the other two who were in my guard, that would be fantastic.'

She patted the man, almost condescendingly, on the arm to release him from her hold, and he stepped away, bowing as he did. 'Yes, Your Majesty. Straight away.'

As he left the room, she took her seat at the head of the table. *Should I get them to bow to me?* she thought with a wry smile before sitting herself on the largest chair. 'You may all be seated, and we shall get this meeting underway. Before we leave this room tonight, we will be at war with Carnelia!' It was a bold statement to make, and it certainly had the impact on the room she intended. Her smile extended to everyone as she started to regale them with the lie regarding the ambush on the road to Carnelia.

Halfway through the meeting, Gordun re-entered with the three guards, including Commander Isrith. She smiled at them as she slipped her hand inside her robes and stroked the orb concealed within the folds. The three men continued the fiction that she had initiated, with the help of the powers of the Glimmer, and implanted into their memories.

'We were camped on the edge of the river; this was our fifth day of travel,' Isrith began at the behest of Endellion. 'We'd spotted numerous Carnelian scouts tracking us over the last two days. Concern was raised as to why they were keeping their distance. I asked our scouts to attempt communication with the soldiers. To open a dialogue. I sent the scouting company, led by Sargent Tirez, who was on that duty, out with three other men into the woods to make contact.' Isrith lowered his head for a few seconds, reliving the false memory. Endellion held her smile at bay. 'They never made it back.'

'If you will excuse me for a moment, I need some fresh air,' the queen stated. 'I have lived this story and have little desire to live through it again.'

'Of course, Your Majesty,' was the resounding chorus from all present, as each of them stood to mark her leaving.

Once outside the room, she made her way around the corner, away from the prying eyes of the guards at the doors. The moment she was out of the line of sight of anyone, she stroked the glowing orb again and her features shifted. She returned to her original form. She relaxed as she leaned against the wall, giggling at how easy all this turned out to be.

~~~~

Cassandra/Endellion hadn't noticed Alexander outside the council rooms. He had been lurking, hoping to get a moment with his sister. She had ignored him since her return from her mission, and that wasn't like her. They were the best of friends, and she was all he had left of his family.

He watched as she walked from the room. He shrunk back into the shadows of the corridor. He wanted to call out, to run to her, to wrap his arms around her and hug her, but he shied away. It had been less than a day, and he knew it sounded silly, even to himself, but he felt like she was a different person since her return.

As she rounded the corner, heading away from the council room, he debated with himself before following her.

Leaving it for a moment, as he didn't want to be caught stalking the queen, he then hurried after her, turning the corner she had just turned. He was astounded to find that there was no sign of his sister anywhere. The only person he could see was an old woman resting against the wall.

She ignored him, lost in her own thoughts. She was giggling to herself like a drunken man.

'Excuse me, ma'am? Can you help me? I'm looking for my sister,' he asked, interrupting her moment. He was a naturally shy boy, but he always tried to channel everything Anthony and Cassandra taught him when addressing the citizens of Azuria. He could never grasp the concept that he was the prince and that the people loved him.

The old woman snapped from her reverie at the sound of his voice and glared down at him. He shied from the stare. The corners of her mouth turned down as she leered at him. 'And exactly how am I supposed to help you with that?' she spat.

He shrunk away from the nasty woman, He wanted to run from her, back around the corner, back to his chambers. *I could wait for Cass there,* he reasoned. But, once again, he channelled everything Anthony had taught him regarding who he was and

112

the role he must play in the kingdom. He took a deep breath and summoned his princely bravado. 'I was wondering if you had seen her, as she would have passed you merely seconds ago.'

The old crone sneered down at him. The glare in her eyes looked dangerous. He'd never seen her before and would be very happy if he never saw her again.

'And just who is this sister of yours, brat?' she growled. 'And how would I know if I've seen her or not? I don't know you from Glimm!'

She began to advance slowly upon him. There was menace in her gait. He didn't know what to do, he'd never been spoken to in such a way and couldn't believe that a woman working in the castle, as she obviously did, wouldn't know who he was or who his sister was.

'Y-You, you don't know me?' he stuttered, backing away from the witch.

'Why? Should I?' she snapped.

'I, I think so …' he stuttered. His back hit the wall behind him, surprising him with its proximity. The malice of the situation had been lost on him, and for the first time ever, he felt scared in his own castle. 'She's your queen. I'm Prince Alexander!'

The woman's eyes widened, and a new brightness shone from them. After a moment or two, she began to laugh. Alexander saw her face physically soften and the malice in her eyes recede. She bowed to him. 'I know who you are, my prince. I was toying with you. Yes, I did see your sister. The queen hurried off in that direction seconds before you came around the corner. She looked to be in an awful rush. If you hurry, you might catch up with her.'

'Thank you …' he replied, obviously waiting for the woman to inform him of her name. After a short while, when it was obvious the name would not be forthcoming, he hurried off in the indicated direction.

~~~~

Endellion watched as the troublesome little brat scurried off, turning only once to look back at her. Even from the short distance, she recognised the cold, cynical look in his eyes. As soon as he was around the corner, she stroked the Glimmer, and her features changed back into Cassandra's. *So that's my little brother. I must remember the level of devotion he has to his sister. He will be an ally.*

As she walked back into the room, everyone stood. She motioned them to sit and for the soldier who was currently addressing the council to continue. He nodded and resumed his meticulous but subconsciously crafted tale.

'Commander Isrith and I were back-to-back, there must have been four of them left. Our dead were scattered all over the camp. The commander gave me the order, and I ran at two of our assailants, cutting down one where he stood before rushing the other. Isrith had done the same. Two of the craven attackers ran off into the bush, their tails were between their legs. We attempted to chase them down, but they must have known the terrain better than us as they had disappeared. We returned to camp and alerted them to the threat. We spent a long night guarding the queen … before they came.'

The second soldier took up the tale. 'I was guarding the queen's tent when it happened …'

From the corner of her eye, Endellion noticed the door to the room creep open. Anthony nudged her arm and pointed at the worried face peering through. She forced a smile and waved at her brother.

This small gesture brightened his stature and she grinned inwardly as he beamed towards her, waving his hand as a return gesture.

When she called him over, indicating the empty seat behind her, she could almost hear a silent squeal of delight coming from him.

'You do realise I haven't been ignoring you, Little Brother,' she whispered into his ear. 'But this matter required my full attention straight away.'

The boy nodded. 'I understand. But I have missed you, Sister. I'm glad you're home.'

Endellion looked around the room, from face to angry face. All of them were listening intently to what the surviving guards had to say regarding the Carnelian attack, and the second attempt on their queen within a few weeks. She sat back, barely stifling a grin, enjoying the warm glow running through her.

'So am I, Prince Alex,' she whispered her reply. 'So am I.'

By the time the meeting was over, some hours later, and the councillors and dignitaries were filing out of the room, Azuria had *officially* put a war with the Kingdom of Carnelia on the table. Two unprovoked attacks upon the royal family had proven enough. Something had to be done about the threats from their troublesome neighbours.

Endellion remained in the council room. Alexander was asleep, resting his young head on the table. She allowed herself a moment to enjoy the smile she had been hiding for too long. Her plans were coming to fruition.

It's almost too easy, she thought.

28.

THE REAL QUEEN of Azuria was worried. The original cache of supplies that had been left was dwindling, and the bowl that she had been hanging out of the window to collect rainwater was dry.

There had been no rain for the past two days.

She stared at the bowl of what had been cured meats and dried fruits but was now just another empty bowl. It was exactly how she felt right now.

Empty!

She was worried for her health, she was worried about the lack of water, she was worried about what the witch Endellion was doing to her kingdom. But most of all, she was worried about Alex. Every time she thought about *her* talking to him, guiding him, laughing with him, a stab of anger laced with emotion and pain lanced her. She could only hope that her brother had seen through the witch's disguise somehow and disposed of her.

Deep down in her heart, she knew it wouldn't be the case. Somehow, she knew Endellion would be manipulating everything and everyone to her will.

She threw herself onto the bed and buried her head into the pillowcase. She cried, not for the first time in the weeks she had been here, and she knew it would certainly not be the last.

As she thrashed on the bed, anguish spilling from every pore, she kicked out. Her leg connected with a small pile of clothing stacked on a small chest at the end of the bed. The stack fell, and something solid hit the floor and rolled. As it was the only distraction she had from the dark depression hanging over her, she sat up to see what it could have been. Hope filled her. Could it be food she hadn't noticed all these days?

It wasn't.

At first, all she saw was a small wooden box; and for a moment, she couldn't remember what it was or where it had come from. But then she saw the lid hanging open and a faint blue glow issuing from the other side of the room.

Then she remembered. It was the parting gift from Alex.

Wiping the tears from her face, she leant over and picked up the small ball. She had expected it to be colder than what it was.

The moment she touched it, her thoughts flew out of the window and through the air towards Azuria. A tear welled in her eye before eventually becoming so fat that it broke the protective damn of her lid and trickled slowly down her face.

She closed her eyes, and …

~~~~

She must have fallen into an unexpected sleep, as she found herself somewhere else. Only everything felt so real. There was a stuffiness in the air, like the place hadn't been lived in for a while, or even visited. It was dark and cold but was not uninviting.

It felt alive and somewhat welcoming.

As the gloom lifted and her eyes adjusted to the darkness, an altar came into view in the centre of the room. There was something adorning the top, something she couldn't quite make out. Curiosity overwhelmed her and—mostly from boredom at being stuck in the same room for weeks and the fact that she was enjoying this strange dream—she felt the urge to investigate.

On closer inspection, she saw it wasn't one thing, it was two.

On closer inspection still, she noticed it was two human skeletons, each with what looks like a ceremonial dagger protruding from their ribcages.

The sight of this double murder, or suicide, didn't scare her. Strangely, she felt drawn to it. An overwhelming feeling of understanding flooded her.

She knew that she was not alone in the chamber.

The hairs on the back of her neck stood on end, and her skin tightened as goosebumps covered it. She wanted nothing more than to turn around, to confront whoever or whatever was behind her, but fear had overtaken her, and she couldn't move.

Then a blue light shone from the gloom.

It was the same cold blue that had radiated from the metallic ball, Alex's gift. The fear that had consumed her only moments ago dissipated, and she relaxed into the blue haze. It comforted her. She felt it was speaking to her, soothing her, telling her everything was going to be all right.

She summoned up her courage and turned. Her eyes remained closed as the rational side of her brain screamed, telling her she really didn't *want* to see who or what was causing the glow, but her emotional side was yelling too, telling her to embrace whatever the light had to offer.

She opened her eyes … and screamed.

The man standing before the altar took her by surprise.

The shrill noise echoed through the empty chamber, bouncing off the unseen far walls. The man was smiling at her. There was something about this smile that told her she could trust him. Even though he looked wild, not to mention dangerous, with his long grey hair merging with his unkempt beard, his deep, dark eyes told of learning and knowledge well beyond the realms of her understanding.

She smiled back at him, though she could feel her heart pounding ten times faster than it should have been.

The man's smile grew as he held out his hand towards her.

In it was the source of the blue light.

It was the Glimmer. The same one Alex had given her. Its glow seemed stronger somehow. It didn't look dangerous, but she shied away from the offered hand. The man implored her and extended his reach further. Tentatively she accepted the orb, wrapping her fingers around its warmth.

In the blink of an eye, she was back in her prison, lying on the bed with her own blue orb in her hand.

'Glimmer?' she questioned. 'From the stories?'

A noise snatched her from her thoughts. It sounded like a bird cawing in her room, as if it was in some distress. She cast her gaze across the room just as two large birds took flight out of the window, soaring away into the blue sky above. As she watched them leave, a jealous thought escaped her. *Off they go to live their best lives in the wide world while I rot in here. Wherever here is.*

She climbed off the bed making her way towards the window to watch them go. As she leaned on the sill, her foot touched something. It was cold and wet. She pulled away from the alien item and looked down.

There was a mound of fruits, berries, and nuts on the floor. There was enough to feed her for the rest of the day, and maybe tomorrow too if she was careful. Enough to crush and quench her thirst and possibly stave off the horrible death she had envisioned for herself.

Not caring where it came from, she dived in.

With her face covered in juice and her stomach filled for the first time in a while, she lay back on the bed and closed her eyes, thinking about the odd, vivid dream she had experienced.

Sleep came easily for the first time since she had been held captive. This time, there were no dreams, just simple, beautiful thoughts of her kingdom and, of course, her brother.

29.

OVER THE COURSE of the last few months, bizarre and inexplicable events had been plaguing the Kingdom of Carnelia. Some had been so bad and so strange that King Thaddius believed there had been an omen, or even a curse, put upon the land.

He was in his council room, a room not unlike the one Endellion commanded in Azuria, casting a worried figure at the head of the table. The others present wore uniforms with the red of Carnelia emblazoned over their chests.

They were fighting among themselves.

'Something needs to be done. These attacks are becoming more frequent.'

'Attacks? What makes you think they're attacks? They're strange and random, I'll grant you that, but by what magic could someone conjure attacks of this nature?'

'They don't seem random to me. Is it coincidence they have only started happening since Azuria ceased communications with us? Am I paranoid, or could this be the truth?'

The two arguing men turned their heads towards Thaddius, who was holding his head in his hands.

He was deep in thought.

He was thinking about dogs. Wild dogs, to be precise.

Roughly three weeks ago, a small pack of wild dogs had run amok through the kingdom. This in itself was nothing new for Carnelia, they had always had their share of stray dogs in the streets. The smell of meat from the butchers attracted them, as did the aromas from the various bakers within the town.

So, a pack of dogs sniffing around here and there was nothing to worry about. But there had never been anything like what happened that day.

The pack was maybe fifty strong and came as if out of nowhere. But the people, the great Carnelian public who witnessed the incident, would attest to the fact that they were almost … organised.

They tore through the main street of the town, knocking down stalls and stands from the market. Anything that spilled was devoured within seconds. They bit and snapped at everything in their path. Pets, domestic animals, men, women, children, everything was prey. They ransacked many a baker's property, spoiling and eating the products. Several of the butchers tried to barricade their properties against the onslaught only to find there were too many of them, and human barricades didn't offer anywhere near enough protection against waves of hungry hounds.

The attack lasted almost two hours. After that, the king's guards were dispatched to run the dogs off the streets. Many a rider and horse were attacked and bitten.

Once it was under control and the dogs had been either run out of the town or destroyed, the counting of the damage had begun.

In total, five civilians had died from wounds suffered in the attack; at least two of them had been partly eaten. Three children were reported missing, feared dead, maybe even devoured. Countless pets and other animals were dead. There was extensive damage to numerous butchers' and bakers' stalls and livelihoods, and other establishments were ruined. The toll on the livestock was devastating.

Open wounds from bites and scratches were bandaged or stitched as best as could be managed, and everyone went to their beds that night shaken but relieved that the ordeal was over.

The very next day, the pack returned. This time, the numbers were estimated to be doubled. King Thaddius wasted no time releasing the full force of his guards onto the city streets. There were to be no mercies on the crazy troublemakers today. The orders stated that every wild dog was to be destroyed on sight.

And they were, but not before an even larger number of adults, children, and pets were slaughtered by the unrelenting savages.

By the time the pack had been hunted, brought under control, and eventually dealt with, it was estimated another thirty civilians were dead, most of that number consisting of children.

Graves were dug, funerals were arranged, and buildings were repaired. The city was in a state of great shock. The walls around Carnelia were searched meticulously, and any holes in the defences that would allow any further attacks from the feral pests were blocked.

Life slowly began to return to something akin to normalcy.

For a short while at least.

A few days later, the domestic animals in the city, the ones who had been attacked by the dogs, began acting funny. They began turning feral themselves. Dogs, cats, geese, horses, even cows began to attack civilians in the street. The populace, already scared by what had happened with the dogs, panicked, and once again, the king's guards were deployed into the streets of Carnelia, again to slaughter animals.

There were no resulting deaths from these attacks, but there had been several people savaged.

Then, an even stranger phenomenon began to pass through the city.

There was talk of the humans, the ones who had been bitten by the animals, beginning to act peculiar themselves. Attacking strangers in the streets, biting them, throttling them, killing them at random.

There were even reports of savage cannibalism.

Once again, the beleaguered king's guard were sent into the town to keep the peace. There were reports of vigilante groups patrolling the streets, dispatching their own forms of justice on the suspected perpetrators of the attacks. Many were injured and arrested, but many were also killed.

Times were strange indeed and seemed to be going from bad to worse.

These attacks were not the end of it. The worst, most horrific part of it was yet to be played out.

It began as a rumour, but as the last set of rumours turned out to be true, King Thaddius took no risks and acted immediately upon the stories being whispered through the city.

The dead were returning to life.

Not all the dead. It was reported that it was only the ones who had been savaged by the infected animals or the infected humans.

King Thaddius had initially dismissed the report as flights of fantasy, scaremongering in the pubs and taverns of the city. There was no way that dead people could rise from their graves and attack the living.

That was what he thought until he witnessed the phenomenon for himself.

He and the queen were taking a moonlit stroll through the grounds, heading towards the graveyard where their ancestors were laid to rest. They usually enjoyed this exercise during the darkening nights of Autumn. They passed through the royal graves, paying tribute to the kings and queens of old before entering the newer resting places.

The king's guard were behind them at a respectable distance. Far enough away to offer privacy but near enough to offer protection that, considering the recent activities, might be required. So, feeling secure in their own lands, King Thaddius and Queen Halia enjoyed their stroll, talking politics and frivolities, however the mood took them.

The night was clear. There were no clouds in the sky, and the silvery light shining down from their zenith was more than enough to illuminate their parade through the well-maintained plots. They were laughing and holding hands. It was something they hadn't had time to do of late, but tonight was a well-earned break from the trials of leadership.

'I sometimes forget the beauty of the land we live in,' Thaddius said. He looked up towards the leaves on the trees, which were changing from green to orange, and smiled. 'When my father was king, I would watch him rule. Flitting from one meeting to the next, always busy, always doing this or doing that. I don't think I ever once saw him stop and take the time to smell the roses.'

Queen Halia stopped and picked the largest pink bloom on the nearest bush. She offered it to her husband. 'Here, why pick them yourself when you have people to do it for you?' she laughed.

Thaddius accepted his wife's gift, offering her a chuckle.

'I see what you mean,' he said with a grin. 'However, he never slowed down. That is not a trait I want to continue, not now we're headed into the Autumn of our years. Once this Azurian thing is over and everything returns to normal, I'll take you away for a week, or maybe even two. We'll travel in the royal yacht and explore. What do you say?'

'I'd say that it would be wonderful, my husband. But what of Bernard? What of his schooling?'

Thaddius shook his head. 'The boy is old enough to look after himself. He's lazy and his head is full of adventure. He needs discipline in his life, and us taking time off may be just the tonic he requires.'

'Well, I'd like to see that happen, of course, but do you think now is the right time?'

The king mused on his wife's retort for a few moments before laughing and taking a step off the path towards a particularly large rose bush, just a little nearer the fresh graves.

'Be careful, my King,' Halia warned.

Thaddius smiled.

As he bent to pluck the large red flower—he wanted his wife to smell the fresh perfume of the petals—something strange happened, something that changed Thaddius's mind about the rumours that had been circulating the kingdom.

The moment the flower was plucked from its stem, the earth beneath it began to rumble. Thaddius was confused. He stopped what he was doing and watched as a small heap of soil was displaced. His initial thought was *moles,* but it was well out of season for them.

The next thing that happened was an ear-splitting scream from his wife. His attention was snapped away from the shifting earth as he turned to see what she could be screaming about.

The sight he was greeted with would stay with him long after the phenomenon was over.

His wife was being wrestled to the ground by what looked like a woman. The attacker was dressed in shabby, dirty, and ripped clothing. Her hair was matted and filthy, and her skin was grey and lifeless. She looked like she should be dead.

'GUARDS!' was all he managed to yell before whatever caused the earth to erupt beneath the rosebush reached up and grabbed him.

A cold, ghastly hand gripped him with an inhuman strength. Its freezing fingers dug into the sleeves of his robe, tearing them with dirty, sharp fingernails. Thaddius couldn't breathe, let alone shout for help. His throat felt like it was swelling, closing, sealing off his windpipe, stifling the air that he needed to alert his men.

Thankfully, the guards were more alert than he ever gave them credit for.

125

He fought the thing from him as a head appeared from the ground. He tried to step away, pushing the thing's snapping mouth as far away from him as he was able. The last thing he wanted was to be bitten by that germ infected mouth. Suddenly, the head toppled off onto the ground next to him. The vice-like grip on his arm was gone, and Thaddius watched in horror as it flopped to the ground with a wet slap.

He turned, quick as a flash, just in time to see the monster that was attacking his wife also fall to the ground headless in much the same fashion as the first.

'Quickly, Your Highness, we need to get you home.' The soldier threw his arm around the king and dragged him to his feet. Without another word, Thaddius found himself being hauled through the cemetery, back towards the castle. His wife was behind him, doing a better job at running than he.

'What … what was that?' He stuttered the question, even though in his head, it sounded rational and clear, regal even. The answer he received sent his head reeling.

'That was the dead, sir,' the soldier answered, quite out of breath. 'We didn't believe it ourselves at first, but it's true. The bodies of the people who were bitten by the dogs or the other … things are rising from their graves. There's been reports all over the kingdom.'

Thaddius looked back at his wife, who was obviously shaken by her ordeal. 'Are you all right, my queen?' he asked tenderly, a lot more gently than he felt.

'What was it?' she asked, looking at her husband, her eyes wide and her bottom lip quivering.

He wrapped his arms around her and could feel her body shaking beneath his embrace.

'We don't know, but we're going back to the castle this instant. The guards will deal with them.'

Halia didn't reply, she just held onto him. The guards escorted them back to the castle with their swords drawn, ready to defend their royalty. The journey wasn't without its peril, as they were attacked several times by similar ungodly things.

One attacker came at them from the front in a slow, encumbered lunge. Both the king and queen were able to get a good view of who it was.

'Oh my …' the queen whimpered from where she had buried her head into her husband's cloak. 'That's my cousin, Galen. He was savaged by the dogs on the second day; he didn't last the night. Why would he attack us?'

It was the king's turn to not answer as he protected his wife from seeing her cousin's severed head bounce off the path ahead of them.

For the next few days, there were more reports of the dead rising and attacking the living. In a few frightening cases, it was also reported that the people who had been attacked had begun to show signs of rapid decay and even a taste for human flesh themselves.

It took a while, but eventually, the guards, assisted by the petrified populace of Carnelia, had dug up all the bodies who had been attacked and severed their heads. Then they had to deal with the living who had been bitten. They were imprisoned, for their own safety and the safety of the kingdom. They were monitored, and if they showed any sign of turning into one of those monsters, they were dealt with, swiftly.

The ugly phenomenon passed, and things eventually began to return to normal. This is how they ended up here in the council rooms, arguing about how the Kingdom of Azuria was to blame for nasty magic hoodoo that was upon them.

King Thaddius had had enough.

'And now, there is no noise coming from the kingdom at all. They've closed all channels of communication with the outside world.' One of the councillors was shouting across the room, anger evident in her voice. 'It's time we took up arms. It sounds like a precursor to invasion to me. I would urge that we set the vanguard around our borders. We need to protect what's ours.'

'I second this proposal. If the Azurians want war, I say we give them what they want,' another councillor shouted back across the room, the heat of the debate obviously bringing her blood to the boil.

'What about the strange magic? If it is them and they have a sorcerer, how do we combat that? You have all seen what has been occurring in this kingdom over the last few weeks. My king, we should attempt to open dialogue with them before we jump to conclusions.'

'You are right, Petrie. All this talk of conjuring and magic is conjecture, and dangerous conjecture at that. If we were to send a vanguard to Azuria, then it would have to be under the pretence of something other than why they have frozen us out.'

A man entered the room during the debate. The door opened just a crack and he did his best not to be seen by anyone as he cowered along the wall, heading towards where the queen was sat, silently watching the proceedings. He offered her a small piece of parchment, bowed low, and made his way back out of the room in the same manner which he entered. The king observed this and watched his wife's face change from concern to shock in the blink of an eye.

'What is it, my love?' he whispered as the hot debate raged around them.

'It's what we've been looking for, my king,' she replied. Queen Halia then stood at the head of the table, and the rest of the room fell silent. She cleared her throat, getting everyone's attention. A few moments later, all eyes in the room were on her.

'I have just received some very serious news. If it is true, and I have no reason to disbelieve it, then it could be the reason for the Azurian freeze and the reason for us to go there.'

She took a moment or two to allow this to sink into the congregated councillors.

'It seems Queen Alverna is dead.'

A silence descended over the room. From her vantage point, she watched as the men and women looked from face to face, silently hoping someone would ask a question. When none was forthcoming, she continued.

'There are no details in this message other than the fact that they have appointed her sixteen-year-old daughter, Cassandra, as Queen of Azuria.' She put the note onto the table and looked around the room at the troubled faces before her. 'I believe we should send an envoy. To offer our condolences and respects for such a great woman. We can also take the opportunity to gauge what is happening in their kingdom.'

There was a murmur around the room.

The king stood to accompany his wife. The room fell silent again. 'Ladies and gentlemen of the council, it seems we have the beginnings of a plan here. If this news is true, then we have an opportunity that we can exploit for our own peace of mind. If the news is correct, then we will have saved face with a valued ally. If we are wrong, then we can tell them we are acting on misinformation and apologise to them. I propose we take this path. All in favour of the queen's mission, please raise your hands.'

Most of the hands in the room went up on this insistence.

'Those against …'

The two councillors who were arguing and shouting earlier put their hands up, along with another three.

'So, on a majority vote, it is agreed. We send a vanguard to Azuria with the condolences of our great nation for their loss.' The king went to sit down, but he stopped midway and stood up once again. There was an enigmatic smile on his face. 'I propose that our son, Prince Bernard, should head this vanguard. It will show the Azurians we mean peace and we mean no malice towards them.'

Once more the room was awash in agreeing murmurs. King Thaddius smiled as he sat down next to his wife. He patted her hand and looked around room. 'Ladies and gentlemen, I now propose we close this meeting.'

Murmurs again as the members of the council began to gather their notes and shuffle out of the room, each taking their time to pay respects to the royalty present.

When they were alone, Halia turned to her husband.

'What troubles you, my lady?' he asked with a tender tone.

'Why send Bernard? He's a boy, he's likely to fail.'

Thaddius shook his head and smiled. 'You're right, he is a boy, but a boy needs to grow up. This mission will make a man of him.'

'But if we're wrong about this, then the Azurians are bound to see it as a precursor to invasion. They'll lock him up, most likely kill him.'

'Bernard is past the time of testing. He'll not be alone. I'll send Sir Ambric with him. He is master at arms, and I cannot envision him letting anything happen to the boy. I'll inform Ambric that he will be the leader of the expedition, but he must allow Bernard to believe he is in charge. If anything happens that is out of the boy's skills, then Ambric is to take over the reins. Bernard is an excellent warrior; what he lacks in discipline he makes up for in willing. He needs to learn diplomacy too if he is to rule one day, and one day he will. Believe me, wife, this is the best thing that we can do for him.'

The queen moved her hand from beneath the king's and released a long sigh. 'So, it is our only son we send to Azuria then?' There was scorn in her voice. It was obvious she hated the idea of Bernard so far away from her.

'Yes, my love, and may the Glimm themselves watch over him.'

Halia took a moment to answer him, when she did it was merely a curt nod.

That was all Thaddius required.

The decision was made.

The king and queen made their way out of the council room hand in hand. They were followed by the royal guards as they made their way towards the royal residence. There, they would find Prince Bernard and relay to him the good news regarding his upcoming mission.

~~~~

Two days later, Prince Bernard, closely accompanied by an older, grizzled man with a thick, dark moustache, was dressed, packed, and ready to depart.

Sir Ambric hadn't been happy at the prince's choice of guard. It was made up mostly of his friends from school, scattered with a few seasoned troops. Ambric thought their experience was light for a mission such as this, but his remit had been to give the boy enough rope to hang himself with before reeling him in and saving his life.

The king and queen were there to see them off, along with an assorted crowd, mostly from the village.

As tradition dictated on these occasions, Prince Bernard tipped his sword to his father before making the horse bow to his mother. Then, to great aplomb, the gates to the city were opened and the company drove their horses out into the big, wild, and dangerous world.

Queen Halia wiped a tear from her eye as her husband nodded.

30.

CASSANDRA, STILL IMPRISONED in her circular room, had counted out close to forty days since she had been locked up. Fresh water had been collected using the bowl now that the rains had come, and she had been able to fashion herself a small toilet using a second bucket and some other parts of the table that she had broken up.

She was surviving physically, but she could feel her mental health deteriorating. This was mostly due to where her food was coming from. She thought she was going mad when she had heard scratching and scurrying in the middle of the night, and the next morning there had been a fresh supply of food.

She hadn't been ungrateful for it, just confused.

When she did sleep, her dreams were vivid, plagued by visions of wild old men with grey hair and beards, all of them wearing white muslin robes wrapped around their skinny bodies. In each dream, they had been offering her something, sometimes they were even jumping up and down in excitement and frustration for her to accept the offerings. Sometimes the thing they were offering was a blue glowing ball, other times, and these were the upsetting times, it was a vision of Alexander dressed in purple clothing. Each time, he looked happy, smiling. This cheered her up, but ultimately, she would wake in her prison not even knowing how many miles away from her beloved brother and kingdom she was.

Each time the men in her dreams tried to communicate something to her, the frustration on their faces was easy to read. Cassandra didn't know how to break through the invisible wall that divided them. Occasionally, especially when the offering was Alexander, she would rant and rave herself, mimicking the frustrations of the old men. She would bang her fists on the invisible barrier that separated them.

She knew they were trying to tell her something, she recognised by their urgency that it was something important; and it frustrated her to distraction that she couldn't communicate with them.

The one stable of all the dreams was the blue glow. It was the same blue that tinged her hair and the hair of the people of Azuria. The glow was constant, either emitting from the metallic ball offered or from Alexander's head, or sometimes it was just in the background creating an atmosphere.

In these dreams, she searched frantically for something to write on, anything to allow communication with these men, but there was nothing in the large hall except the altar and the skeletons upon it.

Whenever she awoke, she had all the time in the world to ponder the dreams. The strange thing was that she had never been one to dream as a child. There had been the occasional nightmare, especially after her father had died, but they were never anything as vivid as these.

The men were determined for her to receive the orb they were offering, but try as she might, she just could not break through the invisible wall between them.

Tonight, she thought. *If the dream comes again, I'll be ready for it!*

~~~

There were three of them, all dressed alike—not the same, but similar. One had a miniature Alexander in his hands. The boy was happy playing with his toys. Another man held the blue glowing ball and was attempting to hand it to her. The third was not looking Cassandra's way. His back was turned, and he looked like he was having a heated conversation with someone else.

Instead of trying to take the ball this time, she slipped her hand inside her gown. Because she knew this was a dream, she had no idea if this was going to work. After a moment's fumbling, she relaxed as her fingers found the warm globe. She pulled it from her gown and held it up. In all the time it had been in her possession, she had never seen it shine so brightly. The cobalt pulse illuminated her wide eyes and smiling lips.

With effort, she drew her eyes away from the prop and looked at the men beyond the invisible wall. The two who were looking at her were grinning.

Something different happened.

It was a sound like air being drawn into a room. A whoosh. It came from everywhere, bouncing around the darkness that surrounded her. Other sounds began to echo too, and smells began to filter in.

The sounds were voices resonating around the empty chamber, and the aromas of age and dust assaulted her senses. She didn't know if she wanted to gag or dance. She gazed at the ball in her hand before looking at the men before her. The one who had been offering the ball was now empty-handed. A kindly smile that looked filled with relief was etched across his face. He reached out and touched her forehead. 'Sleep now, child,' he said in her tongue as her eyes grew heavy. 'You have accomplished much.'

Before she fell into slumber, she saw the third man *was* pleading with someone she couldn't see. This person was bathed in red glow, similar but also opposite, to the blue!

31.

ALEXANDER WAS IN a strange place. Not physically. Physically, he was in his own room, playing with his toys. They were in the middle of an epic battle, with the Azurian army playing off against the mighty foe that was the Carnelians. It was something that had been quite a theme between him and his friends over the last few weeks.

Especially since his mother …

He didn't like to think about that. Or the time Cass disappeared for a whole week. He had thought he would never see her again and didn't know how to feel about it. He had been glad for Anthony's guidance and counsel during that time, but thankfully, she had come back.

He thanked the Glimm for that.

The strange place he was in was in his head. Things were just not fitting into place anymore. Anthony and his teachers said it was to do with the loss of his mother and the stresses created by the increased responsibility it had caused. But he didn't know what any of that meant. All he knew was things were not the same. *Even Cass.* A deep down, ugly thought had occurred to him. It was one he didn't want to admit having, but it niggled at him, forcing him to acknowledge it. *Maybe* especially *Cass! How did she get down that corridor so quickly? And how did she get back into that council room without me seeing her?* These thoughts had been plaguing him ever since her return. They

135

mixed with the memory of the old woman he'd seen in the corridor. There had been something about her that he didn't like. It was in the way she hadn't recognised him and was so quick to deny seeing his sister run past her.

One of the main questions that had been plaguing him, burning him even, was: why hadn't she been to his room to see him these last few nights? She had always come to play beforehand before she went to Carnelia.

He wanted answers, but he didn't know what questions to ask. All he knew was there *were* questions, and he was determined to find them.

He picked up his favourite soldier, the captain of his army, and looked at it. 'I'll ask her tonight at dinner,' he said to the toy. 'I'll ask her straight what's going on, why she doesn't play with me anymore.'

He thought about the orb he had given her as a leaving gift and how it glowed blue. He wondered where it was right now. Absently, he put the captain of his Azurian army down and stood up. With wistful eyes, he made his way to his chest and removed something before returning to his toys.

He took the captain and covered him with what he had in his hands before placing it back at the head of his army. Then, he stood and walked out of the room, turning the knob on the gas lamp as he did.

He left the room dark.

The leader of the Azurian army was drying. The purple paint hardened as it sunk into its wooden body.

32.

THE WEEKS CONTINUED, and Endellion had been productive. Since her return as Cassandra to the Kingdom of Azuria, she had wasted no time in setting her plans in motion. Within the first few days, she had begun raising the levels of paranoia as to what Carnelia was doing, reminding everyone how they had killed her mother, possibly her father, and had tried their very best to kill her too.

In short, she was advocating her war to whoever would listen, and of course, she knew the people would listen.

Nightly meetings were held in the council chambers, and she did her best to attend every one of them.

Her whining, pathetic brother would mope around at given every opportunity. He would ask her to read him stories or to come and see him in his chambers, even if it was only for a few moments. He told her he missed her, and loved her, and wanted some time for themselves.

Can't that miserable little brat see the kingdom is on the breech of war? I don't have time to mollycoddle a baby. I have plans to bring to fruition!

As she opened the door to the council chambers for another meeting, everyone stood. 'As you were,' she commanded, taking her seat. Everyone followed her lead.

The council was made up of old men, she had replaced all the younger, liberal, free-thinking councillors with the

137

warmongers she recognized. Grizzled old men who had read about the glories of war with Carnelia but had only experienced the frustration of minor skirmishes with rogue nations and free roamers. The thought of war made these men salivate. Endellion could almost taste the testosterone levels rise every time she mentioned the possibility of a full-blown conflict with their biggest rivals.

'The Carnelians are hungry for this. It is a war of their own doing. They are the aggressors.' She knew these men would love it even more if they thought they were on the righteous side. 'They were salivating as they cut down our men, they were in a kill frenzy. There were many of our brave brothers and sons calling, no… not calling, *crying* for mercy. A mercy that was in the hands of these butchers, a mercy that would not be forthcoming.'

The men grumbled and shouted at this tale, banging their fists on the table in frustration.

'I saw one cut the ears from a wounded Azurian soldier. The madman weaved them onto a chain that hung around his neck. His comrades cheered him on as he proudly displayed his trophies. His victim died, choking in a pool of his own blood, watching his murderer dance.'

She would start every single one of her meetings with an outright lie like this. The tales had been too many and too embellished to make any sense in such a short conflict, but the war-hungry old men lapped them up like thirsty dogs drinking the blood of the hunt.

'This cannot be tolerated,' one man shouted as he stood, he was holding a flagon of wine in his hand, and he raised it in his shout. The red liquid sloshed from it, dripping down his hands.

Endellion looked on with a hidden smirk. *Very symbolic,* she thought.

'We should march on Carnelia at once,' another drunken man shouted, slamming his wine down on the heavy table before him. This shout was greeted with cheers from the others.

Everyone, with the exception of Endellion, was drinking, the alcohol making more of the decisions than the once sharper brains within the room.

She was wearing a beautiful, flowing blue gown and looking every inch the beautiful princess, she was mimicking. When she stood, the older men quietened, resting their over-used goblets on the table. A respectful silence fell in the rowdy room.

'It is my solemn duty as your queen to proclaim our beautiful realm of Azuria must prepare for war. We must call in our generals and our armies, we must arm them, every man. The Carnelian threat has been dangling over our heads for far too long. We are proud. We are formidable. We are Azurian!'

The men in the room were roused to a fever. Each jumping and shouting, hailing their queen as the best they had ever had. The queen who would go down in history as the savour of Azuria.

She allowed them to continue their celebrations before taking them up to yet another level. The servants had been briefed to keep the flow of wine coming fast and sweet. She took a goblet herself and stood from the table, raising it into the air. This time there was no respite from the cheering.

'We will not sit idly by and wait for their next move. We are proud Azurians. We will march on our enemy. We will take them by surprise. Our revenge will be swift, and it will be merciless.'

More cheers came from the drunken councillors.

'We will need to fortify our city. If our brave soldiers are marching on the scourge of Carnelia, then we cannot, and will not, leave our mothers and babes unprotected. Those dirty, cowardly Carnelians will no doubt lead a counterattack when they know the lion's share of our forces are defeating their men in battle. We will surprise them. They will not find an unprotected Azuria for them to occupy. They will find an impregnable kingdom with the resources to protect itself from their filth.'

The blood lust was deep within these old warriors, they had been out of war for far too long.

She sat back, taking a sip of wine. She winced at how strong it was. Once she swallowed, a wry smile spread across her lips.

~~~~

Endellion left the rowdy room. She had set the councillors the task of drafting the articles of war. A document that was required to be forwarded to all councillors before conflict could be formally declared. As most of the members of said council were present, salivating over each other as to how they will announce it, she didn't need to be there anymore. She excused herself to take care of some business that was closer to home.

33.

ALEXANDER WAS WIDE awake when he heard the door handle to the chambers turn. His heart began to pound. The only person who didn't need to knock before entering was his sister.

As the door pushed open, he heard the squeal of the metal hinges complaining. He didn't know if he should call out to her or allow her to enter her own chambers and get herself ready for bed before surprising her by bursting into her room and jumping on the bed. She had always loved a surprise pillow fight. *I wonder if she let me win all those times before?* he asked himself. He positioned his head to listen so he would know when the best time was to attack her.

But something disheartened him.

She was talking.

Who is she with?

Alexander was more than a little upset. *If she has a visitor in our chambers, that is not befitting my sister, or my queen.*

The real underlying feeling that he was experiencing was jealousy. He didn't want to know why she thought bringing someone back to their chambers was acceptable, especially when she couldn't take the time to come and see him.

He pushed his blankets away and slid, silently, out of bed. He made his way through the gloom of his own sleeping chamber, towards the ajar door to their shared living quarters. A thin light fought its way through the door, it was just enough for him to be able to see her moving about inside.

To his relief, she was alone; or at least he thought she was.

She was having a one-sided conversation, and she sounded strange. He couldn't tell if she was angry or excited.

He continued to watch. The light from the living quarters that was making it into his room had a red tinge to it. It made him feel strange. There was something about it, something wrong, something that told him it shouldn't be there. Unperturbed, he pressed his face to the crack in the door and watched. Normally, knowing that Cassandra was there, that he wasn't alone in his chambers, would soothe him. He liked to hear his sister potter around, it reassured him she was safe and that she hadn't left him like their mother had done.

Tonight, though, Cass wasn't pottering. She was dressed in her nightgown, and she was kneeling at the side of her bed holding something in the air. Whatever it was, it was the source of the red glow in the room. To Alex, it was similar to the orb he gave her on her departure from Azuria. This made him smile for a moment before he realised *that* ball had shone with the blue of Azuria, not the red of … Carnelia!

He stepped away from the door. He wanted to hide in his bed, to pull the covers over him and sleep, forgetting all about the red glow. However, his natural, youthful curiosity wouldn't allow it. It forced him to look. He needed to see what was happening. He needed to know why his beloved sister had been ignoring him since her return from her expedition.

'And so, it is my command that it be done,' she spoke aloud. As she did, the ball's glow dimmed and she brought it back down onto the bed. The room visibly darkened, and for the first time in his life, Alexander feared Cassandra. He didn't understand why, but the fear was there.

In the returned gloom of the room, he watched her lift her head. He didn't understand how, but he knew she was smiling, either to herself or to whoever she had been talking or praying to.

Either way, he didn't like it.

'Brother?' she whispered in the gloom, not turning her head.

Alexander stopped breathing. He could taste the fear coursing through him. It tasted like blood, like when he cut his lip. His body began to shake uncontrollably, and for a terrible moment, he thought he might lose control of his functions and an embarrassing accident would occur.

'Alexander,' she called. Her voice was sweet, like it used to be. 'I know you're there. It's OK, you know. You can come in if you need to.'

Her words were whispered with such kindness that he felt compelled to enter the chambers and run to her. A wave of apprehension overcame him as he looked on the bed and saw the glowing orb.

'I can see you, sweet brother. Come, let us talk. I feel like I haven't seen you for a year.'

He pushed the door open, exposing his hiding space. His head was bowed, and his arms dangled, swinging left to right. He felt embarrassed being caught spying.

'Come, Alex. Let's talk and play. I feel events are taking me away from you, and you are growing up so quickly.' She held her arms out to him. It was an invitation he so desperately wanted and needed.

~~~~

A smile broke on his young face.

She noticed it lighting up his features, giving her a glimpse of the man, and the magnificent ally, he would soon become. The next thing she felt was the full strength of a ten-year-old running into her open arms. He almost knocked her over in his eagerness to embrace her. Then there was wetness on her shoulder as she felt his body tremble beneath her enfolding arms.

'Oh, Cass …' he sobbed. 'I'm so glad we're still friends. I've missed you all this time.' He hesitated for a moment, not sure if he should carry on with what he was about to say. 'I … I miss Mother too,' he continued.

'There, there, Brother. Don't cry now. I'm going to need my big strong brother in the days and weeks to come. There'll be some hard times for Azuria, and in hard times, a queen needs soldiers and princes she can rely on. She'll need strong warriors to help her and keep her safe.' She moved his shivering body away from her, holding him at arm's length.

Her Cassandra face smiled at the snivelling little wretch before her. *How pathetic are young boys really?* she thought, but her face gave a most beautiful smile. 'Will you be that strong warrior prince for me, Alexander?'

Wiping the tears from his face, he managed a crooked smile, and his dark eyes lightened for a moment. A confused and shaky sob, that might have been a laugh, escaped him as he looked deep into her eyes. As he opened his mouth, thin chords of saliva threaded between his lips. 'Yes,' he gushed at once. 'Yes, Cass. Of course I'll be your warrior prince. I'm your brother and your protector. I'm the strongest and bravest of them all. Of all Azuria.'

He buried his moist face back into her shoulder. This time, there was no weak shudder from his body, she felt his strong resolve, like he had just grown up, matured even, within the last couple of seconds.

'I know you will.' She grinned through her Cassandra façade. 'I know you will, my prince.'

34.

PRINCE BERNARD OF Carnelia had grown bored by the slow mission he had been sent upon as his debut. He was irked and hard done by with the fact that Sir Ambric had been granted second in command status. He had been allowed to hand pick much of his command but had no say in the role of his advisor. His only constraint was that the company had to be at least a thirty to seventy spilt with men that Sir Ambric approved of as opposed to everyone who Bernard selected. It had resulted in a mixed mission, young academy recruits mixed with older, seasoned guards.

The whole situation made Ambric unhappy and uneasy. As a group, they had been briefed on the urgency and importance of this mission and the dangers that were associated with it. The possibility of war between the two kingdoms hung on a successful negotiation between Bernard's party and the Azurians.

Ambric did not hold the chances of success as high, mostly due to the frivolity of the younger members of the party. He had been a special guard for longer than anyone in the army cared to remember. Many had tried to guess his age, but there were widening differences. The consensus was that he was somewhere in his late fifties, but there was no one who would clarify that, and Ambric himself was stoic when it came to his personal life.

'I live my life in service to the Kingdom of Carnelia' was always his stock answer when anyone asked him anything about himself.

But there was one thing that everyone knew about the thick-set older man. He was the best soldier Carnelia had. This was a fact, and it had never once been in dispute. He had led many battles with rogue nations and outlanders, he had taken many injuries, yet he had always come back victorious.

He wore his dark, red tinged hair long, usually tied back, but always with some hanging over his face to hide the scars he had received in many battles. If challenged on them, he would often tell the young recruits that he loved and cherished every one, then told them they should too.

'But why hide them?' they would undoubtedly ask.

'Because, if I was ever to be caught and tied up, I would have at least one last weapon to brandish on my foes.'

This always caused a laugh, but Ambric never laughed. Not at the prospect of war anyway.

This mission was proving too much for him, though. The thought of babysitting this motley gang of young, over-privileged reprobates turned his stomach. *If it does come to war and these are all that's left to defend Carnelia, then I* will *rise from the grave and do it myself,* he found himself thinking on more than one occasion. Although he would never have said it aloud, he thought it was short sighted and almost a folly of the king to send a such a youngster as Bernard to negotiate something as potentially explosive as this.

The young man and his friends didn't seem to understand the importance of an early night and an early rise. They preferred to stay up late drinking ales and singing loudly into the night. What they were doing was giving their position away to anyone within a five-mile radius. On more than one occasion, Ambric had risen at his normal time, usually ten to fifteen minutes before the rest of the duty, only to find the sentries fast asleep at their post. When he had challenged them and put them on discipline duty, he had been overruled by the prince.

It was rapidly becoming an impossible situation. The boy would never in a hundred years become a soldier, never mind a leader or a king. He was treating this expedition as if it were a vacation.

~~~~

'But the mission is such a bore, Ambric. I need release.'

Ambric and Bernard were standing toe to toe in the prince's tent. The older, squat man stood a good three or four inches shorter than the younger man, but lack of height had never troubled him; in fact, he had always used it to his advantage. Tall people always underestimated short men. 'This mission is of the utmost importance. We are going to Azuria to give our condolences for the passing of their queen. While we are there, we'll find out why they have closed their borders to all—'

'Sir Ambric. I respect you and all you have done for the Kingdom of Azuria,' Bernard interrupted with a patronising tone that made Ambric want to slap him. 'But I assure you, sir, I oversee this mission, and I say we *will* make camp and we *will* hunt. I know the only reason I've been sent on this ... folly is because my father, the fool that he is, deems I'm in need of discipline. Well, I say I might as well be cooked for the goose as for the gander, eh? The men need recreation.'

'Your men need discipline,' Ambric snapped. 'Your men get recreation every night. Your sentries sleep on their duties, you sleep late, and you sing too loud. We need to get to Azuria as soon as we can.'

The prince put his hand on the older man's shoulders and smiled. Ambric's fingers twitched at the smug look on his face. 'Do I need to remind you who you are, Sir Ambric, and who you answer to?'

Ambric licked his lips. He was fighting the urge to complete his orders, to take control of this expedition as the king intended. But he knew if he did, the prince would never learn anything and he would lose respect from his peers and subordinates alike.

The prince smiled again, Ambric could see that he thought victory was in his grasp. 'I thought not. Now, my men will hunt, and we will do it today. You can stay behind and guard the camp, Sir Ambric. We need to hunt fast; therefore, we can't have any old men slowing us down.' The prince turned and disappeared out of the flap of the tent, leaving it to waft in the breeze.

'This is not how this mission is supposed to go,' Ambric mumbled to himself as he followed the youngster out. 'It's what happens when you put boys in charge of men's work.'

35.

CASSANDRA HELD THE glowing blue ball in her hands. She had been holding it for maybe an hour, although it was difficult to tell in her timeless prison. She had stared into it for days, attempting to unlock its mysteries. Each time she gazed into its depths, she searched for a pattern, something to show how it worked.

All she had received for her hard work were random light patterns and a splitting headache.

'How was the man in the dream able to speak to me?' she mused. 'All I'd done was pick up the ball.' Her own voice seemed strange to her. She had not talked to, or even seen, another person since the witch Endellion had left her up here alone. She knew that she needed to speak aloud to make sure that her voice got exercise. She'd heard of people being locked up for too long losing the ability to speak altogether.

Day was dawning outside, and Cassandra was hungry, hungry and more than a little bored. *Maybe not bored as such, more ... frustrated,* she thought as she put the ball down carefully on the floor next to her bed. As she lay her head on her pillow, her thoughts cast back to the dream of the old men. 'Could the ball have caused the dreams? Is there some magical power to the thing?' It was an enigma to her, a frustrating puzzle. The men in the dream obviously held importance to the thing. It was something akin to a full-time obsession. Other than the faint blue glow, Cassandra could see very little physical interest in it.

She put her hands over her eyes in a vain attempt to block out the rising sun that would very soon be streaming in through the windows. She also tried to ignore the rumble in her stomach. She had very little food left and knew the phenomenon of the little critters bringing her food would probably not last forever.

After all, she wasn't living in a fairy-tale.

She could hear scratching coming from the window but didn't know if she was dozing off and the noise was in her subconscious or if the noise was indeed real. The last time this noise had occurred, she'd found a parcel of nuts, fruits, and berries beneath the sill. She threw herself towards the opening and hung her head out, searching.

There was no one.

But there was some*thing*.

A small stoat was perched on the windowsill. It was sitting up on its hind legs, looking at her. It sniffed the air a few times before darting off, back out of the opening it had come from. Cassandra watched it escape, fascinated as it clung to the steep, smooth walls of her prison.

'I wish I could do that.' She chuckled as she turned towards her gift. She threw herself on the package like a savage, giving no care as to where it came from. After making short work of the fruit and the berries, she grudgingly left the nuts. 'For later,' she said.

This had happened again and again over the weeks that she had been stuck in the room. Although, her saviour wasn't always a stoat. One time it had been a large black rat, another time it had been a bird, but the end-product was always the same. A bundle of nuts, fruits, and berries. They had obviously been foraged from the forest.

Initially, after filling her belly, she thought maybe the witch Endellion had sent the animals to bring her food, but after pondering on it a while, she concluded that it must have been someone else, someone less malignant.

'Thank you, little stoat,' she shouted after the fleeing animal.

It stopped and looked at her as if listening to her voice.

It was then that she realised she was holding the Glimmer, and it was glowing a brighter blue than usual. Her eyes flicked from it back to the stoat. 'I love the berries and fruits, but next time could you bring me some meat and some wood to create a small fire?' She laughed at herself for talking to the animal. 'I really could do with some fat and bone to give me strength, to plan an escape.'

Cassandra chuckled at her silliness as the stoat broke its trance-like stare at the Glimmer, then scurried back down the wall to the freedom of the forest.

She flopped onto the bed. Even though she was still hungry, she knew that she would have to wait 'til later to finish her bounty. 'You could have stayed for a small while too, Mr Stoat,' she whispered as a tear welled in her eye. Her last thought before sleep overtook her was of Alexander.

~~~~

A few precious, dreamless hours later, Cassandra awoke hungrier than ever. As she stretched, saliva built in her mouth and her stomach complained about its lack of activity. The thought of the nuts lifted her dark mood.

The light streaming in through the window illuminated something else by the package that the stoat had left. It took her a while to make out what it was, but in the end, it was her nose that gave it away.

There were more nuts and fruits, but this time there was something else too, something exciting. It was a dead animal.

She got slowly out of the bed and crept over to where her deceased, unexpected guest lay. It was a small chicken; its neck had been broken. Next to the bird was a pile of wood kindling that was big enough to allow the cooking of the chicken.

She scratched her head. It was one thing to be brought nuts and fruits of the forest, it was another to be brought an animal and a means to cook it.

Using only her hands, she tore the animal's corpse to pieces, into chunks large enough to cook. She then rubbed the sticks together, creating a small fire from the dry kindling. She took her water bowl and placed the chicken in it, using the fruits and nuts to flavour it.

Less than an hour later, she had a chicken dinner complete with gravy juice and nuts to garnish. She left no part of the animal, *or gift,* to waste. She sucked the bones clean and stored them to one side to boil later before drinking the remains of the gravy from the still warm bowl.

She fell back against the bed, her belly full and her mood satisfied. A silly smile broke on her lips as an absurd thought passed through her head. *How did that animal understand me when I told it I needed meat?* 'I must be going mad up here.' She laughed and climbed onto the bed. 'Stoats can't understand humans, and you just can't go about ordering them to do things for you.'

With the lovely chicken dinner laying blissfully heavy on her stomach, she yawned and stretched on the bed.

Sleep came fast and easy.

'The stoat understood you,' the familiar voice echoed through the darkness of her sleep. 'It obeyed you via the Glimmer.'

When she opened her eyes, she was not surprised to find herself in the darkness, not of her dreams but of the cavernous chamber she was now used to. The two skeletons lay on the top of the alter, still together in their death embrace for all eternity. She turned to see the three men. They were smiling towards her, and a comfort from their presence spread through her. It was almost as if she belonged here now, wherever *here* was. She looked down at her hands and noticed for the first time that she was holding the Glimmer. The glow from it was fierce, but the feel of its surface against her skin was warm and comforting.

'You are in possession of a Glimmer. It is one of the most powerful objects that a mortal such as yourself can possess.'

Another one of the men took up the tale. 'We were known once as the Glimm. We were an ancient order. Our history could be traced back over thousands of years. We followed the teachings of The Great Lord Glimm. His presence and powers were part of us, as we were part of him.'

The third man continued. 'Unfortunately for us, and for our loved ones, we became engrossed in our work and our studies. Our numbers dwindled, it was a natural regression, but was accelerated by our own selfish motives.'

The first man moved forward and gestured towards the two skeletons on the altar. Cassandra's eyes followed. She regarded the emaciated men with the daggers between their ribs. 'This is me. I along with my brother were the last of our kind. We knew the magic of the old ways would die with us, so we preserved it, our essence, if you will. We encased the full extent of our powers into Glimmers. Knowledge, wisdom, and magic. They were forged into two orbs. One of which you now possess.'

She lifted the ball and looked at it. The glare from it should have hurt her eyes, but it did the opposite. It made them feel better, more alive. Like radiance was flowing into her. 'What do I do with it?'

The man whose skeleton was laying on the altar looked at her. The humour and levity that had been abundant in his eyes and smile left abruptly. 'You survive …' he demanded.

'Yes … survive,' the second man continued. 'It has already sustained you. Our order and our magic had a great affinity with nature. You needed meat to survive, the Glimmer instructed the stoat to get you some. The stoat obeyed.'

'Why is it that you plague my dreams? Why not come to me in the hours of daylight? Do you crave your Glimmers back? Will they restore your order and bring you back from the dead?'

The three men laughed at the questions. Cassandra didn't; her face was serious.

'No, child. Our time is long past. This time is yours. We...' the man stifled a laugh, '...plague your dreams, as you say, because we want the Glimmers used to bring peace and harmony to the world. They were forged for good, not for ill.'

The third man then spoke again. 'But, alas, we are as much servants of the Glimmers as the animals are.'

'Servants?' Cass asked; her interest had spiked during this conversation.

'Yes,' he continued. 'We are servants. The ones who hold the Glimmers can command from us all we have to give. Our knowledge, our powers, and our magic.'

'What powers do you speak of?'

'Our kind conquered the elements, we deciphered nature, we mapped the spans of life and death. Our powers are vast, the sum of thousands of years.' The man then hung his head low, and a sadness tinged his features. 'Alas, to our own shame, we could not conquer our own naivety. We thought we would last forever.'

'So ... I have all these powers now, right here, at my fingertips?'

The man whose body was on the altar took over.

'Yes, child, you do. But count the figures on the alter. There are two of them. One is me and one is my dear bother.'

'What do you mean?' she asked looking deep into the glowing blue.

'It means there are two Glimmers, my child. The other, the sibling to this one, is being used right now, as we speak.' The man's face fell. 'The user is an abuser. It is doing the work of ill right now, and it pains us.'

Cassandra looked at the men, all three of them. Her features began to stretch as realisation dawned. 'Endellion,' she whispered. 'Endellion has the second Glimmer, doesn't she?'

'Yes, child. It is Endellion who is custodian of the red Glimmer. She has become a powerful user of the magic we possess. But her heart is black, and there is little or no light in her soul. We understand that you have been the victim of her Glimmer yourself.'

It was Cassandra's turn to drop her head. 'A little more than just a victim, I'd say. She has taken everything from me. My mother, my brother, my home, and my kingdom.'

'We are sorry for this. But there is something you should know. When we forged the Glimmers, we made a single mistake. They were meant to be individual sources of power, but something happened in the genetic make-up of them. If a person were to be in possession of both Glimmers, then that person would be *the* most powerful entity in this world. A power that may rival The Great Lord Glimm himself. It would take a strong-willed person to tame them and to be the harbinger of a brand-new era. If that person were to be dark willed, then the future would be very bleak indeed.'

'Is Endellion strong willed?' Cassandra asked, dread filling her heart.

'We cannot say ...' he continued.

Before she was able to ask any of the thousand questions that had suddenly rushed into her head, the men began to fade, as did the room.

As did everything.

Cassandra fell into a deep and otherwise dreamless sleep.

36.

ENDELLION WAS IN Cassandra's chambers. She had made doubly sure that Alexander was out of the way. He was in school and wouldn't be back until the end of the day. That gave her a few hours to herself.

She'd had an idea. It was something that had popped into her head just recently. She remembered reading about the phenomenon when she was a youth, not really believing it, thinking that it had only been a horror story written to scare the housewives before they went to sleep at night. But now, with her new abilities, harnessing the power of the Glimmer, she was realising there was little that was impossible to her anymore. This thought gave her the impetus to begin her adventure, and now, based on what she knew she could do, she had every intention to see it through to the very end.

The bloody end.

'I command you to bring forth black rain. My will is your command, and my will is for you to do my bidding.' She was in the centre of the room; her Cassandra disguise had been dropped, and she languished in her original form. Her eyes were closed, and the red orb was illuminating the room.

Her surroundings began to swim around her. She had performed this many times and relished the dizzy feeling that accompanied it.

When she opened her eyes, she was surrounded by three men, each had long, wild grey hair that mingled with their beards. Their scrawny bodies were wrapped in filthy muslin gowns that looked like they hadn't been washed for millennia. Each man regarded Endellion with unbidden loathing.

'Do as I say, I command you,' Endellion snapped. The old man's head was bowed low, and his shoulders were hunched. She was repulsed that she could see his collar bones covered only with a thin film of pale skin.

'The black rain is very powerful, very dark magic. We would be remiss if we didn't implore you to rethink its use. Once it has been deployed, it's devastating powers cannot be revoked.'

'Do I not hold the Glimmer?'

'Yes, you do. I am erring you on the side of cau—'

'Don't talk to me of caution,' she interrupted, cutting the man off mid-sentence. 'I am the custodian of the Glimmer, and hence your magic. I *demand* the black rain!'

'The Glimmers were forged to endorse peace, love, and understanding, not for war and ill will towards man. The kingdoms of Azuria and Carnelia were meant to be bastions of knowledge and wisdom, not of bloodshed and slaughter. You pervert our work for greed, revenge, and misplaced judgement. I implore you one more time.' The man dropped to his knees before her. 'I beseech you to reconsider and to acknowledge the consequences these actions will bring.'

Endellion's face appreciated the Glimm's actions. *Just where you belong,* she thought, unable to stifle the laugh building inside her. It flew out of her mouth, as an involuntary bray. 'You speak to me of consequences? You, who allowed your kind to die due to your own perverted lusts for knowledge and power. You are not to lecture me on consequences. I demand you give me the black rain. The people will kneel before me, much like you are doing now.'

The Glimm looked around the dark chamber, towards his colleagues, before realising he was still on his knees. He got up slowly, dusting himself off.

'The Kingdom of Azuria will be fortified. I will rule with an iron fist with the help of my firefly army. I will take the blood of the young and the innocent.' She reached out, grasping the glowing Glimmer. She threw her head back and laughed. It was an evil, maniacal laugh. 'I will become stronger, more powerful than the Great Lord Glimm himself.'

The three men exchanged looks. They were trapped. This was a situation they had no control over. There was nothing in their powers they could do about it.

The Glimm who had been on his knees stepped forward from the other two; his head was low, and his shoulders drooped. His eyes held the look of a broken man, one who was beaten and lost. 'As you wish, my lady. The black rain will be yours.'

Endellion sneered at the small gathering before her. 'I know it will …' Her voice was low and dangerous. 'I will not thank you for giving me something that is already mine.' She twisted the Glimmer in her hand, and the men, the altar, and the dark chamber around them blinked from existence.

She was back in Cassandra's chambers. She stroked the Glimmer, and her features began to melt and twist. Within a few moments, Endellion was gone, her repugnance replaced by youthful beauty.

37.

PRINCE BERNARD WAS enjoying his hunt. He was also relishing the distaste he read in Ambric's face at their folly. They had been on the trail of a wild boar for two days, and he felt he was getting close to the nest. The boars of these woods could grow to almost eight arms in length and sometimes at least half that in height. They were ferocious beasts with short tempers, and anyone who got in the way of their long, razor-sharp tusks would be very lucky if they lived long enough to tell the tale. Bernard had only seen them mounted in the Carnelian museums. They had always fascinated him, and he had long held dreams of hunting one.

They had caught the trail on the first day. The prince, due to his ignorance of the woods, didn't know it was piglet season and the boars would be plenty as they patrolled their patches, fiercely protecting their young.

The hunt had spooked the boar earlier, and it had led them on a merry chase through the forest.

Ambric sat atop his mount at the peak of a hill. Even though it was small, it gave him an unobstructed view of the children charging through the trees below. The men he had picked for the mission were mounted behind him. The disdainful look on their faces spoke volumes of what they thought of this hunt and this mission.

Ambric knew by instinct that the boar had gone to ground. He also knew the beast was female, and that she was leading the hunt party on a merry trail, confusing them, to best protect her piglets. He also knew that Bernard and his party were ignorant of this fact. He had tried to tell him last night around the fire, during another free drinking session, but the prince was loath to listen.

'Sire, we are a full day out of our route. We're going to find it difficult to keep the timescales in check as it is. We must give up this jest,' he advised the youngster. Alas, he was old enough and wise enough to know when he was pissing in the wind.

'Your kind are all about the mission, Sir Ambric. If you don't look up every now and again, life passes you by. I intend to grasp every second I have and live it to the fullest.'

'Sir, there is more than just a mission about this trip. This is about peace between two great nations.'

Bernard got up from the fire and carried his metal plate away from Sir Ambric and sat with the younger men. Ambric shook his head, finishing his food alone.

That was the night before, and the boy still would not listen to reason. Ambric knew that he had the remit to take control, if need be, but he wanted to give the prince the benefit of the doubt.

Give him a chance to learn something.

He knew that underestimating the sow, especially as she protected her younglings, would likely result in serious injury, maybe even death, but he would keep out of it for now, determined as he was to teach these young boys a serious lesson. He would grieve for whoever was the unfortunate one to die, as he did the loss of any Carnelian brother, but life and death are serious lessons to learn.

The prince had split his hunt party into two flanks, and they were advancing, far too fast and far too cock sure for Ambric's liking, on the sow's lair. He watched Bernard give a signal before both flanks charged.

A flock of birds lifted from the trees as the squealing of the defensive sow tore through the midday air. Ambric tutted and shook his head.

He watched with an air of amusement as the copse of trees the sow was using as her lair began to shake. Birds flew out, panicking as they flapped away in every direction, attempting to escape the terror of the charging army and the ill-fated pig.

Ambric turned away from the game. He'd seen enough. He signalled for his loyal men to return to camp and get the fires ready for the evening meal. *There'll be a lot of hungry bellies tonight,* he thought. *And hopefully, some pig meat.*

The second scream to rip through the air was not from any sow Ambric had ever heard. It was human. It sounded like a woman, even though he knew there were none within the company. He turned back towards the trees as the scream stopped abruptly. The branches and leaves had stopped moving too. He knew his fear had come true. Someone was wounded and, by the sounds of it, badly.

What happened next, happened fast.

The sow dashed out of the copse of trees. This was Ambric's first view of the beast, and he was awed by its size. It was almost as large as one of the guard's horses. It was hampered in its run by something dangling from one of its trunk-like tusks. It didn't take Ambric long to realise that the thing dangling was the source of the scream. It was one of Bernard's men. From this distance, he couldn't make out who it was, but whoever it may be was as good as dead already.

The beast rampaged from the bushes, obviously in two minds as to flee the marauding pack or to protect her young still in the lair. She was tossing her head, attempting to rid herself of the restriction hanging from her tusk. The silence from the man told Ambric all he needed to know. The sow had taken a Carnelian life.

Eventually, the corpse slipped from his impalement and the sow turned on him. She kicked at the dirt behind her, lowered her head and charged. His already dead body was trampled, mauled into a pulp within seconds.

Ambric closed his eyes and offered up a small prayer for the soldier.

Suddenly, the hunt pack burst out of the trees, and the sow squealed again before dashing off in the opposite direction.

The pack gave chase.

Their blood was up, and the fever of the hunt was on them.

The way they're charging, there'll be more of that party who won't see another morning, Ambric thought, shaking his head.

As if hearing his musing, the beast abruptly changed direction and charged at one of the breakaway horses. The steed saw the advancing beast and recoiled, throwing its surprised rider. The man hit the floor hard, and Ambric watched as he attempted to get up, dazed from the fall. Without knowing what was happening, he was tossed into the air. Blood flowed from two wounds, one in his neck and the other from his leg, as he hit the floor, flopping like a ragdoll. The blood began to pool around him, thick, fresh, and dark. The boy attempted to get up, checking himself for a weapon. Ambric guessed he didn't have a clue what happened.

The pig bore down on the man so fast and so ruthlessly that Ambric was sure he died on the very first pass. It may have been the second, as the magnificent beast turned on its hind legs and trampled him again. This time, she was not so fast and was able to stop closer and turn again for a third. What was left of the boy below her muscular legs and trotters had stopped moving independently. The remains were merely flopping each time the sow stomped on them.

The hunt pack fell back into the chase, and the sow got wind of them. She squealed and abruptly changed direction. This time she was heading for the camp. Ambric tutted. He turned his horse. Anticipating her destination, he attempted to ride down the hill to head her off and possibly save the camp from the beast's rampage. As his horse galloped down the steep incline, he realised he was going to be too late. The pig had gotten ahead of him with the rest of the pack on its heels.

It hit the camp like a tornado.

The ferocious animal made small work of the tents on the edge of the camp. Her tusks ripped through canvas like it was parchment, not even slowing her down. In fact, they seemed to enrage her even more, giving her impetus to ransack and destroy. Ambric pushed his courser, hoping to catch up with the beast but knowing he was already too late. The sow had made it into the centre of the camp, and the damage it was doing was already irreparable.

With dawning horror, he watched as the raging beast made it to the fire in the centre, where a meal was already roasting on the spit. It ran full tilt into the pit, knocking the roasting animal from its mount and into the flames. Hot fat and fire spat everywhere, landing on the torn and wrecked canvases of the ruined tents, instantly igniting them. Within moments, the camp was an inferno and the beast was turning, its murderous eyes beset upon the chasing pack. Ambric had had enough; he put a final spurt of speed on the horse, removed his longsword from its sheath with one hand, and prepared for a battle.

This wouldn't be his first.

The sow began to charge the pack. Ambric, forever battle ready, could see the fear in the boys' faces as the protective beast stampeded towards them. He turned his steed and matched the sow's speed. He jumped gracefully from his mount onto the back of the animal. Without a second to lose, he sank his weapon into the pig's neck. Instantly, her back legs buckled. It stumbled, squealing like a baby, tossing Ambric from his hold. He was equal to the fall and readied his body to take minimal impact, all the while priming his longsword to finish the animal in as humane and painless a manner as was possible.

Fixing himself, he charged and struck the thrashing sow deep between its eyes, pushing with all his might, avoiding her slashing tusks while attempting to penetrate her thick skull. Once through the bone, the heavy steel did its job and the beast fell instantly. A death rattle wracked through its body before it lay still, allowing him to relax. His tired body fell back against the beast as he breathed a sigh of relief.

He shook his head as he regarded the burning ruins of the camp.

The prince and the rest of the hunt pack eventually caught up, and Ambric watched as they dismounted their steeds. Bernard walked towards him wearing a smile that spread across his whole face. His eyes brimmed with hero-worship and awe. He was clapping.

'Sir Ambric, that was the single most heroic thing I have ever witnessed in my life. What a takedown. Could you talk me through your moves and the thinking behind them?'

Ambric stood, as he did, he pulled his longsword from the animal's head and wiped the blood onto his tunic, then turned towards the smiling prince. His eyes blazed brighter than the ruined tents around him. He watched as the rest of the pack dismounted and attempted to douse the flames.

Ambric knew this was a futile gesture, they were already ruined, their contents lost.

Rage was boiling inside him, rage for the tents and their camp, rage for the unnecessary loss of two lives, and rage for the impudence of the prince in his disregard of his duties and responsibilities. He knew he had to be careful in his response, but the time had come for him to take control of this mission.

With one deft punch, Ambric knocked the young boy on his backside. 'Prince Bernard,' he growled, 'your folly has cost us dear today. Not only have your childish actions cost us two men, but they have also caused the destruction of our camp.'

Bernard was on the floor, holding his jaw, his eyes told Ambric everything he needed to know. The boy had not expected the blow and didn't know how to deal with it when it came. 'What of it?' he asked, checking his hand for blood. There was some, not much, but enough to scare him. Ambric knew how to punch for maximum effect. 'If those men were stupid enough to allow a beast to better and kill them, imagine how they would have been in a time of war. They would have died in that too, no doubt, mayhap even taken a few of our own with them. We are Carnelian soldiers; we can sleep under the stars for a few nights—'

'Bernard … be quiet, child,' Ambric snapped.

Bernard stopped talking and looked at the older man. The men, Bernard's men, stopped what they were doing, watching the drama unfold before them.

'I have had enough of your childishness.'

Bernard's face fell, his brow furled, and his thickening lips tightened. He had never been spoken to like this by anyone, much less a subordinate officer. 'How dare you lay your hands on me,' he snarled, only now realising what had happened. 'I am your prince *and* your superior officer. You will apologise, Sir Ambric, or I'll have these men take you prisoner and you will answer for your treason back home in Carnelia.' He scrambled up from the floor, his hand on the hilt of his sword, his face earnest, and hurt.

Ambric did nothing. He never moved or allowed any emotion to show on his face. Everything that Bernard needed to know about this situation was written in his dark and unmoving eyes.

'My prince …' he spoke low, and there was more than a hint of danger in his tone. Bernard could hear it, but with his men behind him, it was obvious he didn't fear it. 'You *were* in charge of this mission, and I allowed that on the behest of your father. But your childishness and immaturity have put this most important assignment into jeopardy. Do you not see the devastation of the camp?'

At Ambric's invitation, Bernard looked at the ruined tents and the men doing their best to salvage what they could.

'Your father gave me remit to take command whenever I saw fit. I gave you rope, my prince, and proved it just enough to hang yourself with.'

'Men,' Bernard shouted, sounding braver than he looked. 'I command you to seize this treasonous bastard and hold him until we get home to Carnelia. I command this as your prince and heir to the throne.'

Some of the younger men moved forward to obey Bernard's commands.

Ambric looked at them. He counted fifteen men.

A metallic noise rose from behind him. He knew the men he had handpicked would back him. The noise he heard was their drawing steel. He knew there were seven of them, eight including himself. Ample odds.

'It would seem we have a stand-off, my prince. As a betting man, who would you put your money on? Your group of youths, still green behind their ears, or my men, less than half your numbers but each one a veteran, and loyal?'

Bernard, his longsword half drawn, looked at Ambric through squinted eyes. He stopped midway through stepping forward towards his adversary, his eyes darting between the stoic faces of the seven men, all of them now bearing arms, and Ambric, who had not even reached for his steel yet. A change fell over his face as the bravado and the smarm of youth collapsed in an instant, replaced by indecision and fear.

'Is … Is this true, Ambric? Are you taking command from me?'

'I am, my prince. This mission has become a joke. We are four days ride from our purpose, and now we have no supplies or means to cover our heads from the elements. I need you to show more of the traits of your father and allow me to do my job, one that, in my opinion, has just become somewhat grave.'

The prince looked around the burning camp as if he was seeing the devastation for the first time. He turned to his men. Each had re-sheathed their weapons, and all of them were looking at him, some sheepish, others he could see were already with Ambric. Eventually, he turned back to the warrior before him. He noted that Ambric still had not moved from his original position. He dropped his eyes. He breathed a deep sigh and spoke. 'I yield, Sir Ambric. I apologise for my childish behaviour.'

The tension that had spread through the band of men was suddenly lifted as Ambric offered his hand to the prince before him. 'Good man, Prince Bernard. You have learned a great lesson here today. One of humility. It is a great trait in a leader. Unfortunately, it has cost us two men who would have made great soldiers. Come with me and learn how to command an expedition. I will pass leadership back to you only when I see worth, but right now, we have to address this situation.'

Bernard accepted the hand with a face that was solemn and contrite.

'Why do you think our predicament so grave, Sir Ambric?' he asked, trying his best to sound authoritative after what had just happened.

'Because we are four days off our route and all the mapping I had done has burned in these fires. I'm afraid we are lost, my prince.'

'Lost?'

Ambric looked at him. There was no scorn in his look, only that of a leader teaching a subordinate. The power had truly shifted, and Ambric could see it, although he took no pride in it. 'Yes, lost. I do not know this terrain. That was why I was making maps.'

'Can you not navigate by the stars?'

Ambric laughed. It was a rare thing to see, and most of the men, including the ones he had hand-picked himself, turned to witness the event with a certain awe. 'Prince Bernard, I am a master at arms, not a master at sea.' As suddenly as it appeared, the mirth on Ambric's face disappeared. 'We must hope we left tracks we can use to help get us back on course. The going will be slow, but if we work together, only then, we can do our best.' He pointed to some of the men before indicating the large dead beast lying on the floor of the burning camp. 'Butcher what you can from the beast. Salt the meat and collect the blood. It will be our sustenance for the next few days. At least we will not go hungry or need to hunt. It will gain us some ground that has been lost.' He addressed the whole camp next. 'Everyone, salvage what you can from the remains of the camp, we leave in two hours.'

Ambric turned from the rest of the men and walked to his still burning tent. He poked about in the inferno with his sword, hoping to find anything that was salvageable from the mess.

'Sir Ambric?'

He was surprised to see Bernard stood at his side. His eyes were shifting from left to right, and it was obvious he didn't want to make eye contact. 'Sir Ambric, I am truly sorry. I was not ready to lead, and I led this expedition into trouble. My actions killed two of our men. I will bow to your lead and command.'

Ambric put a heavy hand on Bernard's shoulder and looked at him. 'In the last few minutes, you have shown me more leadership qualities than you have in this whole mission. A good leader must first be a good follower. I believe, in time, you will be a great leader, Prince Bernard … and that time is near.'

38.

CASS WAS FLYING!

She was soaring high above the tree-tops and through deep valleys between majestic, snow-covered mountains. She followed paths made by crystal clear lakes that were teaming with fish. Unknown villages, towns, kingdoms, passed below her as she continued to ride the eddies of warm air. The wind blew through her dark, blue tinged hair. She had never felt so alive in her life.

She was free.

Free of her responsibilities, free from the Kingdom of Azuria, free from her family ties, free from the confines that she had made for herself, but most of all, she was free from that horrible prison. She had been in there a long time. How long? She couldn't answer that; each day had merged into another.

The wind turned into rain, and she felt fresh, cleansed. Most of all, she felt new. A new Cassandra had emerged from her confines.

She adjusted her position and swooped towards the yellow field below. Several cows, grazing in the fields, ran from her attack, and she laughed out loud.

She then soared back into the darkening sky.

An odd sound cut through the roar of the wind in her ears. It was almost alien to her, but familiar too. It was something she hadn't heard for a long, long time.

It was the sound of human voices.

It sounded like children.

'Help us. Please help us.'

Cassandra fell out of the bed, bumping her head on the hard floor. For a second, her vision shook, and she wasn't sure where she was. Then her focus returned, and the room, the one that had been her home and her prison, came back into view.

'A dream,' she spat, the disgust in her voice deeply evident. *If only there* was *someone here to hear it,* she thought, sadness tinging her thoughts.

She picked herself up from the floor, rubbing her head and intending to get back into the bed she had fallen from, when she heard a now familiar noise coming from the window. *Gifts,* she thought, bringing a small smile to her face.

She spared a glance over, curious to see what kind of animal it was this time. She was completely unprepared for what was there. She staggered back, shocked and more than a little scared by the vision perched on her sill.

It was the largest bird she had ever seen in her life.

It was so big that all it could do was perch outside the window. Its head was almost the same size as the window itself, and its immense body was concealed by the walls as it couldn't fit its bulk through the small hole.

Petrified of the magnificent creature, she stepped even further back, falling onto her bed. She scrambled as far into the wall as she could, trying to make herself as small as possible. The magnificent creature turned its head, and one beady black eye peered inside the window. It flicked around, taking in the room until finally focusing upon the quaking figure of Cassandra cowering against the wall. An enormous sound issued from outside. She knew it was a squawk, but in these close confines, it sounded more like a roar.

She had heard tales of birds like this, swooping down from the sky, taking babies from their cribs, never to be seen again. The memories of these tales did not help her now as she reached along the wall trying to escape the attentions of this behemoth. Her hand brushed on something that was at the head of her bed.

It was a small wooden box.

She looked at it, and an idea occurred to her.

She remembered what the old men in her dream had told her about their command of nature and of animals. Without taking her eyes from the beast at the window, she grabbed the box. Careful not to make any sudden movements and spook it, she opened the lid. The blue glow escaped its confines and illuminated the room.

The bird's cold eye left Cassandra and considered the box. Another scream emitted from outside, making her jump. She dropped the box, and the Glimmer rolled along the floor. The bird's eye followed as it trundled. Cassandra could see its fascination as the sphere came to a halt. The huge animal never once looked away from it.

Feeling brave, she edged off the bed and crept to where the glowing orb had come to rest. Not taking her eyes from the beast, she gripped the Glimmer. For a split second, the old men in the dark chamber appeared, and a ghostly whisper came from everywhere at once.

'Take the Glimmer. Use it. Command the bird ...' it said before the ghosts, if they were even there in the first place, disappeared, leaving her alone in the room with the monster.

Grasping the Glimmer for dear life, she waved it left to right, watching the huge eye in her window follow it with rapture. She edged towards the opening, glad the bird was ignoring her movements and fixating only on the orb. Once she was close enough, she reached out her free hand and stroked its soft feathers. A musky smell arose from its body; it wasn't bad, but it wasn't something she thought she could, or would want to, become accustomed to.

'There you go,' she soothed. 'There you go, my lovely.' She leaned out of the window, and for the first time, she caught a

171

better look at the beast. She marvelled at its huge beak, but not in a good way. The smooth ridges and sharp tip looked lethal. *This thing could snap me in two,* she thought with awe. She stepped back and admired it, trying to see its full majesty, most of which was still outside the room. *I bet this thing is big enough for me to ride on its back.* As the thought passed through her head, the Glimmer began to glow, and the bird stretched its wings. It manoeuvred itself on the ledge, giving her access to climb onto it.

Her body shook.

Dare she?

What do I have to lose?

She slipped the Glimmer into the folds in her gown and looked at the back of the bird before her. Its tail feathers poked through the window, and without thinking, she reached out and grasped them. The tremors that ran through her body were twofold. First, she shook in fear of this beast turning on her and killing her instantly, and second, from the thought of escaping this prison and getting away from the room that she had become resigned to dying in.

Gingerly, she clambered onto the monster's back, her arms and legs gripping anywhere they could. The feel of the magnificent beast's muscles beneath her was a wonder, and she second guessed her actions.

By then it was too late.

The bird pushed away from the window, spreading its wings. Their span was more than impressive as they flapped in the breeze.

She closed her eyes, expecting to fall. Instead, she felt herself lift. She felt the wind in her face and tears in her eyes.

After a few moments of frantically holding on for dear life, Cassandra began to enjoy the ride.

Her dream was breaking.

This time, she really was flying!

39.

THE DUNGEON WAS dark, and it was rank. But to Endellion, it felt rather homelike. She had dwelt in worse, more dangerous places, and the stink was nothing compared to some places she had lived over the years. The stench of decay and hopelessness was almost physical the deeper she travelled into the darkness.

It suited her needs well.

The dim light from the torch the jailer held was barely enough to illuminate the treacherous walkway they were navigating. The steps were thin, wet, and in parts, slimy. She had an idea what the slime could be, but right now it wouldn't be prudent to think too much about that. It didn't bother her too much, although if she were still in the guise of Cassandra, she would have a lot of explaining to do. As she was currently Endellion, doing this work with the Royal Carnelian Seal to prove it, then there were no issues and, best of all, no questions.

What the dim light did keep from her, however, was the filthy, desperate hands that reached out of the stinking cells trying to grab her. Dirty, thin, barely human claws extended from the darkness, flapping like fish out of water, their extra-long fingernails raking at anything they could gain purchase on.

When one of them grasped her arm, she didn't even flinch as she flicked it away from her and back into the hellish abyss from which it had come.

'How many men did you say you needed, ma'am?' the jailor asked in a thin, reedy voice, a voice that suited his look entirely. He was small with very little hair, what he did have had grown long and wispy. His skinny, bowed legs made him look even more absurd than his top half did. He was a man suited to his place in the world.

'The queen said that ten should suffice. They need to be fit and healthy, not like the majority of the scum you have holed up in here. I need fresh men.'

'What crimes are you looking to punish, ma'am?' he asked, turning towards her; his devious smile, illuminated by the dim torch, made him look even more impish, more hideous, than he had earlier. His malignancy was enough to put shivers up even Endellion's thick skin.

'Oh, don't worry yourself too much about that,' she replied, smiling in the darkness. 'The queen just needs them fit and active. You'll be handsomely rewarded for your service to the crown, and for your silence.'

'Well, that's something we both needn't worry about then. I'm loyal to the throne … and to my pocket.' He turned away and continued down the slimy steps.

A dirty cackle could be heard from him in the darkness. She heard the laughing stop for a moment as he hocked in a disgusting sound from deep inside his chest. He then lowered his torch and spat something thick onto the floor. Endellion was compelled to watch as grasping hands reached out of small holes in the doors to either side of the phlegm and grabbed at it.

Disgusting, she thought, *exactly what I need.*

The jailer continued to cackle as he continued down the dark steps. 'Just a little bit further down here, ma'am. Watch your step. We got a new batch in last week, deserters, I'm told. Caught out in the woods, they were, poaching the queen's game and greens. They won't have been affected by their stay yet. They should be fit enough for your needs, whatever they may be.'

They reached a door that was no different to any of the others they had passed, but the vile man stopped and jingled a huge set of keys that had been hanging from the waist of his ill-fitting trousers. He also produced a wicked looking club that had been otherwise concealed. He looked at the club and then at Endellion. A smile spread across his filthy face. 'You can't be too careful, ma'am. Most of these prisoners would eat you as soon as look at you. You have to show them who is in charge.'

He selected a key and opened the door. Like a rat charging into a sewer, he ran into the room, randomly lashing his club in the dark. She watched with interest as the prisoners cowered away from the dim light of the torch, and from the arc of the vicious weapon.

Endellion stepped inside to a chorus of moaning and crying. The jailor had made it to the other end of the cell and was using his torch to light another on the far side. The dim light from that one, conjoining with the light from his original, gave Endellion the ability to see everything she needed. There were maybe twenty men cowering into the walls on either side. All were shackled, and some were bleeding from various wounds. The stink was worse than she had experienced in the hallway. She hadn't thought it possible, but here she was experiencing it for itself.

Within the flickering light, she could see that the prisoners were naked and filthy, but they seemed to be in good physical condition to serve her purposes.

'May I?' she asked the jailer as she stepped up to one of them.

'Be my guest,' he replied with a grin.

She took hold of one of the prisoners by his long, matted hair and pulled his head back. She ran her hand down his body, feeling his muscles, all the while nodding her approval.

'These are perfect for the queen's requirements. I'll take ten of these men right now.'

The jailer looked at her and shook his head. As he grinned, Endellion saw the rotting remains of teeth. Even though she was used to ugly sights, she had experienced worse than rotten teeth in her days, this sight disgusted her more than anything. The man was truly loathsome.

'Are you crazy, woman?' he chided. 'If I were to let ten of these men loose right now, they'd overpower us both, kill us, and make good their escape in moments. No, you can have them one at a time. It will take a little while to get them out, but it will be safer.'

Endellion reached into her cloak and produced her Glimmer. The red glow outshone the dim light of the two torches. Everyone, prisoners and jailor alike, were transfixed by it. Wide, dark eyes tried their best to absorb every bit of red light they could.

'Not these men … they will be as good and gold.' She raised the Glimmer into the air and spoke one word: 'OBEY!'

All the prisoners in the room stopped cowering and sat obediently against the damp walls of the cell. The jailor looked around, his eyes wide at whatever magic the woman had spoken.

'You may unshackle ten of these men, they will cause you no harm.'

He looked at her, fumbling at another set of keys hanging from his hip. Without taking his eyes off the mysterious woman and her glowing orb, he reached gingerly for the first man. He touched him as if he were handling a wild animal, expecting it to bite or attack him. He removed the shackles and watched in wonder as the prisoner stood still by the open door. He quickly moved on to the next one and the one after that.

Before long, ten men were freed and were waiting obediently by the cell door. Their blank faces were staring ahead of them as if it was the most ordinary thing in the world.

'What manner of magic is that thing?' the jailor asked as he put his keys back on his belt. He leered in towards Endellion, his greedy eyes not moving from the Glimmer she held. 'You can tell me. I can keep a secret. You know that now, don't you?'

'Bring the torch,' she commanded as she turned towards the ten naked and dirty men before her. 'Everyone, outside the cell now.'

The jailor marvelled once again as the men obeyed her without question.

'If I could get my hands on one of those …' he spoke absently as he locked the door before moving to the front of the line, holding the torch before him. 'My job here would be so much easier.'

He led the troupe back up the stairs from whence they came, through the corridor of dark cells.

'Stop,' Endellion commanded, and the line of men obeyed her. She held up the Glimmer again and said one word. The jailor, sensing that something was about to happen, came back to look at the glowing ball again.

'Cassandra,' Endellion said.

The old woman's appearance began to melt away, replaced with the beautiful, youthful appearance of Queen Cassandra. The jailor checked his torch to see if it was causing him hallucinations. Happy that it wasn't, his attention diverted back to his queen. 'What are you?' he whispered, his voice barely registering in the damp corridor.

Endellion smiled Cassandra's sweetest smile. 'For you, my good man, I am death.'

She grabbed the keys hanging from his waist and pushed him with her other hand against the doors to the cell behind him. Thin, wraithlike hands reached out from within, grabbing and clawing at the surprised jailor. Endellion laughed as the long, dirty fingernails of the wretched creatures raked across his skin, tearing his clothes, cutting deep into his greasy flesh.

'Open,' she commanded, and the door to the cell unlocked and swung inwards. The jailor's face was a mask of horror as he fell into the open cell.

The door swung shut behind him and clicked as the lock snapped into place, trapping the unfortunate man inside. The screams were horrific as they poured from the darkness. They were closely followed by moans and the sounds of tearing.

There was one final plea. Endellion was not sure if the man was shouting in any language that she knew or understood, but she got the message it was trying to convey.

The dirty jailor wanted help.

Returning to her Endellion features, she laughed as she illuminated her way to the front of the line of prisoners. She guessed there would be no help or mercy coming that vile man's way any time soon.

40.

ALEXANDER WAS IN his chambers. He was playing alone, as he mostly did these days. With no Cassandra to keep him company, his evenings had become almost solitary. All his friends had to be home before darkness fell, that just left his wards, and they were never any fun.

His toy army, led by their new purple leader, was lying in wait for the Carnelian's who were walking into their trap. He had a feeling this time the mighty Azurian guard may not win.

He jumped as the door to his chambers slammed against the wall, and he knocked over half of his army in the process. His fright turned quickly to delight as Cassandra rushed into the room.

'Alex, do you fancy a ride out with me tonight? I have something I want you to see. It's something that will make you into a man and the kind of knight that I'll need as my most valued protector.'

Alexander jumped from the floor, his toys instantly forgotten. He knew it was late and he had to be up tomorrow for school, but Cass was his queen, his legal guardian, and, most of all, his sister. He knew he couldn't pass up this adventure.

'Yeah. Where are we going?'

'You'll see when we get there. This is going to be a night you'll never, ever forget. Bring warm clothing as we're going to ride so fast, you'll likely get cold.'

Alexander was already one step ahead of her, having pulled on his riding boots and a heavy Azurian tunic. 'Let's go,' he shouted, not bothering to conceal the delight and excitement on his face.

~~~~

They rode fast into the night. Alexander was on his own horse, trailing slightly behind Cassandra's white steed. The wind in his hair was exciting as the dark countryside blurred past them. He had never been out this far before, and his heart was racing at the prospect of what they might be going to see. He never once felt scared. He was with his sister, and he could count ten guardsmen riding with them.

He thought it strange that not once through the ride had any of the guards spoken to him, or to Cassandra for that matter, but he thought it might be part of the night's entertainment. He didn't mind, he was riding far too fast for conversation anyway.

Eventually, they stopped to water the horses, and Alexander got a chance to talk to his sister. 'Cass, where exactly are we going?' he managed to puff over his heavy breathing. The wild ride had stolen all his breath from him.

'We're going to ride until the sun rises. Maybe another half an hour.'

Alex looked up into the sky and noticed for the first time that it was lightening a little. He smiled. 'So, I take it I won't be going to school tomorrow then?'

Cassandra looked at him and laughed. 'No, Alex, you cheeky monkey, you won't be going to school tomorrow. You'll be learning a valuable life lesson out here tonight, with me. Come now, we must ride again, we have a mission to complete.' She turned her attention to the guardsmen who were watering their horses. 'You men,' she shouted with an authority that he had never heard in her before. 'Get back on your mounts, we ride again in five minutes.'

Without further prompting, all ten men got back on their horses, and the party continued their way, riding into the emerging morning.

Alex was lost in his thoughts, thoughts of bravery and chivalry, about the kind of king he would be and how the kingdom would be run when he was in charge. Cassandra broke him from his reverie with a loud shout.

'We're here,' she called as her horse slowed.

He brought his horse to a halt right behind his sister's and watched as the ten men of the guard did the same.

The silence of the men unnerved him, it was eerie and creepy. He had never witnessed such silence between members of the guard. There was always *some* banter between them, or even orders, but not this time. This time there was complete silence, each one as stoic as the next.

Alex didn't like it, not one bit.

Cassandra announced they were here, but he had no idea where here was. He watched as she dismounted and commanded the ten men to do the same. Each of them obeyed and stood before their steeds ready for whatever order she was about to give.

'Alexander. To me,' she ordered.

He obeyed as silently as the guardsmen.

He watched as his sister pulled something from her robes, something small and glowing. It was the ball he had given her on her departure all that time ago, but it was red, not blue. *Strange,* he thought. *The red ball again. I wonder if it* is *the same one I gave her.*

'I call upon the face of Glimm,' she shouted, holding the glowing orb before her. 'I challenge your powers and your knowledge. I command you to make the blackest of rains to pour narrowly on the heads of these men.'

As she spoke, whatever spell the ten men had been under broke. They flopped as if they were puppets and their master had cut their strings. Each man looked around as confused as the next.

'What's happening here?' one man muttered aloud.

Another joined him in his queries. 'Who are you?' he asked, looking directly at Cassandra.

With his heart pounding, Alexander stepped forward, drawing his sword from its sheath just a little, enough to threaten the man. 'She is your queen, soldier, and you will address her correctly.'

The soldier looked at the little man and laughed. He then drew his own sword and pointed it at him. 'You want to play soldier, little man?' he asked. 'I bow to no one or no realm. I'm a free man,' he spat.

'You weren't so free this morning,' Endellion interrupted. 'When I pulled you out of that stinking prison. You were ready to die in there. Are you ready to die out here?' she asked, holding the glowing red ball towards him. 'Alex, come here, my brother, you must witness this. It's part of your education. You will not become a knight of the realm unless you are able to watch this until the very end.'

He turned from the laughing soldier and looked at his sister.

'Alexander ... To me,' she commanded.

He re-sheathed his sword and obeyed her.

The other soldiers had drawn their weapons and were looking around the terrain. Alexander could tell they were calculating the best ways of escaping this situation.

'Bring the black rain,' Cassandra whispered as she gripped the glowing red Glimmer tighter in her hand. Alexander could see her knuckles turning white.

The boy looked at the sky as the early morning light began to dim; it was turning dark again. Murky clouds began to roll in from nowhere. They clashed with the lighter ones before banishing them in favour of their own dark malevolence. The soldiers were looking at them too, all of them dancing, nervously holding their swords ready, as if they could sense something coming, something bad.

As Alex watched the phenomenon, he leaned back into his sister's skirts, almost as if seeking refuge. What he saw terrified him, but he tried his best not to allow his sister or the men to see this fear. It was proving difficult. 'What's happening, Cass?' he whispered, hoping that whatever was causing the black clouds wouldn't hear him, wouldn't find him, and therefore, wouldn't come for him.

'Don't you worry yourself, Little Brother, it is not for you. This is for the enemies of Azuria. These men are not soldiers anymore. They are deserters, scum, and cowards. This is what happens when you challenge the throne. Watch, my knight, watch this until the bitter end.'

The clouds swirled around the small group of soldiers. Alexander gripped his sister's gowns as he watched them whip around above the men. The soldiers looked to have forgotten all about escape and were now transfixed on what was happening above them.

Alexander looked at his sister. She was grinning, her eyes were wide and excited.

'Rain,' she whispered.

The boy looked slowly back to the clouds above the scared men.

The skies opened, and he watched in wonder as black, oily raindrops began to fall.

They fell only on the men.

He watched as they landed on their shoulders and heads. There was something about this rain he didn't like, and he suddenly wished that he was back in his chambers, getting up, looking forward to breakfast and to school. That scenario seemed much more pleasant than the one he found himself in now.

The men were drenched in the thick, greasy rain. It became difficult to see their blue uniforms beneath the blackness covering them. All Alexander could make out was the whites of their eyes and their teeth.

The teeth were vicious, the eyes were wide and crazed. He was petrified, he had never seen men change moods so quickly. They'd transformed from men desperate to escape to men who were blood thirsty and angry.

Within an instant, and without provocation, they turned on each other. He had never seen such ferociousness or violence in his short life. They were screaming and shouting, swinging their weapons, punching and kicking. A few had discarded their swords in favour of using their hands, elbows, feet, and teeth to attack and kill their comrades.

Covered as they were in the slick rain, Alexander found it difficult to even see them as men anymore. There was more feral animal in the fighting that ensued than free thinking, rational human beings.

A severed head covered in black rolled out of the melee before them. Cassandra pulled Alexander out of the way of it. His young eyes, seeing far too much for his age, stared at it as the rest of his body recoiled from the sight.

'Don't touch it,' his sister warned.

As if I was going to touch that thing, he thought in response; he had wanted to say it aloud but found himself unable to speak.

Other body parts began to emerge from the melee at an uncanny rate as the men continued to tear each other to pieces.

Alexander slid further behind his sister, sickened by the whole ordeal. He pulled at her robes, attempting to bury his head into them.

Endellion, in the guise of Cassandra, grasped him. Squeezing his face forwards, she forced him to witness the savagery before him. 'You *must* watch this, my brother. This is your lesson for today. Death is an inevitable part of life, especially if you are an enemy of Azuria.'

As he watched, his heart searched for Cassandra. It couldn't find even a trace of his sister; to him, it was as if she wore the face of a stranger, an old woman, a hag even. His thoughts rolled back to the mean old woman he'd bumped into the night his sister had left the council room.

The thought wasn't allowed to wallow.

'You have to watch, Alex. This is life. This is *our* life now. We are at war, whether we like it or not.'

He watched the performance unfold before him with tears in his eyes, trying his best to hide them.

After ten brutal minutes, the sky began to brighten and the thick clouds that had brought the black rain began to dissipate. The fight slowed, most of the men were dead or dismembered. Normal, light rain began to fall in place of the darkness, washing away the oily mess, leaving rivers of blood in its wake.

It was a hideous scene.

He wanted to run away but knew Cassandra would chastise him. She would be disappointed. It would be a sign of weakness, and she wouldn't allow him to be a knight. His pale face looked at her, his eyes filled with horrors that no ten-year-old boy should ever witness.

'Oh, Alex. I wish hadn't seen that but doing so has made you stronger. You are no longer a child, my brother. You are now a knight of the realm, a true grown man. You will be my personal guard, Alexander. The highest knight in the kingdom. You will swear an oath to protect me and the realm. You will be privy to secrets, the first of which you have just witnessed. No one can know about the black rain. Do you understand me?'

His brain was still trying to process what he had just seen. He stared at her and nodded. His mouth moved, attempting to vocalise what he was thinking, but all he could issue was a stutter. 'I-I hear you,' he whispered.

Endellion smiled and pulled him closer and hugged him. 'I know you do, Sir Alexander … I know you do.'

41.

THE GROUND WAS getting closer, and the wind in her hair was getting slower. Cassandra could tell the falcon was tiring beneath her. She watched as the massive wings slowed, catching another eddy of air beneath them. It carried them on for a further few miles, but human and bird alike knew the flight couldn't last much longer.

A clearing in the woods opened below them. It looked big enough for a bird of this size to land safely. She reached into her robes for the ball hidden within. Careful not to drop it, she whispered into it, not knowing if she needed to put it up to her mouth or not. 'Land,' she whispered.

The large bird began to slow. It angled its huge body towards the ground, and she closed her eyes as the trees rose to meet them.

The great bird performed a perfect landing.

As soon as she felt solid ground, she slipped off the beast's back and lay on the grass. 'Oh, thank the Glimm,' she whispered, spreading her arms wide, allowing the long grass to tickle her skin. She opened her eyes and was shocked to see the huge bird was still there. It was looking at her, its dangerous beak was pointing at her. She smiled. 'Thank you, brave bird,' she said, feeling a little silly talking to an animal, but it seemed to understand. It squawked, a roaring screech, before spreading its wings and taking off, seemingly happy to be rid of its burden for the day.

Cassandra marvelled as it rose into the clear blue sky. She closed her eyes and stretched out again before opening them and sitting up rather suddenly. She looked around, and her short-lived positivity slipped as she realised that she had absolutely no idea where she was.

As there was nothing she could do about it and she was exhausted from the flight, she lay back and closed her eyes, relishing the sun rising above and the solid earth below.

It wasn't long before she fell asleep and once again found herself in the dark, empty chamber with three old men standing before her. There was something different about them this time. They had always seemed happy to see her and to help, but today there was a strangeness about them, they seemed almost … sad.

'Child,' the first man spoke, 'you must learn the ways of the Glimm. You will learn to help yourself.'

'What do you mean? Help myself?'

'You must learn the ways of the Glimm,' he repeated. 'Master the Glimmer and help yourself. This is our guidance.'

'Help myself to do what? How do I learn to use the Glimmer?'

'The second Glimmer is being used as we speak. It is bringing dark magic, the worst kind. We are powerless to prevent the person bringing this darkness. This person will cause unrest, unbalance, and death. You must learn our ways. We can see good in you. Only you can stop this person before it becomes too late. You must bring back harmony.'

'How am I supposed to do that? I don't even know where I am.'

Cassandra could read the desperation in the man's voice. He was twitching and nervous, he kept looking behind him as if expecting to see someone there. She followed his gaze and saw another three men working around the altar. Their body language told her they were unhappy about whatever it was they were doing.

'The Glimmers are destined to be together. Whomever can conjoin them will have unlimited and untold power. You *must* help yourself …' The men, the altar, and the chamber became thin, and everything around her became translucent. This was her cue to wake up.

She was aware that the sun had moved a little during her visit to the altar, and she was also aware that the grass beneath her had grown a little colder, but there was something else she was aware of too.

A shadow had grown over her.

She opened one eye, half expecting to see the terrifying bird back again, maybe this time it was hungry after the flight and in need of a little Cassandra-flavoured snack.

It her took a few moments to realise it was not the bird, but what it was, was much scarier.

A person was blocking out her sun.

They were clad in chainmail from head to toe. Whoever it was, they were looking down at her with weapon drawn.

Silhouetted as they were with the sun behind them, she could not make out any features, but she could tell it was a male. Looking around, she could see that the man wasn't alone either. He had friends, a lot of them.

'Identify yourself,' the shadow commanded.

By his voice, she fathomed that it was more of a boy than a man. That made her situation a little more dangerous. Men usually had honour, boys were impetuous, or so Anthony, her counsellor, had always advised her. *I'll have to keep my wits about me,* she thought.

'My name is Cassandra. I am Queen of Azuria. You need to identify *yourself.*'

The boy shifted slightly, allowing the light from the sun to hit her eyes. As she squinted, his features became focused, allowing her to see who was questioning her. Her heart fell as she noticed his dark hair was tinged with red.

Carnelian guardsmen, just what I need right now.

'That's a pretty big claim for a wretch asleep on the grass in the middle of the woods, miles from her kingdom,' the boy continued in a mocking tone, holding a hand out towards her.

She took the offered hand and dragged herself up, dusting her filthy gowns as she did. She ran a hand through her hair and realised when it got stuck halfway through that she had not bathed in a long time. *I must look a mess,* she thought.

'I asked who you are,' she countered, ignoring the boy's last statement, attempting to make herself look and sound more regal than she suddenly felt.

'Well, if you're the Queen of Azuria, then I'm Prince Bernard of Carnelia. The difference between us is that I can *prove* who I say I am. Can you offer me the same assurances?'

The words hit her hard. Her eyes went wide, she could feel anger building inside her. 'I can, but ... but you must go first.'

'Young lady, it may have escaped your notice that I'm wearing the uniform of the Carnelian guard, and if you look at the insignia on my sleeve, it is the royal seal.' He cocked his head as he turned to point out the insignia. 'Only members of the royal family are allowed to wear such a thing. Other than that, and the fact that we are marching with the Carnelian banner, I would say that my credentials speak for themselves.' He stood back and looked at her, arms folded and a smug grin on his face. 'Your turn.'

She thought about using the Glimmer at that moment, summoning a great falcon down from the sky and commanding it to remove all these men from her presence. She took a deep breath, attempting to calm herself. She remembered her dream, the old men telling her that the Glimmer must only be used for good, that plus the fact she didn't know how to use it properly anyway, she thought she was more likely to summon an alligator and get them all into trouble.

'Listen, sir ...' She spat the 'sir' part shrouded in sarcasm. 'I *am* Queen Cassandra of Azuria. I was on my way to your kingdom to ask the questions as to why your guardsmen ambushed, attacked, and killed my mother. I was accosted by a witch who imprisoned me in a tower and has taken my identity. I fear for the Kingdom of Azuria and for the frail peace between our nations.'

Bernard shook his head and looked at the floor, half-heartedly attempting to conceal the humour he was finding in this situation. There were a few sniggers from the men—*or boys,* she thought—behind him. 'What is this folly you talk of, child?'

She became enraged at his tone. 'Don't you *dare* call me child,' she snapped. 'I am Queen Ca—'

'What *is* this folly you talk of, child?' Bernard cut in, not allowing her to finish.

'You annoying cretin. Did you not listen to what I just said? It is no more folly than you traipsing around the woods, boys pretending to be soldiers. Your people are at risk as much as mine are. I'm sure Azuria will by now be plotting war against you. The witch who imprisoned me will have seen to that.'

Bernard's laugh was filled with smarm. She could see he was enjoying this confrontation. He raised his eyebrows and smiled a lopsided grin. 'Cretin, am I?' he asked, shaking his head. 'You talk in tongues, girl. My people have been plagued this last year, plagued by strange phenomenon. All of them since your kingdom closed its borders. If you are who you say you are, we say that it is *you* aggravating hostilities between our nations.'

Cassandra watched the humour leave his face as he shook his head. 'We did not kill your queen. Carnelia and Azuria are, or were, allies, in trade and other business. It is my mission to travel to your kingdom, to give my condolences for the loss of your queen and find out what is happening.'

'If your words are true, then I fear it is both our kingdoms that are being duped into a war neither wants nor can afford.'

Bernard sighed as he leaned forward to take hold of the filthy girl before him. As he spoke, he rolled his eyes towards his men. 'That's as may be,' he whispered. 'But I don't yet know who you are. By the blue tinges in your hair, I see that you are Azurian, but until we can be sure …' He signalled to his men behind him, four of whom moved forward at his bidding. 'Restrain this wretch. If you truly are the Queen of Azuria, I will apologise later. If what you are saying is true and our kingdoms are in peril, then at least you will be safe in our custody.'

As the men restrained her, Cassandra thrashed, attempting to wriggle free of her binds. Alas, they were too strong for her, especially in her weakened state, and her arms were easily pinned behind her back, tight ropes binding her hands and waist. 'How dare you bind the Queen of Azuria! You will regret this, Prince Bernard. I'm no wretch. I'll have your head for this outrage.'

Bernard was heading back towards the trees, to where they had tethered their horses. As the girl began her tirade, he turned to regard her, the same smug smile prevalent on his face. 'I'm sure I'll have time to reflect on my mistakes at leisure, ma'am. But, for now, please don't make me gag you too. We need all the rope we have right now.' He turned away from her and addressed his men. 'I need the counsel of Sir Ambric regarding this. We may need to go back to Carnelia to report it post-haste. We'll need to take this young … lady with us.'

The troupe laughed at his small craic as he walked off, disappearing into the trees.

I'm not your young lady, Cassandra thought. *I'm the same age as you.* The dark colours beneath her eyes contrasted deeply with the red flush of her cheeks. She harrumphed as she was dragged unceremoniously towards the trees.

42.

'ALEXANDER, WHERE HAVE you been?' Anthony scolded as the boy strolled into the throne room. He was dirty, his clothes were covered in mud and other substances that the older man couldn't easily identify, but he had his suspicions. 'You should have been here at eight thirty sharp. Just because you are the prince, it does not give you leave to pick and choose your schooling.'

The boy walked past his counsellor without offering him a second look. His wide eyes were unblinking, his face had a pained expression that Anthony didn't like. He kept on walking, almost as if he were somewhere else. 'Prince Alexander, are you OK?' Everyone turned to see what was happening as the throne room was usually kept so quiet. Murmurs were heard as the boy continued towards the exit to the royal chambers on the other side.

Anthony followed the boy, attempting to get his attention. He cursed as Alexander made it to the door before him and he heard the lock click as it closed. He turned to see the faces of the class looking at him. Concern and amusement at what had just happened covered all their faces.

He clapped his hands, getting everyone's attention. 'Continue with your work,' he demanded. One by one, they returned to their duties, leaving Anthony wearing a worried expression.

43.

ENDELLION MADE HER way to her chambers via the back passageways. She had made it her duty to learn all the secret corridors, false doors, and secret entrances in the castle that she could. She didn't want to be seen or questioned by anyone today, so she had removed the guise of Cassandra and moved unmolested through the corridors and public rooms, enjoying her anonymity.

Before she went into the chambers, she did a quick change back into Cassandra, just in case Alexander was still awake. She seriously doubted he would be. She checked his room anyway, but before she peeped her head around the door, she heard the heavy drone of his snoring.

The boy was in an uneasy sleep, his head was twitching, and his brow was furrowing. Endellion smiled as she watched him. The youth had witnessed much for his tender age, *perhaps too much,* she thought, grinning. Careful not to wake the sleeping child, she slipped away from the door, closing it gently behind her.

'It worked ... it worked,' she sang, dancing in glee across the living chambers, holding the glowing red ball to her chest. 'The black rain really worked, just as the ancient texts said it would.' Her Cassandra features began to melt away once again, to be replaced by the former beauty that was a rapturous

Endellion. 'With that in my arsenal, this mission is going to be so easy.'

The glimmer in her hand began to glow a deep crimson, and her little dance was interrupted by a tap-tap-tapping at the window. She stopped and looked towards the source; a smile—an affectionate one for such a weathered face—widened, as did her eyes.

'My beauties … come in, my beauties. I have an important job for you.'

The window opened and in flew two fearsome fireflies. She threw her hands in the air and welcomed the beasts as if they were her very own children born from her womb. The insects hovered around her, and she tickled their thoraxes in affection.

'You will fly and capture me ten Carnelian men. They must be captured alive. This is very important. I need them for the night after next. They are an important piece in my puzzle.'

The fireflies buzzed around her once more, and she revelled in their affections. 'Fly now, my beauties, do my bidding.'

The Glimmer in her hand glowed once more, and the insects left the room the same way they had entered.

She sat on the small chair by the window, rubbing her hands together, laughing.

44.

CASSANDRA COULDN'T BELIEVE her bad luck. She had gone from being imprisoned in a horrible tower to being in shackles, traipsing through the woods with a bunch of boys playing soldiers. She had been tied and unceremoniously dumped onto the back of a horse before being strapped, too tightly, and led off in the centre of the pack. Her back was in agony, and her feet were beginning to tingle with painful pins and needles.

She noted with wry amusement that their party had been travelling in circles for the last few hours. She had seen the same gnarly oak tree three times. The way it was going, she was about to witness it for a fourth. Nobody knew where they were, and she saw no evidence of a map to follow.

Why are they travelling so light for being this deep into the woods? She thought about saying something to Bernard, offering him her skills in tracking and reading the natural navigations the woods offered, but then thought better of it. It might have exacerbated her current predicament even further.

Bernard's horse pulled up next to hers, and the arrogant young man looked at her. There was a strange mixture of cruel amusement and anger in his dark eyes. 'Tell me what you smirk at, my queen.' The last two words were spoken mockingly, and the soldier who was pulling her horse's rein laughed aloud. Bernard looked at him for back up and smiled.

'Nothing, my prince. I was just thinking that I was glad to be in such safe and knowledgeable company. I trust that we'll be in Carnelia by this time tomorrow night.'

Bernard blew breath from his nose before urging his horse on towards the front of the pack.

Cassandra smirked; she loved small victories.

~~~

Ambric was at the head of the pack. His eyes were squinting at every possible landmark they could see. From time to time, he would ride off to look at a large tree trunk. There, he would inevitably release a deep, resounding sigh before riding back, shaking his head. The journey towards the path they had deviated from was not going well.

'Sir Ambric, are we truly lost?' Bernard whispered as his horse sidled up to the older man's.

Ambric looked like he had something in his mouth that didn't agree with his tastes, and he spat onto the floor in disgust. He exhaled deeply through his nose before answering. 'I believe we are, my prince. I had made accurate maps of our deviations, but now they are lost, I see my folly. I should have made incisions in the trees. I've tried to follow the stars, but I'm not learned in that art. I believe we are in for a long trek.'

Bernard slowed his horse, allowing the older soldier to move ahead of him. He knew it was his fault, due to his insistence on the hunt deviation and for the destruction of the maps. He felt foolish and young and not deserving of his position within the troupe. As he dropped further back, not wanting to talk to anybody, wanting only to get lost in his own thoughts, a faint sound snapped him from his reverie. It was a light buzzing.

The noise was not much different from the other noises of insects and such that he had gotten used to, but there was a disparity. For some reason, the buzz sounded almost …

determined. He looked up to the sky, wondering if anyone else in the pack could hear it too.

Apparently, he was the only one.

He caught up to Ambric again, who was still looking for landmarks. 'Sir Ambric, do you hear that sound?'

Ambric didn't look at him as his eyes continued to scan the foliage around them. 'I do,' he replied.

'Is it me, or is it getting louder?'

'Prince Bernard … Prince Bernard.' The shout came from the centre of the pack, and the youth snapped his head around to see what the fuss was about.

The soldier who was tethering Cassandra was attempting to keep her quiet, but there was something in the girl's face that made him want to listen to what she had to say.

She looked scared.

He dropped back and matched her horse for pace. He rolled his eyes, mocking her as he spoke. 'What is it now, Your Highness? We have a lot of ground to cover, and we can't cater for your every—'

'Will you shut up and listen to me?' she snapped. 'That noise we can hear …'

Bernard recoiled from the surprise of being told to shut up by his prisoner. He closed his eyes and held a gloved finger up to his mouth. 'Did you just tell me to shut up?'

'That noise we can hear,' Cassandra continued, ignoring the prince's indignation, 'I've heard it before. It's fireflies.'

Bernard looked at her. He squinted his eyes and shrugged his shoulders. 'Fireflies? What of it?'

'They're giant fireflies. Huge, mutated. We need to get to cover. They took out my entire royal guard in a matter of minutes.'

'Giant fireflies? Do you take me for a fool, wench?'

Cassandra's eyes moved past the prince and grew wide as she stared into the sky. 'Look,' she said, attempting to point with her face due to her shackled hands.

Bernard turned to see where she was gesturing. His own eyes grew wild, and he backed his horse away from her. The steed had seen the sight at the same time and reared up, spooked by the unnatural spectacle.

The sky was almost as dark as night, which he knew was at least three, maybe four hours away. When the darkness began to swirl, he knew they were in trouble. Whatever it was swarming above them broke formation. They split, allowing sunlight to stream between them, allowing them to see what they were.

Giant fireflies.

~~~~

As Cassandra watched them, they headed straight for the pack. A shiver ran through her as she saw the dangerous stings protruding from the ends of their bloated, glowing bellies. Her thoughts flashed back to the horrendous day of the attack and the hellish journey with the witch to her prison.

'I told you,' she shouted above the drone of the insect's wings. 'We have to get to cover, those things will tear us all apart. They're fast and deadly.'

Bernard turned away. 'Cut the girl loose,' he shouted towards the soldier tethered to her. The man obeyed; producing a large knife, he severed Cassandra's bonds.

~~~~

'Ambric, can you see—' Bernard shouted.

'I see them fine, Bernard,' Ambric interrupted. 'Everyone get to cover,' he shouted to the company, making his voice loud enough to be heard even at the back. 'I don't know what these things are, but it's clear they're heading our way.'

The company stopped, and all of them looked to the air, much to the chagrin of Ambric.

'Get to ground!' he screamed.

Most of the men took heed of this sound advice, but not all.

He dived under the cover of foliage, then peered out, only to see several men with swords drawn, ready to fight the huge devils. 'You men …' he yelled. 'Get to cover, now, you fools. That is an order.'

Each man either ignored him or did not hear him over the sickening thrum of the insects' wings.

The scene was one of chaos. Horses were bolting left and right, some were running back along the path they had just travelled, others were attempting to bolt into the foliage, most of them getting stuck.

It will be a hard task calming them down later, Ambric thought as the massive beasts from the sky began to descend.

Cassandra tried to hide her eyes from what was about to happen, but because she knew the men standing out in the open ready to fight were about to die, she couldn't. 'You have to get those men to cover,' she said, more to herself than to anyone else. As she started to crawl out of the foliage covered ditch, an incredibly strong hand grabbed her by the shoulder, pulling her back into the deep cover of the brambles. She turned to see an older man, the man she had heard referred to as Sir Ambric, looking at her. His weather worn and battle-scarred face regarded her for a few moments, and she saw an understanding in his eyes. A pride in the fact that she was ready to help his men.

'You stay with Bernard. If you are who you say you are, then we need you alive. Someone must sort out the mess between our two kingdoms. I'll get the men.'

With that, he leapt out of the cover, running towards the battle-ready soldiers.

The fireflies were swarming above them, and each man was swinging his sword in vain attempts to battle the hovering monsters. Ambric's quick assessment of the scene told him that these men, his men, had no chance against a foe like this.

He grabbed at the soldiers as he ran through them, hauling two of them into the undergrowth. They offered little resistance to the manhandling, happy to be out of the way of the threat. The next two did offer resistance, however. They reeled around, brandishing their swords towards the lunatic who was attacking them. Ambric disarmed the youths with ease, pushing them both back into the safety of the ditch.

A single firefly swooped low and buzzed him. A swipe of his drawn sword cut the insect's sting in half, dowsing him in a thick yellow fluid. The beast fell from the sky, uttering a high-pitch scream. He watched it fall. Even in his heightened state of alertness, the wonder of what he was fighting was etched on his face. His awe turned in an instant to horror as another beast swooped him from behind.

He braced himself for the agony of impalement as he offered up a small prayer to the Great Lord Glimm himself, offering him a warning of the imminent arrival of a fierce warrior into his realm, when something unexpected happened.

The insect wrapped its legs tight around his body, restricting his movements, forcing him to drop his sword. The beast then picked him up, high into the sky, then flew off with the surprised warrior in its clutches.

~~~~~

Bernard stood and was just about to shout Ambric's name when Cassandra grabbed his tunic and pulled him down. She forced her hand over his mouth. His eyes stared into hers as she shook her head. Her eyes, looking back into his, told him to be quiet, relayed to him that there was nothing he could do for his friend now.

Both Cassandra and Bernard watched in silence as the fireflies descended on the other men in the opening.

All of them were taken in much the same way as Ambric had been, and they were flown off, restrained within the strong insectoid legs.

As they watched them go, they could see Ambric struggling. He had somehow gotten his hand on a small dagger and was still in the fight.

He was slicing and thrusting at his captor, and eventually, one of the creature's legs fell from its body. With more manoeuvring space, he altered his grip on the weapon and managed to thrust it upwards, into the bloated belly of the creature.

Everyone watched as the monster carrying their captain faltered in its flight before releasing its hold of the man. They watched Ambric fall from a great height, surely to his death. Cassandra looked away.

Another firefly swooped in from the swarm and caught the falling soldier. The second beast wrapped its legs around the warrior, tighter than the first, before sweeping up to fall in line with the other retreating monstrosities.

Everyone was silent as they watched the fireflies leave with their cargo. It was then reported to Bernard that ten men in total had been taken, including Sir Ambric.

'What do we do now?' Cassandra asked in a whisper.

Bernard looked at the young lady before offering an answer. *What would Ambric do?* he thought. 'I believe we should wait here until dark. We need to know those things are gone. Then we regroup and move on.'

'To Carnelia?' Cassandra asked.

Bernard was still looking in the direction the fireflies had flown. 'Yes, home to Carnelia.'

Cassandra bowed her head and averted her eyes. She knew she had to ask the question. 'I'm sorry, Prince Bernard, I offer no condescension with this question, but do you even know where Carnelia is?'

Bernard turned to look at her. The misery in his eyes answered her question long before his mouth did.

'No!'

She reached deep into her robes and brought forth the small metallic ball that had been hidden within the folds. The deep blue glow was beautiful, and Bernard's eyes were immediately drawn to it. 'What is that?'

Cassandra smiled at the ball. 'This, Prince Bernard, is a Glimmer!'

'And just how is that toy going to help us out here? Will it bring Ambric back?' he snapped.

Cassandra was already ignoring him. She had sat back against a tree with her eyes closed.

45.

INSTANTLY, SHE WAS back in the dark and empty chamber of the Glimm. The same three men who had been in her dreams, and always seemed to be there, were once again standing before her. The same two skeletons were on top of the altar, and the same daggers were sticking out of their ribs.

In the background, there was a fourth man; he was once again on his knees, talking—or pleading—to someone she could not see.

The first man stepped forward, blocking her view of whatever was happening behind him. 'My child,' he greeted her with an uneasy smile. 'It seems you have found us outside of your dreams. This is a significant step in understanding the ways of the Glimm.'

Cassandra smiled. She liked these men, whoever—or whatever—they were.

'Can you help me?' she asked.

The man looked at her. The expression on his bearded face was blank, his eyes held no humour. 'I do not know, child. Can we help you?' he asked in return.

'I … I don't understand.'

'Can we help you?' the man asked again.

'I don't know what you're asking. We're lost in the woods and need help getting to Carnelia. Can you help us?' she asked again, feeling a little annoyed at the cryptic answers she was getting.

'Child, you need to understand the question. Can we help?'

She stared hard at the man; he only looked back at her. Nothing else happened between them. Cassandra shook her head and took hold of her Glimmer. 'I don't have time for this,' she snapped before closing her eyes, thinking about the forest, lying in the dirt next to Bernard.

When she opened her eyes again, she was back in the woods. Bernard was leaning over her, about to poke her. 'Did you just fall asleep?' he asked.

46.

ENDELLION AND ALEXANDER were in their chambers in the Azurian castle. They were sitting on opposite ends of a long dinner table, both toying with their food rather than eating it. The room was dark, illuminated only by a few candles in the corners. The flames were playing tricks with the shadows in the room.

Endellion, in the guise of his sister, stared at the boy as he chased his peas around the plate. He was looking at the dish, but she could tell his thoughts were miles away. Perhaps in a twilight clearing, watching black rain fall from a turbulent sky.

'Are you enjoying your meal, Alex?' she asked, knowing full well that he hadn't eaten one bite.

'I am, it's just that I'm not really hungry.'

'Well, because you have been through a lot today, if you eat all your good stuff, I just might have a little surprise for you. Would you like that?'

At the sounding of the word 'surprise,' he stopped playing with his food and looked up at her. 'What is it?' he asked, his brow ruffled. 'It's … it's not more rain, is it?'

Endellion shook her head. 'No, Brother, it's not rain. You have had enough schooling for one day. I'm going to show you something that I know you will love. Eat your greens and we'll find out what it is.'

With the excitement that only a ten-year-old boy can produce at the drop of a hat, he began to dig into his food, shovelling mouthfuls of boiled vegetables into his mouth before tackling the pie. Eventually, the plate was clean, and he held it up to show his sister. 'Will this do?' he asked through a mouthful of pastry, spraying more of it onto the table than he was able to swallow.

Endellion laughed, it was a genuine laugh at the little boy's willingness to do anything for his sister, but also at the humour of the situation. She thought the boy's reaction was delightful. She nodded. 'Yes, Alex, that will do.' She held a finger towards the window and put another one to her lips, shushing him. 'Listen,' she whispered. 'I think I can hear them now.'

~~~~

Alexander put his plate onto the table and stopped chewing the copious amounts of food in his mouth. He looked towards where Endellion was pointing. He got up slowly and, sparing one more look towards his nodding sister, made his way to the window. It was already dark outside, but the stars were bright in the sky. He could hear a low hum; even though it was faint, it seemed to be coming from everywhere. He could feel it vibrating in the pit of his stomach and in his back teeth. It wasn't entirely a pleasant feeling, and it made him want to go to the toilet. 'Who's coming? I can't see anyone out there, it's too dark.'

'Look closer, Alex. They're out there, believe me.'

He looked back out of the window, holding his hands to his head to block out the light reflecting off the glass. 'What's that noise?' he asked, only half wanting an answer, his other half was too excited about what his surprise could be.

Sudden movement from outside startled him, and he stepped back into the safety of the room.

Endellion put a hand to her mouth, stifling a giggle.

As the boy looked into the dark sky again, his eyes widened as something odd happened.

The stars began to move.

The yellow lights began to dance in the sky, and the thrum in the air became heavier. His put his hands over his ears and turned to his sister. 'What-What are they, Cass?' he stuttered.

She laughed. 'You'll see,' she teased, stroking the glowing ball in her pocket.

The lights continued to dance in the sky, but Alex fancied they were getting bigger, maybe even closer. The hum was becoming the norm in his head, and his eyes filled with glee.

Then suddenly, they were gone, as was the heavy thrum in his head and belly. His head twitched as he scanned the sky for the glowing yellow balls of light, but they were no longer there. 'What? Where are they?' He turned back to his sister, his face filled with disappointment and wonder. 'Where did they go?'

Endellion stood and grabbed her cloak from by the door. 'I'll tell you what. You wash up from dinner, and I'll go and find them for you. I'll see if they'll come in to see you. How does that sound?'

Alex's face broke into a beaming smile as he tore from the window and grabbed the plates from the table.

Endellion smiled as she opened the door. 'I'll go and talk to them. I'll not be long,' she shouted back to her little captive before closing the door and walking out into the castle.

~~~~

Once she was away from the corridor and out of sight of any prying eyes, she stroked the Glimmer and her beautiful, young face melted away.

She made her way through the castle with no interference. Why would anyone bother an old crone going about her business? It was how she liked it. She found her way back towards the prison in the tower and headed towards the rear of the grounds. The dark and imposing tower cheered her. It was the means to her ends. Since she'd killed the previous guard, she had made her own appointment to the position as chief ward and had taken him under the influence of her Glimmer. He would do as she bid, when she bid it.

'Good evening, ma'am,' the gruff voice from the darkness greeted her on her arrival. 'I think what you're looking for is assembled in the exercise yard. A fine crop too, if you ask me,' the man snivelled as she entered the small office that was used as the lobby.

'Nobody *did* ask you, and furthermore, nobody will,' she spat as she brushed past her appointee. She was in no mood for pleasantries.

The two of them made their way through a series of dark dank corridors until they came to double doors with a thick, rusted chain holding them together.

The jailer unlocked the doors and pushed them open, revealing a small exercise yard that some prisoners were given access to occasionally.

Endellion, her features now back in the guise of Queen Cassandra, pushed past the jailer and crowed as she looked upon the gathering stood in the centre of the yard. 'Excellent … excellent. My fine beauties, you have done me proud.'

In the centre of the yard were ten men surrounded by a circle of fireflies. The men were shuffling and looking around them. They looked lost and angry. Only one of them was emotionless. The only movement this one made was with his eyes as he methodically absorbed every detail of the courtyard.

The fireflies were hovering around the prisoners. Their stings pointing towards them, threatening, goading them to try to take them on. Endellion noted that every one of them wore the uniform of the Carnelian guard, and each had red tinges to their hair, the same that she had in her original form, the tinges that distinguished them as Carnelian. They were all young, with the exception of the one dangerous looking individual at the end of the line. There was something about this man, something she thought she recognised, but she couldn't grasp from where. Paying it no mind, she continued to inspect her prizes.

They will do me fine. The younger, the better, she thought. *It will make them look more desperate.*

The fireflies had separated as she walked down the line inspecting her catch. She was grinning, nodding her approval, when one of them called to her. 'Queen Casandra, how did you get here so fast? Do you have control of these beasts?'

She didn't understand what the man was shouting. She turned to see which one of them had the audacity to address her directly, she wasn't surprised to find it had been the older man.

'You will be quiet! You are now all prisoners of the Kingdom of Azuria. I am Queen Cassandra, and you are now held at my pleasure.'

'What's the meaning of this?' the older man shouted again, ignoring her threat. 'Do you not recognise me?'

Endellion's face turned red, and she snapped her head towards the audacious prisoner. 'Sir, you will not address me directly,' she hissed, glaring at him. 'I do not know you. Do not attempt to play with my emotions. Be assured, I have none to manipulate. Now, you will all avail yourselves with the arms that will be provided to you and leave this kingdom. My fireflies will take you to where you need to be. There, you will be left to your own devices.'

Ambric listened to what the queen had to say. His confusion had risen to the surface. 'My lady, if we are prisoners of Azuria, then why arm us and send us out of the city bounds?'

Endellion walked to the end of the line with a smile on her face. The jailer and the other men watched her every step. 'Maybe you should count yourself lucky, old man. You have caught me in a good mood.'

She faced the older soldier and cocked her head. There was something about him that unnerved her, she hated the feeling of not knowing.

'I left you in the woods not one hour ago. What kind of dark magic is this?' he asked. There was no hint of fear of his situation in his voice.

'You, sir, look regal. You also don't look anywhere near as afraid as the rest of your band of men. Tell me, what is your name?'

Ambric blinked slowly. 'You know my name. We rescued you. You would be dead by now if it wasn't for us.'

Endellion leaned in close. She bared her teeth. 'Tell me your name, soldier.'

'My name is Ambric. *Sir* Robert Ambric of the Carnelian guard.'

A flash of recognition passed through her eyes, and her mouth fell open ever so slightly. She reached into her pocket and stroked the glimmer again. Her features began to shift, and Cassandra's beauty fell away, revealing the aged beauty of Endellion.

Something happened in Ambric's eyes. His brow furled for a moment, it was obviously shock of witnessing this bizarre event, but his face soon softened. It was as if a memory had resurfaced. A long-forgotten memory. 'Endellion,' he whispered. 'But … how?'

'*Sir* Ambric is it now? The last time I had the misfortune to gaze upon your face, you were yet a low officer in the Carnelian Guard and I, I believe, was your prisoner. Ah, how the tables turn, and how the balances of power shift.' Endellion laughed as she removed the glowing red ball from her pocket and held it aloft.

Ambric's eyes were drawn to the thing, and another flash of recognition passed over him.

Before he could say another word, Endellion signalled to the firefly behind her, and Ambric was seized by eight strong insectoid arms.

He turned his head in time to see the other men being seized in much the same manner as himself.

With a flick of the witch's hand, he and his men were lifted off the ground. They passed by the old woman as they were carried out of the courtyard. She whispered something into the ball as they were lifted over the castle and into the dark, cloudy night sky.

~~~~

Endellion, now back in the guise of Cassandra, reached out for the door handle of Alexander's chambers. 'My brother. Are you still awake?' she whispered.

'Yes. What took you so long? I've been eager for my surprise.'

'Calm yourself, my knight,' she continued as she entered the chambers. 'Look out of your bedroom window now.'

At that exact moment, the boy became acutely aware of the deep hum that was in the air. He felt it in his teeth, and his belly shivered with the low vibrations as he ran to the window and unlatched it. He thrust his head out, looking towards the sky.

A small scream escaped him, and he fell back into the room, onto his backside.

Six huge fireflies flew into the room. They grouped around his sister, and their dark, liquid marble eyes regarded him as he lay on the floor.

'Wha-What are they?' he stuttered.

She laughed as she stroked the stomach of one of the yellow and black striped beasts. 'Why, Alex, there's no need to be afraid. These are your new pets. I brought them back from my travels for you. What do you think?'

He hadn't moved from the floor. 'I … I'm not sure I like them,' he moaned.

Endellion pulled a scornful face. 'That's no way to treat your newest, most loyal subjects, is it? These magnificent beasts will be at your every whim. They will not tire, and they will obey you unquestioningly.' She reached over and offered the boy her hand to help him up off the floor. 'Come and meet your firefly army, Sir Alexander.'

He gingerly accepted her inviting hand and got up off the floor.

'Come and pet them. They're harmless to you.'

He reached out a tentative hand and stroked the belly of one of the beasts. A smile spread across his lips. 'Are they really mine?' he asked.

'Yes, my brother, they are really yours.' *But mostly mine, you fool…* She smiled.

47.

AMBRIC'S JOURNEY HAD not been pleasant. His head had been whirling with dangerous thoughts. All he could feel coursing through him was anger and hate. They were strange feelings for him as his training allowed him to channel negative emotions, to suppress them until they were needed, as they would not serve him well in battle.

He was furious with himself for being caught.

His hatred surged when his thoughts turned to the witch Endellion. He wanted very much to kill her and could envision his sword cutting through the tendrils of her neck, feeling her warm life blood gushing over his hands.

He also wanted to kill the vile beast that was carrying him. He wanted to slice the hideous thing until it lay in pieces at his feet.

But most of all he wanted to kill the stupid men who had gotten him into this position in the first place. He cursed them, he spat at their memory. He despised them for failing to obey even one simple direct order.

His rage was all encompassing.

His captors flew high over the forest until a clearing came into view. There, they deposited him and his men roughly onto the ground.

As he hit the floor, he watched the others dust themselves off. Another beast flew in from behind them. This one landed and deposited a cache of weapons.

He seethed as the fireflies rose into the air before flying off into the distance.

The hate and anger were swelling within him. His hands were moist, and his heart was hammering double time against his chest. Something, some instinct, told him the men, the ones who had been under his command, were all out to get him. A voice in his head told him that he needed to get to the weapons cache before any of the others.

He needed to fight these men. To slaughter them. Every single one of them needed to die.

'Kill them,' the voice in his head commanded him. 'Make it look like a battle.'

Ambric didn't know whose words they were, all he knew was they were not his own. He had an inkling that it was the witch Endellion whispering to him, urging him. He wanted to resist, but the thought planted in his head was too overpowering. It was insisting, no, ordering him to kill these men. It wanted him to murder them and leave their bodies where they would be easily found.

Getting himself up from the floor, he rested on his hands and knees for a moment. His fists were tearing at the ground beneath him. He screwed his eyes closed. 'Kill them, Ambric, kill them now. Leave the bodies where they will be found. Do it now.'

'No,' he screamed, pounding the floor with his fists. 'I will not kill my own men.'

As the words left his mouth, something heavy connected with his jaw and his vision went bright for a moment before swimming back into focus. The first thing he noticed was he was on the floor again with the heavy boot coming back towards his face. Even through the agony in his jaw, he was able to grab the boot before it made contact. Using both hands, he twisted it.

There was a satisfying 'oof' as the man it was connected to fell to the ground.

Ambric was up in an instant. The soldier who had kicked him was struggling; his teeth were bared, and the wild look in his eyes told of his readiness to kill. 'Stay down,' Ambric barked, but the man took no notice. The urge to wrap his hands around this soldier's neck, to throttle every inch of life out of him, was strong, and he had to close his eyes and clench his fists to fight the whispering voice that was spiralling within his head. The sound of battle was rising, and as he opened his eyes to survey the immediate scene, his shoulders slumped.

Carnelian men were battling Carnelian men.

Swords and fists were swinging.

He could tell they knew what they were doing and were doing it under their own free will. He guessed the whispers were urging them on too.

Another order barked within his head, and he clenched his fists again, waiting for the moment to pass.

The words were coming hard and fast, and they were making him dizzy.

Kill them, they are your enemy ... Kill them all.

His years of training and his loyalty to the throne of Carnelia would not allow him to wilfully take the life of another Carnelian on the whim of whispers. He shook his head to clear it as another blow came from behind, dropping him to his knees.

The man standing over him, the same man who had kicked him in the face, was brandishing something in his hands.

It was a log.

Ambric was reeling from the blow, and he saw the soldier in double vision, the images merging in and out, creating a dizzying haze. He put his hand up to protect his face from another inevitable swing of the makeshift weapon when something happened. The blade of a longsword erupted through the chest of the log wielding man. His face turned from aggressive hate to

215

shock and surprise within a fleeting moment. Blood flew from his mouth, and he fell to his knees, dropping the log. His eyes met Ambric's, and Ambric thought he saw regret and sorrow within them.

'Thank you, my man,' Ambric said as he attempted to get up off the floor and clear his head. 'I don't know what came over him.' Before he could get fully up, the soldier pulled his weapon from the body of the attacker, discarding him as if he were rubbish and no longer of any use. He grinned as he raised his blood-soaked weapon, ready to strike again.

Ambric was quicker and better trained than the boy before him. He kicked out at his crotch with all his strength. His aim was true, and the boy crumpled before him in agony.

This time Ambric spared no time, he was up in a flash, grabbing the disabled man's weapon as he fell. The voices in his head were whizzing around, commanding him to do unspeakable things, but the adrenaline coursing through his body was, thankfully, drowning them out.

Once again, he looked around him. The men, his men, were still fighting each other, killing each other.

He headed towards the cover of the trees. From there, he watched as his men fought each other until there were none left standing. He bowed his head.

As the last two hacked and sliced at each other, the whispers in his head began to recede, no longer holding any sway over him. He watched in sadness as the last two men fighting fell.

He knew they were both dead.

Bowing his head again, he muttered a prayer, and took a moment to reflect on what he had just witnessed. After a few moments of contemplation, he turned into the thickness of the woods.

He had to get to Carnelia.

He had to warn them about Endellion.

48.

BERNARD'S CARAVAN HAD settled for the night. What was left of the tents had been erected, set up in a way so that those who didn't have shelter over their heads could sleep on groundsheets between the existing tents. Each man would get the maximum shelter available to him during the cold and rather wet night. This meant the camp was small, it was also vulnerable. For that reason, they had a larger than normal watch for the night.

They still had some of the sow they had killed and butchered. Large chunks of the carcass had been roasted over a concealed fire. The smell from the cooking meat and its juices wafted through the camp and made many an empty stomach growl and rumble with a deep hunger.

For many, it was going to be a long, cold night.

Cassandra and Bernard were sat by the roasting pit, a little further away than some of the others, who were warming their hands or offering clothing out to the flames to warm and dry.

'How was your pig?' Bernard asked.

Cassandra looked up at him. It was the first time he had asked her a question without a face filled with smarm. She smiled, cupping her bowl in her hands. 'It was fine. Actually, it was better than fine; it was delicious.' She laughed as she ran a finger around the dish, mopping up the fat.

Bernard smiled and did the same with his. His face was troubled behind his smile, and as Cassandra looked at him, she could see the man within the boy. The man who had been unwillingly brought forth, thrust into a situation not of his liking. But also, the face of someone who would live up to the responsibilities he was now facing. She had also noticed the way the other men looked to him now that Ambric had gone and knew that they were in good but inexperienced hands.

He put his bowl down and looked at her, all the humour of his previous smile lost in whatever thoughts were currently running through his head. 'Cassandra, you said you'd seen them beasts before. Where was that?'

She licked the last of the fat from her fingers and put the bowl on the ground. She stared into the flames, enjoying the way the heat stung at her face in small, sharp points. When she looked at Bernard, her smile was back, but it was tinged with sadness. 'It's a difficult story to tell, but since you asked so sweetly …'

She watched him blush and was more than a little grateful for the cover of the flames to hide her own.

'My mother went riding, off on a hunt, an annual event in my kingdom, and well …' She was still smiling as she turned back towards the flames. 'She never came back. Well, that's not entirely true. She did come back, eventually, what was left of her. All the evidence on her body pointed to an ambush by your people.'

She knew her smile was showing too many teeth, and the tears that were welling were stinging her eyes.

Bernard recoiled as if he she had reached out and slapped him. 'What? Cassandra, I can assure you nothing of the like happened. We would never …'

She smiled again, this time there was a hint of good nature in it. Even though she was still sad, she recognised Bernard's shock at the accusation. She shook her head. 'It's OK. I know what happened. I know your kingdom had nothing to do with it.'

She considered the embers of the fire again, wondering where she should continue the story from. She could feel Bernard stealing more than a glance at her profile in the glow of the fire. She was conscious of the fact that she was dirty, tired, and sad, but her pride would not allow her to shy away from his stare.

'I rode out to your kingdom with an escort of guards. I wanted to open a dialogue with you, to see why you would be the aggressors and architects of war between our nations. Mostly, I wanted to know why my mother was killed in the way she was.' She paused to wipe a rogue tear that had escaped her lids and was currently blazing a trail of cleanliness down her dirt smeared cheek. She took a shaky breath before continuing. 'The first few nights of the ride were uneventful. Peaceful even. Then, from nowhere, we were attacked on the dawn of the fifth day. The whole guard were slaughtered; the horses, the men, everything. It was the fireflies that attacked us. Giant, mutated fireflies. They ripped through the tents and the camp like a hurricane, taking everything with them, everything including me. What I'm about to tell you will sound fantastical, foolish even, but I swear on everything that I believe in, on my brother's life … it is the truth!'

He looked at her, his eyes telling her that he would believe, or at least give her the benefit of the doubt.

'One of the beasts began to change, right before my eyes. It transformed from a firefly into a human woman, a witch. Her name was Endellion. She took me away and locked me in a prison before stealing my image.'

'Your what?' Bernard asked, squinting. 'Did I mishear then? I thought you said she stole your image.'

Cassandra looked at him, there was no smile, no humour, just a stony expression that made her look hard. 'You didn't mishear. She stole my image. I shudder to think what trouble that witch is brewing even as we speak. She is now sitting on the throne as the Queen of Azuria. As me!'

Bernard was silent, he was shaking his head. Even though the tale was mostly unbelievable and far-fetched, for some reason that she could not fathom, she knew he believed her every word.

One of the men brought a pot of hot herbal water over to them. They both held up their mugs, and the soldier poured before walking away.

They sat for about five minutes, both silently sipping their drinks, mulling over the conversation they had just had.

The cloud cover above began to thin, and Cassandra could already see her and Bernard's breath in the air before them.

'Tomorrow!' he said, breaking the silence. 'We'll find our true path. In the morning. The loss of our men has hit hard, but we'll find our way back to Carnelia. Once there, we will put things right between our nations.'

She smiled a sad smile and sipped from her mug. 'I know we will,' she whispered.

Without thinking, Bernard moved closer to her and, reaching out, tentatively put his arm around her. *Just for warmth* ... she lied as she allowed his arm to touch her stiffened body before relaxing into his warm embrace.

49.

ALEXANDER WAS ASLEEP. Talk of the giant fireflies was all Endellion got from him once they had left the room. Her plan had been a success. The boy had bounced back from his lull of seeing the men become savages and hack each other to death to become animated almost to the point of annoyance regarding his new *pets*.

It had taken some time for sleep to come to him, but once it did, she spared no time in making swift her escape from the chambers via the hidden entrance and off into the castle, making sure her Glimmer was with her, of course.

She snaked her way through the corridors, nodding and saying hello to the various passers-by who recognised her, some even wanting to stop and have a conversation with her. She remembered to be quick with a smile and a handshake, ending the conversations as swiftly as possible, cursing herself for not changing back into her natural image—if she had, she wouldn't have to perform so many pleasantries. Eventually, she made it to where she needed to be, a large, rugged door made from thick timber and held onto the wall by well-oiled hinges.

The aged sign over the door read, Officer's Mess.

She knocked before walking in. The warm air and the smell of sweat, alcohol, and testosterone hit her instantly. It was a smell that Endellion liked, it brought back memories of her exile in the woods and some of the company she was forced to keep in order to survive.

All the men immediately stood up, snapping to attention as they realised who their late-night visitor was.

'Ma'am, what are you doing out of your chambers on your own so late at night?'

Endellion smiled, clutching her hand to her chest, feigning fear. 'Oh, I just couldn't sleep. I don't know if it was just my brain doing overtime or if dark dreams were plaguing me, but I couldn't rest without knowing that my castle and our home were fully protected in the event of a surprise attack from those Carnelian scum.' She sat down heavily on an offered chair at a table where a game of cards had been played. 'How many men do we have on guard duty?' she asked as if it were the most natural question in the world.

The soldier who had first addressed her stepped forward; the stripes on his arms told her he was a captain. 'At any one time, ma'am, we have ten men on all four gates of the city and we have ten men in here; we swap over duties at different times of the day.'

'Excellent. That is exactly what I wanted to hear,' she crowed as she lifted the Glimmer out of the pocket in the folds of her gown. The rich glow from the small metallic ball caught the attention of all present. Their eyes were instantly blank as a dreamlike expression filled their faces.

Endellion grinned. The Glimmer in her hand blinked and dimmed.

'Men, I need you all to go to the orchard just outside the city gates. There you will find ten dead soldiers who will be wearing neutral colours and will have fatal wounds from battle. They will be sporting the red Carnelian tinge in their hair. You are to bring these bodies back, making as much fuss as you can regarding them ambushing and attacking you on the edges of our wall, where they were obviously testing our defences. You are to kill two of your own men, and you are to rough each other up, make it look like you have been in a fight. We need maximum exposure for this. Now go, do my bidding.'

The men, without asking a single question between them, took their equipment and made their way out of the door. As they passed, Endellion touched two of them randomly on the shoulder. 'These two are the two to die,' she said matter-of-factly.

As soon as they were out of the mess, their dreamy expressions dropped and they were their lively selves once again, only with Endellion's dangerous agenda buzzing through their heads.

She stood as to leave the mess herself when her head felt dizzy, and her vision became fuzzy. The room around her began to dissolve, and she was surprised to find herself in the large empty chamber of the Glimm.

'What is the meaning of this?' she spat as she looked around the altar room. The two skeletons were still on top of the grand table, and the three old men with wild hair and beards stood before her. 'How dare you summon *me.*'

'We have brought you here to implore to your better nature.'

'For you to put a stop to your current actions and the actions you force the Glimmer to perform,' a second man pleaded with her as he stepped forward.

The third man dropped to his old, bony knees, and Endellion heard the popping of cartilage as he did, marvelling at how beings who had been dead for thousands of years could still have crackling joints.

'You implore to my better nature?' She laughed. 'What makes you think I *have* a better nature?'

The man on his knees looked up at her laughing face. His own expression was the mirror opposite of her mirth. 'I beg and plead for you to halt this course of action, to stop these atrocities. The Glimmers were not forged for such things. They were not made for war but for the spread of peace and knowledge. They work for harmony.'

Endellion stopped laughing as the man spoke. Her eyes sparkled with curiosity. 'They?' she asked. 'You mean there is more than one? Tell me more, old man,' she leaned in so her face was almost nose to nose with the man on his knees, 'and tell me true.'

The man dropped his head low on his chest. Endellion knelt herself so she could be closer to him. She heard rather than felt the breath that expelled from his nose. He stayed like that for a moment before lifting his face to look to his brothers.

They all matched his sorrow.

'There are two Glimmers,' he said with a sigh. 'They were made as equals, both forged from the death of our race and religion.'

'How am I only hearing of this now? After years of your service, you impart this information onto me. Tell me more, old man,' she ordered. 'There is something you are not telling me about this second Glimmer.'

The old man took in another deep breath. 'If both glimmers are held in unison and brought home to the Throne of Glimm, it would render the custodian the most powerful being in all the lands. The very powers of nature would be at their command, infinitely more powerful than they are now. The power over life itself would be a consequence. It would render the custodian ...'

The man stopped talking, he looked up at the others around him before putting his head back down against his chest.

'It would render the custodian what?' Endellion demanded.

The man ignored her.

'Tell me,' she spat. 'What would the custodian of the two Glimmers hold? Tell me now.'

All three men continued to ignore her. She looked around as the dark chamber began to dissolve. Endellion stood. She attempted to grab the man still on his knees with both of her hands, but her fists passed through him. 'Tell me where the second Glimmer is. Tell me, old man.'

Before she knew it, she was back in the empty officer's mess, furious at the Glimm for giving her a taste of something they were not willing to finish. She lashed out at the table. Glass, drinks, and cards flew everywhere in her rage.

'They will tell me,' she screamed. 'I'll find that second Glimmer and make it my own. I will find the Throne of Glimm and rule these lands with an iron fist.' She took a moment to control her temper. A line of drool dripped unnoticed from her bottom lip. 'But first, I will have Carnelia.'

She exited the room. Her overall plan had changed. It had gone from simple vengeance to total domination.

She was laughing as she stalked the corridors back to her chambers.

50.

THE NEXT MORNING, Cassandra awoke alone in her tent. She had felt guilty accepting a tent of her own when so many of the guards were sleeping outside or sharing many a man to a tent, like Bernard was.

She lay on her makeshift bed and listened to the sounds of the camp's morning activities. She drifted away, lost in thought. What had happened between her and Bernard last night? Was it purely to keep her warm, or to console her after the story she had related? Or was there something else happening here?

She shrugged these thoughts away as soon as they saw the light of day. She knew there was far too much to do to be concerned about stupid matters of the … 'What?' she asked herself aloud; she knew the answer, she just didn't want to voice it.

She stretched, allowing her bones and tendons to crack, and got out of the bed. There was a genuine smile on her face.

Reality kicked in with a bump. She was in exile, and she had witnessed, once again, the massive beasts doing their unnatural work. She had assumed it was the work of the witch Endellion, who either had a grudge against her or her kingdom.

These were not good thoughts to start the day.

She wanted nothing more than to lay back on the strangely comfortable bed and fall back asleep. She wanted to forget everything that had happened over the last few months and allow a blissful slumber to settle over her, but her screaming bladder wouldn't allow that course of action.

She climbed out of the bed and, throwing her warm clothes on, ran straight from the tent into the trees.

'Did you have a good sleep, my queen?'

Cassandra was making her way back when she realised the voice had been talking to her. She turned around and saw Bernard struggling with the ropes of the tent next to hers. She felt her face flush but attempted to brush it out of mind. *My queen, eh?* she thought. *When did that happen?*

'Aye, it was pleasant. As pleasant as it could be in the aftermath of the horrors of yesterday.'

Bernard nodded and handed the rope of the tent he was working on to another of the men. 'I know, but today we make strides towards Carnelia. I have already sent scouts forward to climb the tallest trees to try to make sense as to our location. I assure you we will no longer be walking in circles.' He flashed her a smile, and she felt a blush rising once again.

What is wrong with me? Concentrate, Cassandra, there is too much at stake for this folly. 'Right then,' she continued. 'We'd better begin by taking down this tent.'

Bernard jumped to her aid and grabbed the guide ropes. 'Here, allow me to show you how it's done.' He took the pitch line in his hands and pulled it from the ground. In his haste to show off, he didn't realise that it was the main line he was pulling out, the one that kept the tent erect, and therefore should have been the last one removed. The shelter came crashing down around his head, enveloping him in canvass.

She couldn't help herself but laugh. *Listen to yourself, you sound like a schoolgirl, not a queen.* Despite her own reprimand, she reached out a hand to the struggling prince who was thrashing about in the folds. 'Here, allow me to help you,' she snorted.

A red-faced Bernard accepted her hand and pulled himself from the mire of ropes and canvass. 'I … erm, I meant for that to happen,' he stuttered as bright crimson burned over his whole face.

They both burst out laughing at the same time.

She thought that the red of his skin matched perfectly with the tinges of his hair. She then instantly dismissed the thought and walked away to where the fire pit had been lit again.

A number of the men had witnessed the pantomime and were holding in their smiles and smirks. The morale of the camp had been lifted somewhat by the exchange, and a better mood filtered around the fireside.

51.

THE HUB-BUB COMING from outside his window awoke Alexander almost a full hour earlier than he was used to. His confused eyes peered out of the warm blankets towards the window.

He swung his feet out of the bed, stretched, and yawned. This exercise removed every inch of sleepiness from his body, and he felt refreshed and energetic.

The noises continued outside. There were people shouting, horses whinnying, and he could hear heavy things being dragged across the cobblestones. Scratching his head, he got up from his bed and went to investigate.

The courtyard was filled with people. They were mostly soldiers, running backwards and forwards, delivering messages and shouting orders back and forth. Something was happening, and it looked important.

He continued to scratch his head as he turned away from the window and ran towards Cassandra's chambers. 'Cass, wake up,' he half whispered. 'Something is happening outside.'

~~~~

Endellion opened her eyes. It took her a moment or two to realise she was not in Cassandra's form. She looked up and saw the handle on her door begin to turn and a small panic welled up inside her. She didn't want to have to kill the boy, not yet anyway, she had an idea he would be a great asset in the coming months, maybe even years. But if he was going to ruin her plans, then he would have to become another casualty.

She reached underneath the bed and was relieved to feel the small box where she kept the Glimmer when she was in her chambers. A stroke of the ball began the magic that was required to change her appearance. The old Endellion melted away into the youthful Cassandra, not a moment too soon. Alexander charged full tilt through her door and into her room.

'Cass, have you seen what's happening outside? Have you? It looks important, whatever it is.' His face was beaming in the early morning sun. His eyes looked like they had a life of their own. He jumped onto her bed and shook her shoulder.

Oh, it is important, young Alex, she thought. *Very important indeed!*

'What is it?' she asked. Endellion had always been a fine actress, and these last few months had proven to her that she was indeed skilled in this trade.

'Outside … in the courtyard,' he half yelled, the excitement in his voice taking his breath away with it. 'Something is happening. There're soldiers running back and forth, they look rather urgent. I fear something bad has happened.'

No, my child. Something fantastic has happened.

The boy ran out of the chambers, back towards the window overlooking the goings on below. His fingers gripped the sills as he watched with wide eyes. 'Cass,' he shouted back. 'There's a troupe of soldiers who look like they've been in a battle. They've just marched through the courtyard; they've got a trolley filled with what looks like …' he paused to utter a gasp. 'Dead men!'

Endellion smiled, secretly thanking her own little troupe of soldiers for carrying out their mission, albeit unbeknown to them.

'Oh, my Glimm. Cass, you need to see this.'

230

Endellion got out of the bed and made her way slowly towards the window to join her brother. She looked out over the busy courtyard below. 'What is it, Alex? What are you looking at?'

The boy pointed towards the trolley of dead bodies. 'Am I seeing this right, Cass? All those men on the trolley, they have Carnelian hair.'

Endellion pulled her best shocked face, pressing it nearer to the window, so close that her breath caused fog upon the inside of the glass. 'You're right, my brother. It looks like Carnelian colours they are wearing too. We must get down there and see to this as a queen and her knight.'

The excitement dropped from Alexander's face. 'Does this mean we're at war?'

'If it is what I think it is, my brother, then we may well be.'

With that, Alexander left the room, making his way towards his own chambers to get dressed. Endellion watched him go. There was excitement in her eyes.

~~~~

As they reached the courtyard, she cried out to a passing commander of the watch. 'What is the meaning of this? We were awoken to this disturbance. What's happening?'

Anthony was running to join them too, still buttoning his tunic. 'What's going on?' he asked Cassandra, but she ignored him, her focus was on the commander.

He looked like he had been in a war. His tunic was torn and dirty, his face was bloody and bruised, and he was missing a couple of teeth. He looked exhausted, but when the queen addressed him, he snapped to attention. 'Your Majesty. We received a call from one of the sentries on the wall last night. The call stated they had spotted suspicious activity outside the boundaries, on the edge of the treeline. They thought it might be

231

a covert mission. I dispatched the night guards, including myself, to the area to investigate. When we got there, we saw that it was indeed Carnelian infiltrators. We engaged them. We lost two good men, ma'am, but I think we got them all.' He indicated towards the trolley with a proud look on his beaten face. 'We brought them home as proof of this act of treachery and war against the Azurian kingdom.'

Inside, Endellion was singing; everything was happening as she had orchestrated. The actress was winning-over her growing audience. *These people are braying for war. This is the last straw. The Azurian people will not sleep easy in their beds knowing that the Carnelian threat is at their door.* She raised her hands and shouted towards the gathered crowd. 'Good people of Azuria, hear me now as your queen. Today is the final outrage against our good kingdom. First, they kill our queen, my mother, then they make an attempt on my life. Now, they infiltrate our borders for who knows what reasons. To cause chaos or something even more nefarious, no doubt. This very morning, I will call an emergency meeting of the war council. We will *not* endure this torment anymore.' Endellion pumped her fist into the air for emphasis. She looked around at the expectant faces and could have burst with joy. All of them, without exception, were hungry for war, eager and salivating for it. 'Who of you are with me? Who of you follows your queen into battle to stop the aggressors?'

The roar of approval from the crowd pleased her.

'Will you all be with me when we march on the borders of Carnelia?'

The crowd began to go wild. There were cheers and yells and dancing as they were betrayed into a war that none of them wanted.

'WAR … WAR … WAR …' was the chant in the courtyard, so loud that it brought out others from their houses, rooms, workshops, and offices. Very soon, everyone was caught up in the fever of the moment.

'WAR … WAR … WAR …'

Endellion, disguised as these people's queen, stepped back from the braying crowd, her heart beating its own symphony in her chest.

Everyone was laughing and cheering. With two notable exceptions.

Anthony wasn't shouting and neither was the boy standing next to him.

Someone grabbed her hand, and she looked down to see her brother. His small face was concerned, almost sad. The actress within her couldn't contain the smile that was dying to escape her, so she let it break on her face.

'Are we really going to war?' he asked.

She straightened her smile for a moment and looked at him. 'I'm going to the council right now to seal the issue. It looks like it is already a forgone conclusion.' She looked at her brother and knelt, putting her face close to his. 'You will be holding the Azuria banner, my knight. My bravest companion by my side as we march to glory. Do you think you could do that for me, my brother?'

The youth's face broke into a small smile. 'Could I? Really?'

'After what you witnessed the other morning and with your command over our firefly army, I would have no other at my side.'

His smile widened as he turned back towards the crowd. He raised his hand and punched the air above him. 'WAR … WAR … WAR …' he shouted along with the rest.

Anthony looked from the boy to the young woman he had been tasked with counselling. There was no glorification of the warmongering on his features.

Endellion noted this. *Maybe it's time for Anthony to cease his employment with the Azurian Royal Family,* she thought.

52.

THE CAMP WAS packed, and the men were organised and marching through the unfamiliar trees in the woods. Bernard and Cassandra were trotting along on two of the remaining horses. The rest of the men were on their feet, trailing behind them. Two men rode back into the caravan, spoke to Bernard in whispered tones, then left again.

Bernard's demeanour regressed towards dour. 'The scouts couldn't find any landmarks that would mark our way to Carnelia,' he said, breaking the silence between them. Since the events of the previous night and the comedy between them this morning, the day had become rather sullen. Other than a few furtive looks, there had been precious little communication. 'They rode ahead and found a copse of tall trees, they scaled them, but alas, there was nothing of note indicating the way home.'

Cassandra nodded and looked ahead. She was tired and irritable. It felt like they had been marching for days, not hours.

'It seems we have forgotten the teachings of our ancestors,' Bernard continued. 'If we knew how to navigate between the moon and the stars and the positions of the sun, then I think we wouldn't be going around in circles as I feel we are now.' He looked at her and offered half a smile. 'At this rate, we might even bump into the Azurian boarders,' he concluded, attempting a poor joke.

Cassandra returned his smile before turning away and trotting forwards. She wanted to be alone.

~~~~

An hour or so later, the entourage stopped for a well-earned rest. As the men, including Bernard, attempted to build a pit to make drinks and food for the hungry team, Cassandra made her excuses and took herself into the woods. Once out of ear and eyeshot of the men, she fumbled around in the folds of her cloak and removed the small glowing ball hidden within. She closed her eyes and lifted it into the air. Instantly, the trees gave way and a dark emptiness appeared around her. Empty except for an altar and the three men she had come to expect.

'Greetings, my child, how may we assist you this day?' the first man asked with a smile.

'I need your help. We are lost. I need you to help us find our way back to a known path.'

'All you need to do is ask, my child, and we will obey.'

'This is what you told me last time. Will you help or not?'

The man smiled at her; it was a nice smile, a fatherly smile. It was the kind a grandfather might wear as he imparted knowledge to his granddaughter. 'My child, you asked if we could help you last time, but you did not tell us what you wanted help with. We cannot assume that we can help you if we do not know what you require. Therefore, you must *command* us to do something for you. We will offer advisement if we think the command warrants it, but ultimately, you are in control. As you have told me that you are lost and need help to find your way, then we will oblige.'

Suddenly Cassandra was whisked away, up into the air, zooming into the deep blue of a cloudless sky. The wind was in her hair and the ride was exhilarating. She continued her ascent, higher than any bird had ever flown, higher than any living thing could ever hope to travel. The land beneath her became smaller, and the curvature of the horizon more profound. Soon she was in darkness, looking down upon a ball not unlike her Glimmer, but this glowed blue, green, yellow, and white.

'You are here, child,' the Glimm's voice said, echoing all around. As he spoke, the globe before her flashed and pulsed once. 'More specifically, you are here.' Once again, the sensation of wind in her hair took her by surprise as she fell, without actually falling, towards the land below. She stopped over a large green part of the globe, one that was surrounded by blue.

'How did you do that?' she asked breathlessly.

The voice chuckled; it was a joyful sound. 'It wasn't me, child, it was a Glimm called Malchise. He lived nearly five thousand years ago. His talents were the mapping of the universe and the planets. All his powers were entered into the Glimmer that you hold in your hands. I simply tapped into his magic, and here we are.'

'So, in relation to where we are now, where is Carnelia?'

'Here,' the voice boomed again.

The vista below shifted to the south, then stopped, and she could see the whole Kingdom of Carnelia mapped out before her.

'How many days travel would it be?'

'At your current pace, it would not take you any longer than five days. We can guide you in all the ways we can, but you must keep the Glimmer at hand's reach at all times.'

'My lord, I and all my new friends thank you.'

'You need not thank us, my child; after all, myself and my kind have been dead for nearly two thousand years. You need only use the Glimmer for good, and that will be thanks enough.'

With that, she found herself back in the woods holding the Glimmer. She shook her head and gulped. *That was some ride,* she thought as she put the Gimmer away and made her way through the trees, back towards the camp.

'I know the way back to Carnelia,' she announced.

The men stopped what they were doing and looked at her as if she had gone mad.

Bernard's face looked concerned. 'What did you say, my lady?'

'I said I know the way to Carnelia. It's a five-day journey to the south. Can you map that?'

'How do you know this?'

'I'll tell you some day. Come, we need to get moving. South, and in five days, you will be home.'

53.

ENDELLION DANCED OUT of the meeting of the war council. Her every whim had been catered to. The cantankerous, warmongering fools had been salivating to sign her proposal for war with Carnelia.

When she got back to her chambers, she was almost fit to burst. She peeked into Alexander's room to make sure he was asleep. Satisfied, she then proceeded to shed her Cassandra image. She wanted to celebrate this victory in her own form.

As Cassandra melted and Endellion came into the fore, she began to pace backwards and forwards around the room. She could hardly believe what had come to pass. 'After all these years,' she whispered. 'After everything I've been through. My revenge, my life …' She threw her head back theatrically and laughed. It was an evil cackle that, when it escaped her, filled the room. 'It'll take the armies five days to travel there and less than half a day to sack the kingdom. With more than a little help from me and my Glimmer, of course! Oh Thaddius … my revenge will be so sweet. When your precious kingdom has fallen, I'll annex it to Azuria, which I already hold. I'll rule with my firefly army and commit my resources to finding that second Glimmer. Absolute power will be mine.'

~~~~

Across the room, in his chambers, Alexander slept. It wasn't a peaceful sleep. It was plagued with nightmares and strange realities. He dreamt he was walking into a nightmare, quite literally.

He had become detached from the rest of the war party, and he and his horse were surrounded by a thick, undulating black mist. Just above the mist, he could see the towers that adorned the walls of Carnelia. As he dismounted, he noticed he was no longer a ten-year-old boy but had the tall, athletic physique of a man twice his age. As he stood marvelling at himself, he turned to see his sister approaching. But she was no longer his sister. She was an old woman, a woman who he could see had once been beautiful but wasn't anymore. He recognised her face, but he couldn't put his finger on where he knew her from.

Suddenly, without warning, his sister spread her arms in the air, and he watched as she transformed from the old woman to the Cassandra he knew and loved, and then into a huge firefly, complete with a dripping, lethal sting. She took off from the ground and flew into the strange black mist, which parted, allowing her to enter, where she promptly disappeared.

The castle towers and the sky above the black mist were then engulfed in an orange glow. It was as if the whole of the city beyond the mist were on fire.

Then, there was nothing.

Just him, alone, in darkness.

Fear was seeping into him like a cold chill. He looked around but couldn't see anything except for a tiny red glow. At first, it looked far away, but it was getting closer. As it grew, his fear grew in tandem. Before he knew it, the glow was everywhere, it encompassed him.

Petrified, his heart bashed against his chest.

A blue glow accompanied it.

The blue began to throb from within the red, turning the world a deep purple.

He lay on the floor, allowing the purple to wash over him.

His restlessness ceased then as he fell into a deep, soporific sleep.

~~~~

Outside in the grounds of the castle, everything was far from peaceful. The might of Azuria's army were preparing for war.

In a few days, they would march on Carnelia.

54

'THIS WAR IS not justified!'

Endellion, still in the guise of Cassandra, was sitting on the throne looking down at Anthony, who was standing before her in the area the citizens used to ask favours of the crown. Her face was intense, as if she were listening to her counsellor's pleas.

'There needs to be a dialogue. At the very least, we need to send them banners of our intention of war. Otherwise, we are as bad as them. We are proud Azurians, we do not *do* sneak attacks!'

'What would you have me do?' she asked. She was trying to hide her complete contempt for this man.

'I would have you adhere to the traditions of our nation. This is a rash reaction, and I feel the council have rushed their decision. Helped, no end, by your coercion.'

'Anthony, you were counsellor to my father, to my mother, and now to me. Would you want those Carnelian bastards trampling over our good names?'

'No. You know I wouldn't, but neither do I want your good name to go down in history as a butcher. The queen who attacked her neighbours in their sleep.'

'Anthony,' she said as she stood up from her throne. 'The decision is made, what would you have me do?'

'You have the power of veto. You can delay this action until the banners have been sent. Give them the chance to defend themselves, that much they deserve.'

'I have a feeling you are asking me to betray my own people, Anthony.' She spoke slowly and cautiously as she stepped towards him.

'I'm not asking you to betray anyone, just to give our neighbours time to ...'

He didn't finish his sentence as Cassandra removed the orb from her robes. Anthony's face was drawn to it. His eyes widened as he recognised what it was.

'Is that ...'

'A Glimmer? Yes, it is. Do you recognise the colour it glows?' she asked. The malice in her voice was almost palpable.

'R ... red,' Anthony replied, his voice thin, almost a choked whisper.

Cassandra lifted it. As she did, her face began to melt. Anthony's eyes widened at the phenomenon, and he took a step back.

Endellion's features swam into place, and as they began to settle, she took another step towards her accuser.

'It is Carnelian,' she rasped. 'It has been mine for years. Ever since I was ousted from that place. Ever since I was treated like dirt by Thaddius and his bastard of a father. I am Carnelian, and I will have my revenge.'

Anthony stepped back again. He tripped on the step behind him and fell onto his backside. 'What ... What are you?' he stammered.

She laughed as she stepped closer, looming over him.

'For you and for Carnelia ...' she whispered. 'I am death!'

A hum filled the room. Anthony's eyes tore away from the old woman staring down at him, towards the window to the throne room where the sound was issuing.

The most horrific thing Anthony had ever seen appeared at the window. It was a massive, bloated insect. Its emotionless black eyes never left his as it entered the room. The thick sting at the bottom of its curved body dripped with a thick liquid.

'Kill him,' Endellion ordered; there was no emotion in her voice. She ordered Anthony's death as if she were ordering food.

The last thing Anthony saw was the yellow and black striped monstrosity floating over him and then the glow of its body as the sting entered his stomach.

Endellion reached into a chest behind her and produced a knife. It was encrusted with Carnelian decals. She plunged the knife into the man's wounds and twisted it.

'Take his body out of the castle grounds,' she ordered the firefly. 'Dump him not far from the treeline.'

Anthony's sudden death would cement her plans, ending any doubts the people may have been harbouring regarding the upcoming conflict.

~~~~

'But why kill Anthony?' Alexander asked as he and a tearful Cassandra stood at the front of the funeral cortege.

'I do not know, Brother. All I know is that the Carnelian's have sent us a message. They knew Anthony was a trusted counsel to both me and you. It is a message. That is all. A message.'

'Then we must respond to this message with one of our own,' he replied.

Endellion, hiding deep inside the image of Cassandra, smiled as she hugged the boy close. 'That we will, my brother. That we will.'

55.

IT WAS A fine morning in Carnelia. The sun was shining, and the flowers were blooming. The aromas wafting from the gardens were tantalising. Thaddius was stood by the window observing the colours of his garden. He took in a deep breath, savouring the bouquet billowing on the warm breeze. 'Mayhap the long winter has passed, my love,' he declared, turning to his wife, sitting up in bed, eating breakfast.

She looked up and smiled. 'At last. This winter has been too hard. The ordeals we have endured; the dogs and the strangeness in the graveyards.' She took a bite of toast and looked back at her husband. 'Has there been any word of Bernard?'

The king turned away, taking a breath. 'Not yet. Sir Ambric will make sure no harm comes to him. He's the finest commander there is. With his protection, no harm will come to them, I'm sure.'

The queen nodded and continued her eggs.

His face was suddenly animated. 'I've no pressing business today. Could we take a stroll through the mausoleum? It's father's anniversary, and we could pay respects and savour the gardens.'

Halia smiled. 'I'd love to. I've so missed our walks.'

Thaddius grinned. 'Me too. After all the unpleasantness we've suffered, I have rather a good feeling about the future.'

56.

THE THUNDEROUS NOISE of five thousand men ready for war, galloping at speed through the woods was enough to scare any living creature to retreat deep into the forest, back into their holes or burrows. For four days, the Azurian war machine churned its way towards its goal: the unsuspecting Kingdom of Carnelia.

Tearing up the countryside with war banners on full display, the Azurian army was led by their very own Queen Cassandra, with her young brother by her side, both dressed in specially created armour for the occasion. Cast in Azurian blue, Cassandra resembled a warrior queen, and Alexander was every inch the knight he longed to be.

Within Cassandra's armour, nestled inside a hidden pocket, was her Glimmer. It was currently glowing a deep crimson, almost as if it knew the Kingdom of Carnelia was within their grasp.

She had finally gotten the war she was so desperate for.

57.

AMBRIC WAS DOING everything he could to get back to Carnelia. He'd had a modicum of good luck; where the fireflies had taken him was both familiar, and just off the recognised trade routes between the two kingdoms. Even though it had taken him several days, he knew he was making strides. He had slept rough, washed in the streams, and hunted for small animals and berries to eat. He made camp at first dark each night and broke it at early light, making sure to clear any evidence of him being there before leaving. He didn't want anyone to be able to follow his trail.

In all, if his mission to return to Carnelia hadn't been imperative, he might have been close to having fun.

He sourced a tree, the largest he could find, and scaled it with ease. Once at the top, he surveyed his position. There were a few landmarks he had been using, and they seemed a lot closer today. He guessed at another day, maybe two, and he would be home. Once there, he would alert the king regarding the threat from Azuria, or rather, from Endellion. He knew Thaddius would be anxious to hear what he had to say.

As he shimmied down and collected his meagre belongings, he noticed many of the smaller animals of the forest dashing out of the undergrowth, through his camp, and into the heavy foliage of the forest.

Ambric recognised this behaviour. Something had spooked them. Normally, it was a forest fire or a large predator in the area, but from what he was hearing, it was neither of them. When he realised what it could be, he wanted to run himself.

It sounded like a tree falling. He could tell it was loud, but due to the coverage of the other trees, he couldn't gauge how loud or therefore how near the event, whatever it was, could be. The sound came again, this time it was accompanied with a heavy rumble. He had to steady himself to stop being rushed by the animals dashing past him. The rumble became a constant, and he could hear a rhythm within it. It was a rhythm he knew very well.

Horses, he thought, *and travelling fast.*

Intrigued, he dropped his bag onto the floor and re-climbed the tree. Once he was at the top, the rumble was a lot more distinctive, and it was louder. He didn't need to strain his eyes to see the cloud of dust that was rising from the direction of the sound. He estimated it was less than five miles away.

That's a lot of horses to be able to hear from this distance, he thought as he hurried back down the tree. Grabbing his bag, he made it through the forest towards the disturbance. It wasn't difficult to follow, all he needed to do was travel in the opposite direction the beasts were fleeing. They had begun to get larger now too, deer, wolves, badgers, all escaping in the same direction. It was as if they had all made a temporary truce until the large, more pressing threat had passed.

After maybe an hour of scrambling through undergrowth, he deemed himself to be in the path of the oncoming procession, and he found a small trench to hide in. This would be his vantage point, allowing a view of the passing party while remaining hidden at the same time.

After a while, he could see the hooves of the vanguard. He crouched further into the ground, making sure every inch of him was covered. He then saw two things that shook him to the core of who he was.

The first was the Azurian war banner blazing from the lead horse. A horse that was being ridden by a small boy wearing blue armour.

The second thing was the most shocking.

The second horse in the procession was being ridden by Queen Cassandra of Azuria. The same Cassandra that he had left behind in the camp when the fireflies took him. *Or is it the witch Endellion?* he thought. Confusion took him. *Are the Queen and the witch the same person? What is happening here?*

They were heading for Carnelia.

Confused by what he was seeing, by who Cassandra or Endellion was and what her goals could be, he stayed low until the lion's share of the procession had passed. He sprang from his vantage point and ambushed the last of the procession with a well-aimed throw of a rock to the rider's head. His aim was, as was Ambric's nature, true, and it knocked the rider from his courser. Ambric was on the man in an instant, wrapping his arms around his neck, not giving him any air with which to shout for help. After a few moments, the man stopped struggling and Ambric pushed him to one side. He calmed the steed before mounting it and taking off into the woods.

He hoped that one rider would be able to reach Carnelia faster than a fully armed war machine could.

58.

THE MAUSOLEUM WAS majestic in its simplicity. King Leopold had been a man of simple tastes, in death as much as in life. The structure was tall and made from large grey blocks. There were no exterior markings to differentiate it from others in the cemetery, other than the fact that it was the tallest there by far. King Thaddius and Queen Halia strode into the garden hand in hand on the beautiful spring morning. The flowers were blooming, and the scents on the air gave the couple a much-needed lift in their dwindling spirits.

'I do hope Bernard is doing well. I'd have thought we would have heard from him by now.' Halia was expressing concerns she had been brooding over for a few days, but every time she'd voiced them to her husband, he'd swept them under the carpet. Today, she was determined they would talk about it.

'I, too, share your concerns, and I'll send communications to Azuria as soon as I get back to the office. I'll find out how the negotiations are progressing.'

Halia stopped dead in her tracks and looked at her husband, who had himself stopped to smell a particularly lovely looking red rose. 'Thaddius, is there something you're not telling me regarding our son and this mission? You've been avoiding my questions on the matter for a few days now. I'll not take it anymore. If there's something I should know, then I'd rather I knew it than to be left guessing.'

Thaddius continued to sniff the flower. Halia felt he was ignoring her questions. 'Thaddius,' she snapped. 'I'm serious about this. If my son is in trouble, then I need to know.'

He stepped away from the flower and looked at her. The look made her angry, hurt, and emotional. 'Is he dead?' she asked. The question was final, almost as if she knew the answer already.

Thaddius dropped his eyes and shook his head slowly. 'I don't know, my love.'

'You don't know?' It was more of an accusation than a question.

'No, my queen. There's been no communication since he left. They should have been at Azuria days ago, but there has been no interaction at all. None of our outposts have reported seeing them.'

'So, he is dead then?' She threw herself onto a nearby bench and began to weep, her shoulders rising and falling in rhythm with her sobs.

'Come, my love, let's go into the mausoleum. We'll get some privacy from the guards in there.' He looked up towards the sky. The clouds had begun to gather, blocking out most of the day's early heat, casting shadows on the gravestones around them. 'It looks like it might rain anyway. Let's get some cover until the storm passes, and then we can talk.'

Halia looked at him, her stare was of someone looking into a stranger's face. 'You'll tell me everything that you know?' she asked, her eyes wide and hopeful.

Thaddius nodded.

She stood, wiping her tearful eyes. As she began to make her way slowly towards the small door, Thaddius turned to his guards, who had kept a respectful distance. 'Men, we will require some time for restful contemplation. You may use the time for your own amusements. Just leave the skeleton guards on duty and come back in two hours.'

'Very well, Your Majesty. There will be two men on guard, and the rest shall be by your leave,' the commander replied, snapping to attention. As he turned to instruct his men, Thaddius followed his wife through the small door into the mausoleum. As he entered, he took another look skywards, where the thick clouds had turned dark, unnaturally dark.

Almost black.

~~~~

As she rode, Endellion held her Glimmer tight. It was glowing and pulsing in her grip. Her eyes were closed, words were forming on her lips, but she was making no sounds. Alexander watched. He couldn't take his eyes off the glowing red ball. The deep red pulse reminded him of something that had happened in a dream. He dismissed the idea at almost the same moment it hatched.

He turned away from his sister and spurred his horse on a little faster. Apparently, they were not far from their destination.

~~~~

As soon as they entered the tall building, the heavens opened, and a heavy rain soaked everything and everyone around them. Thaddius was looking out of the window. 'I think we got inside just in time. That rain looks like it might be around for a while.'

'I don't care about the rain, Thaddius. All I care about is our son. Is he OK or not?'

The king turned to face his wife. Her body looked smaller than usual, like she was diminished somehow. Was it grief, or worry? Thaddius thought it could be a little of both. 'The truth is, my love, there's a lot going on right now. Azuria has completely closed its borders to us. No one understands why. All communiqués with them are ignored. We're *hopeful* that the expedition has reached their goal successfully. We know they checked in at Outpost Two, but there has been nothing since.'

He turned away; he couldn't stand to see her with such grief etched into her face. Looking back out of the window, he marvelled that even though the situation was difficult, he couldn't help but wonder at the sheer power of the rainstorm they had found themselves in. The water was pounding down; it was so heavy that it had taken on a dark quality. It looked almost as if the rain was dirty somehow.

Or even black.

'Oh, my lord…' Halia stood. All colour drained from her face as she pointed out of the window. 'Thaddius, look.'

The king shook his head and closed his eyes. 'It was because of this reaction I made the decision not to tell you about what was happening. I knew you would worry and overreact.'

His explanation was cut short by a loud, urgent banging on the door. 'Who could that be?' he snapped as he turned towards the door.

'Don't,' Halia shouted.

The yell was so quick and shrill that Thaddius turned to face her. 'What is it, Halia?'

The banging at the door did not let up, in fact, it sounded as if it had doubled in its urgency.

'Don't open the door. Please, Thaddius.'

The way she spoke his name, the shake, and the pleading in her voice scared him more than anything had before. It sounded pathetic, nothing like the strong woman he knew his wife to be. He looked at the door that was now rattling in its frame with the ferocity of the banging. It was then he noticed that the room was almost in darkness. His gaze shifted out of the window. The cemetery was underneath a slick of oily black liquid. His brow ruffled as he attempted to make sense of the situation. He hurried to the window and pushed it open, he wanted to get a better look at what was occurring outside the walls of the mausoleum.

As he pushed the glass, the banging on the door stopped abruptly. Something felt wrong to him. The slick blackness sliding down the window spooked him.

He turned back to Halia when something strong, vice-like, grabbed his arm. He jumped, and in the short struggle that ensued, he was able to free himself from the clasp and quickly pull his arm back inside to safety. One of guards appeared at the window. He was covered from head to toe in the ugly rain that was still falling. All Thaddius could see were the man's eyes and his teeth. The eyes were wild, the red veins of his eyeballs looked thicker than they should be. The teeth were gnashing and grinding.

'Get out here, you fat old bastard,' the guard growled. 'And bring that slut with you.'

The colour drained from Thaddius's face. 'What?' he asked, barely able to get his words out. 'I'll have your head for this insolence.' He took hold of the door handle and attempted to open it.

Halia jumped at him. 'Thaddius, don't,' she whispered.

But it was too late. The king had turned the handle, unlocking the heavy bolt on the small door. Within a second of the click of the lock, he was knocked unceremoniously to the floor as the door was rushed from the outside. Thaddius was helpless as the man, covered in slick back slime, rushed inside.

He was screaming.

The guard either ignored the king behind the door or didn't see him as he ran at the helpless and hapless Halia cowering in the corner of the small room. With a guttural roar, he grabbed her by her hair and dragged her out of the room, back through the door he had just entered.

Thaddius watched all of this happen from the floor.

He watched as his wife was dragged kicking and screaming from their sanctuary, out into the strange black rain that was falling in torrents outside. He let her go. He had been too scared and, to his shame, relieved that it hadn't been him to stop it. 'Fight him, Halia … fight him,' he whispered. 'Please …' he finished as tears rolled down his cheeks.

~~~~

As Halia was dragged outside, a captive of the slick but vice-like grip of the large guard, she was able to get a look around the gardens outside of the mausoleum. They had been transformed from a place of beauty into a dark, hellish nightmare. All the trees and the flowers had been swallowed, coated in a thick black gloop that was falling from the swirling maelstrom of clouds above. It didn't look natural. It looked staged, false somehow. The ground was saturated in the slick blackness. It covered the grass, the benches, the guard who was dragging her, and the other guard on the lawn, the one lying motionless with a dagger protruding from his eye socket.

She was shocked at seeing the body, but the emotion didn't last long. Something strange was happening to her. The oily substance that was now covering her was soaking into her skin. It was a strange sensation. Rain was supposed to roll off skin, not ooze into her pores. Before long, her face was unrecognisable as the guard continued dragging her towards the trees. There were another two guards a little way off. She could see they were fighting hand to hand, looking like they were trying to kill each other rather than sparring. One of them had a longsword protruding from his chest but was fighting on regardless.

As the black rain continued to crawl into her, a change in her attitude took place. She found herself more interested in the fighting men than the fact that she was being dragged through the rain towards her obvious doom. The thought of the two men killing each other spurred her on. She wanted to see their blood. She wanted to watch it gush out over the blackness around them. More than that, she wanted to feel the warm, thick liquid spill over *her*. She longed to feel the flesh of the men between her teeth; she ached to tear them apart and bathe in their innards. A growl escaped her as the man with the longsword poking from his chest grabbed his opponent in a bear hug, spearing him onto the savage blade that was protruding from him. The guard screamed as the blade entered his body. Both men fell to the floor, both impaled on the same longsword like a disgusting parody of a kebab.

Halia enjoyed the show, but how she yearned to feel the gush of the bastard who was pulling her across the floor flow over her. She wanted to scratch out his eyes, she wanted to beat his head until his brains ran pink across the filthy rain slicked gardens. She would leave him there, dying, while she made it back into the mausoleum to kill her fat, bloated husband. Then she would murder and devour every one of their courtesans. She wouldn't rest until everyone in the kingdom was dead … every last stinking one of them.

The guard dumped her onto the floor, and the world began to swirl as a heavy hobnailed boot crunched into her face. It broke her nose, sending blood and cartilage smattering over her face. She managed to roll away from the next blow, and in her savage rage, she leapt at her assailant. He was not expecting the move and had left his face defenceless. Her long, dangerous fingernails found the purchase they were seeking in the soft flesh of his oily face, and she dug them in. The satisfaction of the man's skin parting beneath her fingers, coupled with the satisfying pop as blood ran down his face, was like ecstasy to her. He screamed in agony as another heavy blow hit her face. It caught her in the same place as the last, and the world swam again. She let go of the guard's face, falling heavily onto the thick black swamp that had once been a beautiful rose garden.

Within the blink of an eye, the man was on top of her, sitting on her chest, pinning her arms to the ground with his knees. The guttural snorting coming from her mouth matched what was coming from his as he began to rain punch after punch after punch down onto her face. She kicked and bucked, but he was too heavy and too agile for her to escape.

Soon the bucking slowed, and her struggling limbs began to flounder. The soldier didn't notice, he just continued to strike her again and again. Her black, rain slicked face was distorted, broken, ruined, and death finally came to claim her.

Queen Halia died, beaten to death by one of the men employed to protect her, in the rose garden outside the Royal Family mausoleum.

The soldier who killed her was himself attacked by two men who were oil slicked gardeners. One hit him over the head with a heavy spade. The blow knocking him from the dead queen. The other began to deliver his own punishment in the form of kicks and stomps. A sickening crack was heard as the soldier's skull fractured beneath the man's boots; but that didn't stop him. He only stopped when his partner took the guard's head off with a machete, he normally used to clear the thicker foliage away from the graves.

It didn't take long for these two men to turn on each other.

~~~

All over Carnelia, the black rain fell. Every person, be they soldier, gentrified courtesan, ragamuffin child, blacksmith, anyone touched by the rain was caught in a vicious, violent rage. A mindless fury, a homicidal impulse to kill everyone, sometimes even themselves, coursed through them. The streets ran black and red as neighbour slaughtered neighbour on that fateful day.

Anyone who was dry was spared the homicidal rages but not the clutches of those who were tainted by the black water. Some were slaughtered by their own loved ones, neighbours, or even strangers.

The rain raged for an hour, but the damage was almost complete.

Eventually, it cleared, and a normal rain fell, flushing every trace of slime from the streets and the people. The survivors of the ravages came to their senses, horrified to find remains of relatives or loved ones dead, torn apart, mutilated by their own hand.

Yet this awful day in the Kingdom of Carnelia had one more terrible surprise in store.

59.

AFTER THE RAIN washed away the blackness of the day, the sun broke through again. The tumultuous clouds that had delivered their particular style of death dissolved almost as fast as they had appeared.

King Thaddius poked his head out of the door to the mausoleum that had been his sanctuary through the horrors of the last hour. He looked up to the bright blue sky as the last of the normal rain ceased and the heat of the sun resumed its dominance after its short but eventful reprieve. He looked about. There was death everywhere. Not one person was standing. He had watched as his men, the gardeners, even some passers-by beat each other to death with passion and aggression the likes of which he had never witnessed before, not even in the heat of battle.

Then he saw her.

She was motionless on the grass in his favourite rose garden. There was no blood around her, it had all washed away, but he could see she was dead. Her face was almost unrecognisable. Her identity was only given away by her long black, red tinged hair and the torn, soaking robes she wore.

It was his wife, the woman he loved, the woman he had shared his life with for almost thirty years. It was the woman he had failed; hiding, snivelling, and petrified as she was beaten to death by one of his own trusted guards.

The Glimmer Saga #1

Glimmer

He ran to her, falling to his knees in the muddy grass. He held her in his arms. He pulled her close, her broken face nestled in his neck, and sobbed. He didn't cry only for her passing but for his own inadequacies in protecting her. He wanted to kiss her, but there was not much left of her beautiful face *to* kiss. So, he took one of her cooling hands in his, he lifted it to his mouth, and kissed that instead.

D E McCluskey

60.

ALL AMBRIC COULD see as he approached the perimeter of Carnelia was the walls of the city shrouded in a dark mist. A gloom was descending upon the city from the black clouds above. As he watched, the clouds began to shift and dissolve before his eyes. The lighter clouds beneath the dark ones opened, and he watched as a heavy rain fell, drenching the city below.

Rain had never bothered Ambric, but there was something unnerving about the darkness he had seen clouding the city and how quickly it was washed away by the lighter rain.

It was almost as if it had been by design.

Once the downpour had run its course, he emerged from his shelter and surveyed the walls of the city. He should have been able to see men pacing backwards and forwards along the ramparts. The sentries were ordered never to leave their posts, no matter what the weather. He took his horse around to the main gate of the city, expecting to explain himself, who he was, and what was his business in the Kingdom of Carnelia.

The gates were wide open.

There was not one single man guarding the entrance to the city. He had never seen the like before. *I'll be having words with the commander of the wall,* he thought as he rode his horse through the entrance.

Within moments, his worst fears had come true.

The dead were everywhere.

They lined the street. Everywhere he looked, there were bodies. The manner of their deaths sickened him. Each corpse looked to have been torn apart, either by hands and fists, or hacked to death by weapons and blunt instruments.

He dismounted his horse and drew his sword, ever ready to defend himself and Carnelia against whoever, or whatever, could have caused these deaths.

There were survivors, he could hear them. The sounds of men, women, and children crying came from everywhere. It was an eerie sensation. Then he saw them. They were sparce, dazed, covered in blood, sobbing, cradling bodies as they wailed. A dazed and unbelieving look haunted their eyes, their hanging mouths and vacant eyes told of unspeakable horrors. It felt as if something evil had blown through the city, something unholy, killing most of the populous and leaving the rest to their misery.

'What's happened here?' he shouted at a shuffling man who was covered almost from head to toe in fresh blood.

The man couldn't answer him, he just shied away, never taking his eyes from the sword in his hands. 'Leave me be … devil,' he croaked as he made his way down the street, putting a safe distance between him and Ambric.

'I'm not the devil, friend. I'm Robert Ambric of the Carnelian guard. I need to know—'

'I saw what you did,' the man shouted. 'I witnessed it with my own eyes. You're the devil.' With that, he ducked into an open door down the side of a house and was away faster than Ambric would have thought possible.

He moved on. The deeper he ventured into the city, the more corpses he encountered, with more and more mourners kneeling and wailing at their side.

'Has anyone seen the king?' he shouted to the people on the street. 'I need to find the king. Has anyone seen him?'

The people were either too dazed or too scared to answer him. Most ignored him, others cowered away.

Ambric was confused. He had never seen anything like this in all his years.

'They went to the mausoleum. Him and the queen. They went to give their respects to Leopold on his anniversary,' a small voice whispered. Ambric looked to see a boy hiding in the branches of a large tree. 'They went up there just before the black rain came. Maybe he's dead like the rest of 'em.' The boy shrugged. 'Like the rest of us.' With that, he shimmied further up the tree and disappeared out of sight.

Without another word, Ambric remounted his horse and galloped up the hill towards the cemetery, his heart, stomach, and soul in turmoil.

After a short while and a hectic ride, dodging survivors and corpses alike, he reached the gardens of the cemetery. Once again, the ground was strewn with mutilated corpses. Some had been decapitated, others beaten to death, but all of them were undeniably dead.

There was one survivor sat on the ground. The poor man looked half drowned as he cradled a body in his lap. Ambric had no mood or time to search the grounds for the king, and he would take no cryptic answers from this man. He dismounted and drew his long sword. 'You, sir,' he shouted. 'Tell me and tell me true, have you seen the king and the queen around these parts?'

The old man never looked at him, but he answered. 'Who is asking?'

Ambric edged closer, taking care as the man could have been concealing a weapon. 'I do not take kindly to questions answered with questions. I'll ask you one more time. Did you see the king and the queen?'

'Sir, I am not being insolent. I am asking your name.'

Ambric sighed. 'My name is Robert Ambric, I am a commander in the Royal Guards of Carnelia, and I'm sworn to protect my king.'

The man held the body in his hands a little tighter, and from his position, Ambric could see it was a woman he held. Her clothes were dirty and torn, as ruined as her face. Ambric's heart went out to the man, he was obviously mourning the only thing, the only person, that really mattered to him. He approached him to offer sympathy.

'Leave me be,' the man snapped, cradling the body tighter still.

'I will, but I must know if you saw the king before or during this event?'

The man dropped his head. 'I did,' he snarled. 'Carnelia has a king … no more!'

Ambric's heart sunk to his stomach. 'You saw this? You're sure?'

'I saw it, Sir Ambric. He died right after his wife was killed. There's nothing left of either of them now.'

'It's a sad day indeed, sir.' Ambric dropped the hand that he had held out. All was lost, and what little comfort he was hoping to give this man he needed for himself.

The man shrugged and dropped his head even further. Ambric saw his devastation and wanted to leave him to grieve. 'I'll give you my leave, sir, but you must know, not two hours ride from here is an Azurian war machine. They are headed this way. If you value your life, I'd run now while you still can.'

'I asked you before to leave me be.'

Ambric nodded slowly and made his way back to his horse.

~~~~

As the sound of the horse's hooves made their way from the gardens, the devastated man turned, making sure Ambric had gone. King Thaddius held the broken body of Queen Halia tighter, allowing his tears to wash over his wife's body.

61.

ALEXANDER BLINKED AS he caught his first far-away glimpse of the walls of Carnelia. A shiver ran through his body as he realised that his dream had been realised in two ways. The city walls were surrounded in a black mist. It looked like a thick, oily cloud had somehow dropped from the sky and nestled itself over the kingdom. Something cold passed over him as he regarded the mist, it was not something that he could easily identify. There was a feeling coming from it, a foreboding that he wanted nothing to do with.

The second part of his dream that was broken was the arrival of the fireflies. They appeared from nowhere. One moment there was a strange, heavy thrum in the air, then the next there was a swarm of the magnificent beasts hovering over the heads of their almighty procession.

Some of their men panicked and began to draw their swords and aim their bows at the beasts, but his sister soothed them, telling them they were friends and allies of the Azurian army.

~~~~

The war machine had stopped to rest their horses and to talk strategy before the final attack. Endellion, in the guise of Cassandra, was addressing the army.

'I do not wish you to tell me how to run my kingdom, and therefore, I would not dream of telling you how to run your battle. Here today, we must bring about an end to this feud between our kingdoms. The only way we can safely do that is to take this kingdom as our own.' Cassandra's speech at the head of the procession was stirring. Alexander could see the men yelling and whooping.

'Who is with me?' she shouted.

All the men hollered their allegiance. Their blood was up, and war was coursing through their veins. There would be no stopping them now, they had come too far. They cheered the name of Azuria as they mounted their steeds, ready to make the final march towards the kingdom they now saw as their enemy. Fireflies hovered above them, gaining uneasy looks as they all continued towards the gates of Carnelia.

Cassandra looked down at her brother, who was beaming back up at her. 'Gaze upon the mighty Carnelia, my brother. Drink it in, for today is the last time it will be known as Carnelia. This will be the last time it stands against the might of Azuria. Today we annex this city, we will govern it from our own palace, and one day, my brother, I will pass it over to you, to do with as you see fit.'

Alexander looked at the walls of the city as the black mist began to dissipate. He smiled, even though something still didn't feel right.

62.

AMBRIC RODE HIS horse back to the palace. He was the only traffic on the road, and despite what had obviously come to pass here today, he had not been stopped or hindered once on his journey.

Decapitated and bloody bodies lying on the floor were many, and the survivors were few. *A fine day for an invasion,* he pondered as his thoughts passed onto the witch Endellion who had transformed herself into Queen Cassandra of Azuria. *If she can do that, if she can change her appearance, then what else is she able to do? Could she be responsible for all of this?* The question hung over his head as he approached the palace officer's mess.

Here he had hoped to find some challenge.

He was sorely disappointed.

The door was closed, barred, and he had to rattle at it to get a response from inside. 'Open up in there … Open up in the name of Carnelia. It is Sir Ambric, I have returned, and I am in need of answers.'

He heard the unmistakable sound of nails and wood being removed from the other side of the door. He shook his head in disappointment. 'What do you think you are doing, hiding away in here?' he scolded when the door opened, and several dishevelled men peered out. 'Did you not see what happened here today?' Spittle was flying from his mouth as he shouted at the men.

'We saw it, sir,' one answered. 'Some went to help, but when the black rain touched them, they turned on each other. They rushed back inside, but there was no reasoning with them, sir, they were raving lunatics. Everyone the rain touched was the same.'

'Men, women, and children, sir. Animals too. As soon as the rain touched them, they became barbaric. We dared not venture out.'

'How many are you?' Ambric asked, trying to get a grip on the situation.

'In here? We are one hundred and thirty-two men accounted for, fully armed and equipped. There are also horses in the back unaffected.'

'How quickly can you mobilise? We need to be away as soon as we can. There's an Azurian war machine maybe two hours away by now. We need to leave.'

'What about the civilians that are left, sir?'

'All are free to join us, but we must be ready to mobilise now. We will warn them on the way. Let's move,' Ambric ordered.

The soldiers wasted no time in relaying his orders to the others inside.

Within ten minutes, there were one hundred and thirty-three men, including Ambric, armed and mounted, ready to flee the city.

They shouted and barked at any civilians they passed to join them, to flee the advancing Azurian war machine.

63.

A LITTLE OVER two hours after Ambric encountered the king in the cemetery, the first wave of Azurian guards entered the open gates of Carnelia. Their orders were to slaughter any civilians who resisted their presence, to round up all who yielded and hold them in the courtyard of the palace.

They were also told to locate the king and bring him before Queen Cassandra, preferably alive.

These soldiers will not have an easier victory than they will today. They will be lucky to find one Carnelian with the pluck to resist this occupation after what they have just been through, Endellion thought as she passed into the city.

Within a few hours, the red flag on the main gates of Carnelia was set ablaze. This was Endellion's chosen signal for the rest of the party to enter the taken city.

As she and Alexander trotted their horses around the kingdom, the war banner of Azuria was hoisted up the main flagpole.

Carnelia had fallen!

64.

THE GROUP WAS exhausted. They had been travelling almost non-stop for three days and had covered most of the ground back to Carnelia, following the directions Cassandra had given them.

Bernard was in high spirits, as were the men. Alas, Cassandra could not share their enthusiasm.

'We should be getting our first site of the beautiful walls of Carnelia as we broach this hill,' Bernard boasted as his horse sidled up to hers, snapping her out of a reverie she had fallen into.

'It's just occurred to me, Bernard. I'm still your prisoner. Should I not be in shackles as we approach your kingdom? Do you think I will be welcomed into Carnelia, or will I be thrown into the deepest, darkest dungeons?'

Bernard smiled and tipped his head. He hoped it had been a reassuring smile. 'You know you've earned the trust of Carnelia, mostly by saving its one and only prince and heir to the throne. I would warrant a guess they'll listen to your pleas, and to your story, mine too. You will be free to go and to be an ally of the Kingdom of Carnelia until the day you die.'

She turned away from his bright smile as they were interrupted by the urgency of the advanced rider who was galloping towards them at some speed. His face was pale and serious. 'Sire. You need to come with me and see this.' He threw

Cassandra a look, and she recoiled as if she'd been slapped. 'Alone,' he concluded.

Bernard looked at Cassandra. 'Stay here, I won't be long,' he whispered before taking off in the direction the scout had come from.

The scout whispered something to another of the guard, and they both looked back at her. As the first man rode off to catch up with Bernard, the second man moved his mount closer to Cassandra, signalling another two men to do the same.

'What's the meaning of this, soldier?' she asked. The hackles on the back of her neck were tingling. She had a very bad feeling about what was happening.

'You'll seen soon enough, Queen Cassandra,' the man spat.

She didn't like his tone.

65.

ENDELLION WAS IN the courtyard of the palace. She was surrounded by Azurian guards. They were hauling the survivors before her in groups. Shock and fear were the most prevalent expressions on their cowed faces. She and Alexander were sat astride their horses at the top of the yard, overlooking the groups coming in.

'Are all these people Azurians now?' he whispered, not wanting any of them to overhear him.

She smiled a sinister smile that he didn't like, but he did his best not to show her. 'No, Brother, and don't ever forget that. These people are under the *protection* of Azuria. Their kingdom is now annexed, along with all their lands, to us. Me and you, we now rule everything we see.'

'Oh, good,' he replied, mostly because it was what he thought he should say.

~~~~

Something caught Endellion's eye, or rather, someone. From one of the alleyways into the courtyard, a group of guards were bringing in a small number of prisoners. There was one prisoner she was very interested in talking to, but it needed to be done privately. 'Would you excuse me, Alex, I have a little bit of business that needs to be attended to. Feel free to roam. Go and find the fireflies if you want, they'll keep you safe from any Carnelian scum who might try to harm you.'

As the boy trotted off, looking rather glum, Endellion trotted her horse over to the group that had caught her eye. 'I'll take this prisoner myself, young man,' she said to the soldier who was leading the group. She grabbed an old, ragged man by the arm, pulling him away from the others.

He offered no resistance.

'I'll need some privacy, Commander. You continue cataloguing these prisoners, and I'll take this one inside.'

'As you see fit, ma'am,' the commander replied, nodding his head. He rode away, herding the Carnelians into the courtyard with the host of others.

She took the old man and shoved him through a door into an empty room. Once again, the man offered no resistance.

She closed the curtains and locked the door behind her before turning to look at him. A smile, a genuine one this time, stretched the width of her face.

'So, Thaddius, it has been a long time, but we finally meet again.'

The old man looked at her. The sad, drawn expression on his face lifted only slightly when he saw the young Queen of Azuria standing before him. 'Queen Cassandra?' he whispered in a broken voice that was barely audible over the noise of what was happening outside in the courtyard. 'Why?' he whispered.

Endellion laughed. 'Oh, I'm so sorry, Thaddius. You've never seen me looking like this before, have you? Please, allow me to change into something a little more … comfortable.'

She pulled the red Glimmer from her robes and stroked it. Thaddius's eyes were naturally drawn to the glowing orb.

'A Glimmer?' he whispered. 'Where did you get that?'

'I took it from you, old man.' She laughed as she stroked it. Her face began to melt away. All the youthful beauty smudged, giving way to the aged and cracked form of Endellion's true self.

'What manner of witch are you?' he asked, his voice weary, unimpressed by the magic.

'Do you not recognise me? Do you not recognise your old friend, your lover?' she whispered, her now perfectly formed, original face only inches from his.

The wrinkles on his brow deepened as his eyes opened wider. His jaw fell slack and his vacant expression disappeared.

'Endellion?' he gasped.

'Yes, Thaddius … Endellion!'

In her hand was a small dagger. Without any further preamble, she plunged it into the old man's neck. Blood spurted from the wound as she pushed him away, onto the floor.

The king's expression didn't change. All he did was lift his hands towards the wound as he fell.

King Thaddius of Carnelia died on the stone floor, bleeding out in one of his own courtyard outbuildings.

Endellion wiped the blood from the knife on Thaddius's ruined clothing. As she stood over the spreading pool of crimson that was still pumping from the man's neck, she cocked her head and watched as it ran between the cracks in the stone floor.

As she exited the building, she had thought she would be laughing, but she felt no mirth in this situation. Only a deep rush of satisfaction.

'Commander,' she snapped as she re-entered the courtyard.

'Yes, ma'am?'

'Are the victory banners ready?'

'They are, ma'am, they're in place right now, ready for you to give the word.'

Endellion smiled through Cassandra's face.

The first part of her plan had succeeded.

Carnelia was hers.

'Raise them,' she ordered.

273

66.

AMBRIC AND HIS men, plus a large group of survivors from the black rain, had taken to the rough terrain outside the city walls. They had made camp a few miles out in a defendable area of the woods that Ambric knew well. It was a place he would come to when he needed time and space to think. It was a tight fit for over two hundred people, but it would have to do for now until a plan could be formulated.

There had already been a hunt, and they had come back with plenty of food.

As he sat next to the eerily quiet campfire, eating his share of the spoils, two of his sentries came back into the camp. He looked up at them and saw their faces were grave.

'What is it?' he asked, putting the meat back on his plate, steeling himself for the worst.

'Sir Ambric, you need to see this.'

He put his plate down and stood; he could feel the eyes of everyone present on him as he stepped away from the warmth of the fire. 'What is it, man?' he whispered as the three of them walked towards the trees.

'Up there.' The second man pointed towards one of the taller trees they had been using as a lookout point.

Ambric climbed with the ability and swiftness of a man half his age. When he got to the sentry point, he looked out over the forest, towards where they were set to watch. He drew in a deep breath; it was exactly what he knew he would see, but that didn't make it any less painful. With a heavy heart, he descended much slower than he had ascended.

'Sir Ambric, does this mean what I think it means?' the sentry asked him. His face was sad but with just a small glimmer of hope that Ambric would tell him something different.

Shaking his head, Ambric whispered, 'Don't call me sir! I'm just Robert now, or Ambric, if you will.' He closed his eyes and bowed his head. He reached out and grabbed the shoulder of the sentry next to him. 'Carnelia has truly fallen!'

With a heavy heart, he made his way back to camp. He never thought he would live to see the day when an Azurian victory flag would hang over the gates of Carnelia.

~~~~

Cassandra was surrounded by three men, her horse trapped in a pincer manoeuvre designed not to allow a rider to move. 'What's going on?' she asked, but none of them would even look at her. She attempted to break her horse free from the barricade, but the riders only needed to jostle her back to stop her from going anywhere. 'Why are you doing this? Have I not gotten you all home safely?'

Bernard's horse became visible through the undergrowth as he made his way slowly but purposefully back towards the camp.

'Bernard,' she called out to him, but the prince ignored her. 'Bernard, what's the meaning of this? What have I done?'

Bernard gave her a look that was so pained that she thought her heart might break as she watched him trot off in the opposite direction. 'What is it?' she asked, her voice raised, fearing that something terrible had happened. 'What have I done?'

The rider who had taken Bernard away came back from the direction they had ridden off in. He took one look at Cassandra and sneered. He grabbed the reins of her horse and the three other riders moved aside. 'This is what troubles him, my queen.' The queen part was spoken as if it was a dirty word.

Her horse was pulled through the undergrowth to a small clearing on the top of a cliff. From there, she had a perfect view of the city walls of Carnelia. The rider took her to the edge of the cliff and gestured out towards the castle. 'Is this your doing?' he sneered. 'Have you been leading us on a merry little dance all this time?' He hung his head as he pointed towards what was hanging over the walls.

It was the Azurian victory flag!

Cassandra's vision blurred and her breath became short. 'I …' she gasped, trying to get words out of her mouth, but failing. 'I … I didn't …'

'Leave us,' commanded a familiar voice from behind her. Cassandra and the rider turned to see Bernard making his way back from the camp.

'As you wish, my prince,' the rider said, handing the reins of Cassandra's horse to him. 'But I won't be far. I'll have my eye watching for treachery.'

'Enough, Steven,' Bernard barked, and the man rode away, back to the camp.

When he was gone, Cassandra had managed to compose herself, somewhat. 'Bernard, you must believe me, I had nothing—'

'I believe you,' he said softly. 'You've been with us for the long journey, and before that you were imprisoned. I believe you, but the men back there … they are the ones who will need convincing.'

'You are their prince, their leader,' she implored. 'They'll believe you.'

'Am I their prince? Look on the walls of Carnelia, Cassandra. In my eyes, it doesn't look like it exists anymore. If a victory flag is flying over the gates, that can mean only one thing.' He held his head low.

Cassandra knew what that one thing was.

It was the death of his parents. Most likely at the hands of Endellion in the guise of the Queen of Azuria.

'Sir … the gates are opening. Riders are leaving the city,' one of the men reported, galloping back towards them. 'We must hide, we do not wish to be seen out here.'

Both Bernard and Cassandra turned to see what the man was reporting. Indeed, the gates *were* opening, and a detachment of riders were leaving.

She watched as the soldiers rode. Bernard watched too, his face long and drawn as he saw a woman ride out with them. A girl, actually, and one that looked remarkably familiar.

He looked from her back to Cassandra. They were the same person! 'What is this magic?' he whispered.

Cassandra wasn't listening; she was far too busy watching the riders.

One rider in particular.

It was small boy wearing royal blue armour.

It was her brother, Alexander. Her heart felt like it had smashed to a million pieces.

The Glimmer Saga
#2

The City of the Fireflies

Coming soon from
D E McCluskey
and
Dammaged Productions

Be the first to know when D E McCluskey's next book is available! Follow him on Facebook, Twitter, Amazon, and Goodreads.
Please don't forget to REVIEW!

The Glimmer Saga #1
Glimmer